John's Escape Route

Kerkin's Search Route

SAFE
HARBOR

LEONARD HOWARD
DAVID DERANIAN

iUniverse, Inc.
New York   Bloomington

Safe Harbor

This is a work of fiction. All of the characters, names, incidents, organizations, and dialogue in this novel are either the products of the author's imagination or are used fictitiously.

iUniverse books may be ordered through booksellers or by contacting:

iUniverse
1663 Liberty Drive
Bloomington, IN 47403
www.iuniverse.com
1-800-Authors (1-800-288-4677)

Because of the dynamic nature of the Internet, any Web addresses or links contained in this book may have changed since publication and may no longer be valid. The views expressed in this work are solely those of the author and do not necessarily reflect the views of the publisher, and the publisher hereby disclaims any responsibility for them.

ISBN: 978-1-4401-2876-9 (pbk)
ISBN: 978-1-4401-2877-6 (ebk)

Printed in the United States of America

iUniverse Rev. 03/07/2012

ACKNOWLEDGMENTS

Special and profound thanks to the dedicated efforts of the editors. Their incisive discernment was instrumental in bringing the book to it's intended potential.

For my wife Esther, daughter Susan, Noori, and very good friends Jerry McLaughlin and his family. Thank you for seeing my potential.

Leonard Howard

A very special thank you to Janice Caprelian for her devoted inspiration. Thank you Chuck Andrews for keeping the faith. To my family; thank you so much for your ever-present encouragement.

David Deranian

Acknowledgments

FORWARD

Unresolved loss – a definition of Hell, perhaps?

Finding resolve, closure if you will, can provide the motivation to deal with the suffering of loss. If not, then the sufferer is bound to a life of mere existence, with no hope.

For some 100 years now, Armenians the world over, have carried the burden of such unresolved loss, with children and grandchildren as fragmented remnants of that loss.

It is the unknowing that can drive someone either to despair, or to resolve. To find that resolve, that closure, implies an acceptance, full knowing that what is found out may not be what is wanted, or even hoped for.

Not quite Heaven, but certainly not Hell.

PREFACE

In writing 'Safe Harbor' our focus, through the wonderful medium of an adventure/novel was to:

1. Remind the world that Armenia exists. As Armenians know all too well, many people still do not know where Armenia is located, and that it exists.

2. Remind the world that in 1915 'something bad happened to Armenians', and to some extent, is still happening. Even today Armenia is being blockaded!

A legal definition of genocide was introduced in the 1948 United Nations Convention on the prevention and punishment of the crime of genocide. Before then, the world at large referred to what happened to Armenians in 1915 as massacres. We do not ignore this! Rather the words massacre and genocide were used, where appropriate, based on truthful historical context.

Based on our personal views of the history, it would have been easy to have used the word 'Genocide' from the beginning and throughout the text. However, we as authors strongly believe that it far better to allow the reader to discover for themselves what 'something bad' means for Armenians and the world at large.

However, it would have been a violation of our conscience to not note, in some way, that what happened to Armenians in 1915 was indeed genocide. This was accomplished with a footnote, referring to genocide where the word massacre was used, throughout the text.

Most importantly, we didn't want anything, be it politics or even our own personal beliefs, to hinder the telling of the story as accurately and compellingly as we were able.

To a good read – the authors.

PROLOGUE

Safe Harbor - That of a harbor or haven, which provides safety from attack. - Wikipedia

"Mama ... don't die."

John's voice kept pleading. His mother could hardly breathe now.

"John, go quickly. Please ... take care of your sister."

These were the last words from John's mother when she succumbed to her wounds, by the side of the dusty road, amidst the chaos of the killing that was the fate of the Armenian people.

Just hearing the word Armenia would take John back to his mother's side in that terrible year, 1915. John was only eight at the time, but right then, at the moment of his mother's death, he lost his childhood. There was no time to think about it. With her arms wrapped tightly around his neck, John's six-year-old sister Anna was holding on for dear life. They had to run.

How could I leave my mother?

The remembrance of that day still haunted John.

"Faster Anna, faster."

He yelled to his sister as he held on to her skinny little hand. John had the barbed wire fence in sight as they weaved their way through, trying to dodge the Turkish soldiers. The fear was overwhelming.

John Avedisian and his sister Anna had been part of the horrific fate dealt to the Armenian people, which was the Turkish Ottoman Empire's determination to exterminate the Armenian race from their ancient homeland of 3000 years. They had lived in the Sasun province of the Ottoman Empire. Sasun was located in the fabled Armenian plateau, a highland of rugged mountains and beautiful valleys between the Caucasus Mountains to the north, the Iraq and Syrian deserts to the south, Iran to the east, and Turkey to the west.

The remnant of a once large and powerful nation, Armenia, because of its geographical position made it a point of contention for all the great Near East Empires. The Romans had fought with the Persians over Armenia. This was followed by the Byzantine Empire battling against the ever-present Muslim conquest of the Near East, starting with the Arabs.

Having converted to Christianity in 301 AD, the Muslim conquests put Armenia under religious pressure that increased with the invasion by central Asian hordes of Mongols and Turks from the east, beginning in the 10th century. Armenians held fast to their Christian faith but it was not without cost.

The Sasun province, as part of the Ottoman Empire, circa 1915, consisted of a federation of some forty Armenian villages. The Armenian people living there called themselves Sasuntsis. Fierce Muslim tribes, to whom they were often forced to pay tribute, surrounded them. When they could, Sasuntsis would defend themselves to maintain a semblance of autonomy.

It was against this historical backdrop that John watched his mother die. An older boy had run past and stopped beside John.

"The Turks are coming ... run."

About 10 Turkish soldiers had fast approached. John had not only been scared but also confused. His confusion came from thoughts of a family friend named Ahmed that happened to be Turkish. How different he was from Turks that had killed any Armenian in sight.

Almost every day Ahmed would come into the family bakery to buy some bread. He always had a word about how good a baker John's father was. No wonder, as the smell of fresh baked bread, even from the outside, was something impossible to resist.

Ahmed and John's father were as close to good friends as any two men in this world could be. The politics of the day could make such friendships difficult, but as John saw it, Ahmed had been a good man.

Ahmed would always be ready to play a game with John.

"Add 23 plus 32 plus 29" he would say, some other simple numbers.

"Eighty four" or the other answers came very quickly to John. When John got it right, which he nearly always did, Ahmed would smile, give John a small coin, and encourage the boy to study hard so that when he grew up he would earn not just a small coin, but a large fortune. It was advice that John would hold dear in the years to come.

The last time John saw Ahmed, this kind man had tears in his eyes as he watched Armenian men being shot dead in the street and Armenian women being raped in open daylight. Ahmed cried out to John.

"My poor boy ... please do not curse all Turks for what is being done here. This is not the Muslim way."

Two Turkish soldiers, hearing Ahmed's words, laughed as they hit Ahmed on the head. They knocked him to the ground.

John ran away before the Turkish soldiers had a chance to notice him. As he ran he had thought about Ahmed's statement, that it was not the Muslim way. For John the idea of religion was then vague at best. He knew that Armenians were Christians and that Turks were Muslims. John knew to pray to Jesus every night but didn't know whom the Muslim children prayed to at night. Did they also pray to Jesus, or was it someone else? All he really knew was that Ahmed, a Muslim, was a kind man.

Ahmed's call to Muslim kindness could only be a plea in the face of a newfound nationalism that ran through the Turkish political elite. By the start of the 20th century the Armenians were a casualty of this nationalism. A Christian people ruled over by Muslim Turks for some 500 years, the Armenians, by the end of the 19th century, were reduced to some three million people.

The decimation of the Armenian people was however but a prelude to their near extinction in 1915. The reason this time was not so much religious as it was nationalistic, specifically a Turkish Pan Nationalism movement that envisioned an empire of Turkish speaking peoples stretching from Istanbul in the West to China in the East. Armenia was set directly in the path of this empire. The result; approximately 1.5 million Armenians dead and the rest mostly scattered in a worldwide diaspora.

John's mother would be part of the 1.5 million Armenians killed. She could not know at the time that her children would be part of the remaining Armenian diaspora. Armenian children would often be taken from their families to live with Turks or local Kurds. At times this was an act of benevolence. Many times though, it was a horrific experience, the result of parents being killed in front of their own children. Such was the case for John and Anna. Their father had died quickly from a gunshot to the head when Turkish soldiers had descended on them. A brutal rape, then left for dead, was the fate of their mother.

John and his sister ran in the direction their mother had told them "Run west ... to America ... there you will be safe."

John took his mother's words to heart as he and Anna ran in the direction of the setting sun. Their mother had not spoken again. They saw a fence. People were climbing through it. Soldiers were everywhere. John could hear his sister crying.

John and Anna ran towards the barbed wire fence. A Turkish soldier began pursuing them. As quickly as John could, he squeezed through the fence with the intention of helping his sister through. John tried to grab his sister's hand, but the Turkish soldier was faster. Anna was stolen away from John just as she was trying to get through.

Anna cried.

"John don't leave me."

John tried to get back through the fence but more people were coming through now, knocking him down. When he got up, Anna had suddenly disappeared. Then he saw his only sister being led off by the Turkish soldier. John had watched tearfully as the Turkish solider took Anna away.

Feeling utterly hopeless because of the loss of his sister, only fear now drove him to continue. He began to travel west in the direction of the Mediterranean Sea.

"There are French ships ready to help you get away ...", someone had said.

"Go to Musa Dagh."

John remembered his father telling him about Musa Dagh, that it was a big mountain overlooking the sea.

John had run fast until coming upon horrific scenes he could never have imagined. Dead bodies were everywhere. John smelled the death all around him. He never forgot that smell.

The full moon illuminated the strewn bodies in a ghastly appearance, something John could never have been prepared to see. In a state of near shock, John was petrified. He went into a kind of trance, walking around the bodies, as if they were stumps of wood in his way.

Walking further, John came upon a mound of dead bodies, over 6 feet high. The only way through was to climb over the bodies. He was so scared. His left foot fell in between some arms of corpses. John went into a panic and frantically crawled his way through, coming to the other side onto solid ground. On his hands and knees, John shook in utter fear.

CHAPTER ONE

Safe Harbor - Being saved from a bad fate and allowed to come home. - Authors

John Avedisian was escorted, along with his wife Talah into the New York Plaza hotel. It was the 1944 venue for the Agricultural League of Businessmen annual banquet.

Although only 36 years of age, John was already exceptionally successful in the financial banking of a major agricultural expansion throughout California's Central Valley. The League had recognized John as an exceptional person, not only because of his vast fortune, but also because he used his money to help people where he was able.

John's financial success came not only through thoughtful planning but also from a kind of good luck that can smile on someone at the right place and the right time.

At the age of eight, and having barely escaped the 1915 massacres[1] in his Armenian homeland, John had secured access to a French ship on the eastern Mediterranean Sea near Musa Dagh.

John had made his way to Musa Dagh from Sasun, teaming up with 10 other boys and girls of the same age. They shared whatever food they could scrape together, hiding from the enemy when they had to. Finally after three weeks of travel and surprising help from some Turkish people met along the way, they had reached Musa Dagh. Once there, French ships transported people, mainly Armenians, away from the massacres.[1]

The boys and girls were welcomed aboard and given food. They were allowed to sleep as the ship set sail to Egypt in route to their final destination, France.

Once fed a good meal and well rested, John ventured about the ship in search of anything interesting that he could find. This inevitably led him to a small library of sorts. John always loved books and set out to find one that he could understand, that is a book written in English because, besides Armenian, John had some simple education in English. It seemed however that all the books were written in French. Discouraged and almost ready to give up, John at last spotted a book written in English. The title was, 'California's Central Valley – The World's Best Fruit'.

"Can you read that?" came a voice from one of the sailors.

John felt embarrassed.

"I can read some."

The sailor reached for the book. John willingly gave it to him.

"Would you like me to read the book to you?"

John became excited. His father always read to him. Tears came to his eyes remembering those days.

"Please ... I can understand some English."

The sailor smiled.

"My name is Jacques."

Reading everyday with Jacques, John had been excited to hear of a small town in the Central Valley of California, a place called Fresno. At the farms near Fresno a burgeoning new grape crop was flourishing. John could hardly believe it when Jacques read that some of the newly arrived immigrants that had considerable success in farming were Armenians. In particular, the Armenians were very good at cultivating raisins. At that very moment John decided he would go to Fresno and become a farmer.

His decision to become a farmer eventually led to John's financial success with the result that he was now in New York to be honored by the Agricultural League of Businessmen.

A married couple and a single man approached John and his wife Talah as they walked into the lobby of the hotel.

"How are you John?"

"Good now that I've seen you my friend."

Myron Chersky and his wife Rubina were very good friends of John and his wife Talah. Rubina kissed Talah on both cheeks and then the same with John. Talah could tell by the expression on John's face that he eagerly anticipated a gentleman's discussion with Myron. Taking her cue, she took Rubina by the hand so that the two women could politely excuse themselves.

Myron smiled back politely. "I will only keep your husband for a short while."

Talah responded back.

"I know he does enjoy these conversations with you. Keep him for as long as you like."

As she and Rubina walked away, Talah could not help but notice the striking good looks of the stranger standing next to Myron. Tall, dark and handsome came to mind.

Myron immediately started talking to John.

"What do you make of the Russian advances into the continent?"

"It seems the Nazis are on their way out of Europe which is just fine with me."

Myron, looking a bit despondent at the mention of the Nazis, responded back.

"Have you heard about the Jews? There's a place called Auschwitz."

John put his hand on Myron's shoulder.

"I understand my friend, believe me ... as an Armenian I do understand."

Myron composed himself.

"The Turks are dividing a fine line of neutrality with the Nazis."

John took note of the connection between the Nazis and the Turkish government made by Myron.

"The Russians certainly are making this connection. It won't be long I expect before they invade Turkey."

Myron's interest peaked.

"Do you think there is a chance that Armenians will get back some of their historical provinces?"

John hesitated to answer.

"Who can say? I expect only if it serves Soviet purposes."

Myron motioned to the man, not known to John, beside him.

John was surprised when the man greeted him with the familiar Armenian hello, "Parev."

John responded with the familiar Armenian response for how are you, "Inchbes es?"

John joked to Myron.

"You are surrounded by Armenians."

Myron laughed.

"Excuse me for not introducing you straight away. This is Kerkin. I think you will find him an interesting man. Kerkin has just come back from the Western Armenian provinces."

John's attention went to Kerkin.

"Please continue ... I'm interested to hear about the Old Country."

Images immediately came to John's mind, to the days in Armenia when he barely escaped with his life. How he made it from the Sasun province to the Mediterranean Sea was a miracle in itself. But by taking and rowing a boat over a mile to the French ship with seven other children and then being rescued, John considered this purely a gift from God. He remembered the other two boys who had been with them for most of the journey. Unfortunately they had succumbed to sickness before getting a chance on the boat.

John hesitated then asked Kerkin, "What is it like now?"

Kerkin's demeanor became despondent.

"The Turks are destroying anything Armenian or else converting it to something Turkish. I've seen great churches

either destroyed or turned into mosques. Which is worse ... I
can't tell you. Our ancient Armenia is now called Kurdistan, a
way of saying ... I suppose ... that Armenia never existed. It's as
if Armenians never were there. The Turks want to completely
remove our historical presence from our land."

John asked, "Are there any Armenians still left?"

Kerkin's eyes lighted up.

"Still many. They are hidden ... afraid to say they are
Armenian. Still ... they keep the culture in secret."

Could my sister be alive - in the Old Country?

The question haunted John. He asked Kerkin with hope.

"Have you been to Sasun?"

Kerkin looked at Myron somewhat annoyed.

"I have ... but please ... do not ask me."

John was somewhat surprised.

"Ask what?"

Myron jumped in.

"I told him about Anna."

Seeing John's optimism at the prospect of Kerkin having
been near where Anna could possibly be, made Kerkin uneasy.
He knew that John considered him a link to finding Anna. The
reality of the matter, in Kerkin's opinion, was that if Anna was alive
at all she had likely been completely 'Turkified' or 'Kurdified'. In
other words, she was no longer Armenian. To find her would
not be to find an Armenian, certainly not the sister that John
remembered.

John continued.

"I tried to find Anna but no one could help me. The Turks
wouldn't even let me into the country. They had to know I was
Armenian."

Kerkin looked at John intently.

"You can be sure they knew."

John couldn't hold back his thoughts concerning Anna. As calmly as he could he asked Kerkin, "Could you find Anna? Is it possible?"

Kerkin hesitated.

"I suppose anything is possible ... but given the years and what's happened over there ... well ... who can say."

John persisted.

"But still ... is it possible?"

Kerkin thought back to his recent trip to the Sasun region. The trip was a clandestine mission arranged by the United States army to see which way the Turks were leaning in the war, be it the Allies or Axis powers. For despite the fact that the Turks were initially leaning towards the Axis powers, now that the Allied forces appeared to be winning in Europe the prevailing opinion was that the Turks would ultimately side with the Allies in some official manner. This would be especially important for Turkish interests given the possible impending invasion of eastern Turkey by the Soviet Union.

Kerkin remembered first hand how armed Kurdish Peshmerga militia roamed about during his recent journey to historical Western Armenia and the surrounding regions. Taken captive by a Kurdish tribe, he was interrogated by beating and torture.

The Kurds thought Kerkin was a spy for the Turks. His Armenian heritage was of no use in stopping the beating and torture. Realizing that he was eventually going to be beaten to death, Kerkin became angry deep inside himself about the injustice to the Armenians, both by the Turks and the Kurds. His inner anger burned outwardly for all to see.

As would be expected, Kerkin's reaction initially infuriated the Kurds, but then seeing the anger of this Armenian, the Kurds began to feel for themselves the injustice. It was as if they realized that this Armenian, all Armenians really, had suffered enough. The beating stopped and Kerkin was allowed to go.

Kerkin came back to the discussion.

"You have no idea ... how it is over there."

John persisted.

"Then tell me ... how is it?"

Myron joshed Kerkin.

"I told you he is persistent."

Kerkin was not amused and gave Myron and John a look that he was being manipulated into something. John sensed this and took hold of Kerkin's arm.

"Look ... she is my only sister ... I have an obligation to find her."

Kerkin responded in kind.

"Don't we all have an obligation?"

John was a bit incensed.

"Not like this. Please come over here and at least talk with me. I will tell you about my sister."

Kerkin reluctantly acquiesced. He and John headed to a remote corner as Myron acknowledged his presence was not needed.

John and Kerkin found a table and sat down. A waiter arrived almost immediately to get drinks for the two men. John asked the waiter, "Do you serve lions milk?"

The waiter laughed at the request.

Kerkin jumped in.

"Raki."

Hearing the word, the waiter remembered how the clear liquor of Raki changed to a milky color. He smiled, acknowledging that two Rakis would be coming right up.

As the waiter walked away, John's mind was pondering that day when he had lost his sister.

I failed her.

Almost never a day went by that he did not think about Anna, how he failed his mother's promise to take care of her, no matter what.

How could I have left her?

The guilt raged in John.

Noticing an awkward silence while John was in his thoughts, Kerkin took a good look at the troubled man before him. What he wondered, had this man experienced? How had he managed to survive? He had even thrived in the aftermath of the horror of the massacres.[1] Some like John did manage to keep their minds. Others, even though surviving physically, died in other ways. Everyone had his or her way of getting through, but at what cost?

"Two glasses of lions milk," joked the waiter as he placed the glasses of Raki on the table along with two glasses of water. Walking away, the waiter glanced at the drink turning milky white as Kerkin poured water into it.

John slowly poured water into his glass of Raki to coalesce with his words.

"These years run slow for me."

Kerkin knew what was coming. He had heard many such stories. How a loved one was left behind, usually a child. They were all tragic stories that begged hope or at least closure. The reality, as Kerkin had witnessed too many times, was that there was no hope at all, no kind of closure, simply nothing. Still, sitting there watching this rich young man as he slowly poured more water into the glass of Raki, Kerkin accepted that the least he could do was to hear the man's story.

Kerkin waited for John to sip from his glass then spoke.

"Tell me about your sister."

John slowly looked up.

"She was only six years old."

John with his head lowered, fought back tears.

"I could not get her through the fence. That Turkish soldier ... he took her."

John thought back to his sister, how he tried to pull Anna through the fence, her hand slipping from his. To this day, the memory was too painful for John to bear. Kerkin could see the guilt in John's face. He put his hand on John's shoulder.

"There was nothing you could do."

John had a tear in his eye.

"It should have been me that was taken ... not Anna."

Kerkin witnessed John in that moment, a broken man, filled with guilt over a trauma where nothing could be done. That nothing could have been done was of course the plain truth, but for John sitting there with a glass of Raki in hand, it made no difference. The 'if only' would haunt John to the day he died and that would likely be a day of peace for his troubled spirit.

Women, Kerkin thought, could handle such guilt better than men. For a man, such guilt can only be assuaged by action. Kerkin knew that John wanted him as the instrument of that action. But Kerkin also knew of the hopelessness of such an action. No, Anna was gone forever. There was no hope to ever find her. To give John any kind of hope meant getting involved. That, Kerkin did not want to do.

Kerkin knew what he must do. He looked John straight in the eye.

"You will always love your sister. Do not let the tragedy of what happened to her so long ago tear that love from you."

John was not affected by Kerkin's words.

Kerkin continued.

"The very best you can do for Anna is to love her through your life in this new land with your good fortune and your family. Let them be your love for Anna."

John became almost angry in response.

"Nothing can replace Anna. She was my responsibility."

Seeing the pain in John, Kerkin hesitated to speak. What could he say that would somehow make this man feel better? There was nothing he could say, except to fight back the thought.

Seeing John like that, there was that word 'hope' yet again. Kerkin finally relinquished.

"Look ... I don't want to give you hope that is not there. You must realize the near impossibility of the situation. Your sister is gone. You must face this. There's nothing that can be done."

John persisted.

"I can not ... I will not accept this. No ... I will find a way."

Kerkin couldn't help but admire the insistence of John, that he would find a way. In some way this was Kerkin's own philosophy of life. He was sure that the only outcome of such insistence would be disappointment. Perhaps though, Kerkin pondered the thought, this insistence is what kept John in life. Without it, he would fall into despair. It was this that reached down into Kerkin, bringing something to his consciousness, a kind of unrealistic hope.

John's insistence then prompted Kerkin.

"Are you prepared to really understand about Anna ... whatever that can mean?"

John considered the question.

"Whatever that can mean?"

Kerkin took his glass of Raki.

"Myron was right about your persistence."

He sipped the drink.

"There are maps and reports of the area at my home. Come there tomorrow morning. We can discuss this further then."

Endnotes
1. After 1948 defined as the Armenian Genocide. See Powers, Samantha, "A Problem from Hell": America and the Age of Genocide Harper Perennial (2003) paperback, 656 pages ISBN 0-06-054164-4

CHAPTER TWO

The fates of Jews and Armenians passed through John's mind as he walked with Myron Chersky along an old street in Brooklyn, New York. John liked Brooklyn, with it's borough of neighborhoods that each seemed to have a unique character.

It was the uniqueness, a kind of freedom of expression, that so characterized the United States for John. Memories of when he first arrived to the New Country came to mind. John had come by ship, passing the Statue of Liberty with Battery Park in the distance. That first taste of freedom had stayed with him. He had never forgotten it.

John had stayed overnight at the Plaza hotel with his wife after the charity event. Tired, his home in Fresno seemed far away. He had traveled from there by train. The trip was pleasant enough. The trouble was that he had not been able to sleep.

In a way, the trip reminded him of when he had first come to America. In those days he had taken many jobs, including working at a delicatessen where he had met many Jewish people. John often thought how their history was so similar to Armenian history. A clever people, they were usually dedicated to their adopted country but for various reasons tended to not be fully accepted. Both peoples had ancient cultures and had suffered greatly under foreign domination. Still, Jews and Armenians had a way of bending without breaking, allowing them to flourish despite the odds

John couldn't help but wonder if the terrible massacres[1] inflicted on the Armenian people some 29 years previous would keep Armenians from their lands for 2000 years, the way it

11

happened to the Jews. It was a thought that bothered him greatly. For although the Soviet Republic of Armenia existed, it was only a tiny remnant of what was historical Armenia. If Armenians could not find a way to resettle the Western Armenian provinces soon, then these provinces could be lost to Armenians for a very long time, perhaps forever.

"Kerkin needs a cause. I hope John ... that you can convince him to help."

"Any idea why he is melancholy?"

"Well ... keep this between us ... but like a lot of men who went off to war, it probably cost him his marriage. They sent him to try and help the Armenians in Turkey and as you could imagine ... he became obsessed with the job. He could have stayed home after the first trip and even the second, but he insisted on going back again and again."

They were nearing a crossroad now. John knew that Myron would be going in another direction.

"His wife got fed up with his obsession and went back to Fresno to be with her parents. They had a big argument. She took their son with her."

At least John knew now. He said his farewell to Myron. John continued down the road to where he guessed Kerkin lived.

What was really keeping John tired and at times, down right despondent, were his doubts about ever finding Anna. Try as he may to keep an optimistic spirit, his mind still drifted at times to the melancholy. Especially lately, he seemed to be asking those 'what if' and 'if only' questions about Anna, that if only he had somehow pulled her through that fence, then she could be with him today. He must try and get Kerkin to help him. John was, after all, a rich man. Maybe the money could make the difference.

John took his mind back to the immediate task in front of him, to focus Kerkin on finding Anna. As he walked through the neighborhood, John couldn't help but notice that it was run down, with the housing in significant disrepair. Still, John admired a kind of old city charm that only this part of New York could bring.

Colorful fall leaves covered the streets and sidewalks in a way reflecting the multi-ethnic makeup of the area itself. John came up to a building that brought an immediate sense of familiarity. It was a church with the characteristic Armenian dome of eight sides. This eight-sided dome was indelibly imprinted in every Armenian's mind, a kind of symbolic architecture rooted in the heart of the Old Country.

Kerkin had told John that his home was adjoining the Armenian church. John walked around the perimeter of the church to find Kerkin's home. Rounding a corner he saw Kerkin at a distance picking some kind of fruit from a tree.

Kerkin noticed John.

"The mulberries are just now ripe."

As John approached the garden Kerkin held out a purple berry.

"Try one."

John reached out to take the berry, then tasted it. Memories filled him of his cousin's mulberry trees back in the Old Country.

John savored the taste of the mulberry.

"Shat hamov", very tasty in the Armenian language.

Kerkin put a handful of mulberries into a small bucket.

"They make a tasty pie."

John wiped his fingers on his pants.

"Your wife will bake this pie?"

No sooner were the words out of his mouth than John regretted forgetting what Myron had told him.

Kerkin replied sadly.

"My wife is not here. Come on now into the house."

Kerkin's house was small and dark with not much furniture. It was clear he lived alone. On a table in the small kitchen was a map of Armenia. Kerkin motioned for John to sit down at the table, then pointed to the area on the map labeled Sasun.

"You say this is where you last saw your sister?"

John studied the map, noticing the surrounding cities like Kharpert and Mush, places he could now barely remember. John focused on Sasun.

"This is where we lived."

Kerkin then pointed to Istanbul, the capital of Turkey that lay about 1000 miles west of Sasun.

"You see how far."

Kerkin then pointed south-west of Sasun to the Mediterranean port city of Adana, close to Musa Dagh. Although closer to Sasun than Istanbul, the distance was still quite far, about 400 miles.

Kerkin looked at John.

"You see how far."

John looked at the map discouraged, realizing that getting to Sasun from the Turkish border was an immense challenge, especially in1944, when Turkey was wavering in it's position of whether to side with the Allies or Axis powers in the war.

Kerkin pointed back to Sasun.

"This region is filled with warring Kurdish tribes. They fight for a Kurdistan ... I think mostly because the Turks refuse to acknowledge their identity. The Turks call the Kurds 'Mountain Turks'. A fitting name I suppose for how the Turks used the Kurds to kill Armenians."

John traced a route between Adana and Sasun.

"Are there roads?"

Kerkin opened a cabinet filled with photos. He put them in front of John.

"Have a look for yourself."

John looked through the photos. They depicted very rugged mountains, some snow-capped, others dry and barren. The photos also depicted the Kurdish Peshmerga fighters. They were warlike in appearance, very well armed with knives and guns. These fighters were known through history as fearless men of the mountains. Saladin, the great Muslim warrior who took

Jerusalem back from the Crusading Christians in 1187, was a Kurd.

Looking at the photos of the Kurds, John began to realize the difficulties Kerkin would encounter for any rescue of Anna. To get through the Kurdish Peshmerga would be some kind of feat. Doubts started to run through John's mind about how anyone could get through such fierce warriors.

John looked directly at Kerkin.

"I see why you are reluctant to find Anna."

These words brought to mind Kerkin's own sense of doubt, about anything having to do with what happened to Armenians.

Does it matter?

The question ran through Kerkin as he considered his own personal life in shambles. After the death of his son, his wife had left with their remaining child. He was not sure who he was anymore. There was a time when Kerkin was living a happily married life, with two children. His wife loved him and he loved her. Now they did not even speak to each other.

Was it his emotional attachment to the Armenian cause that drove his wife away? Kerkin saddened thinking about all he had lost. If only he could have realized that his family was his strength. He could have balanced his attachment to Armenian interests with love for his wife. No. Instead he just assumed she would always be there, would always trust him. The consequences were a life lived in one room, with no money. It was only by the concern of the Armenian priest that he even had this. What had his life come to?

Kerkin's state of mind about his current life drifted from moment to moment. Regaining composure he asked John, "Are you happy?"

John was caught off guard.

Why ask me?

Was this some further attempt to discourage him from trying to find Anna?

John responded.

"I'm not sure what it means to be happy. You could say I have a good business, a wife... such things could be said to make a man happy."

Kerkin thought back to his wife and children, no longer with him.

"But there is something missing for you ... your sister!"

John saw a chance here that Kerkin may be reconsidering the search for Anna. What he thought, could he now say, to move the discussion along in the direction he needed?

John picked up one of the photos of a tough looking Kurdish Peshmerga.

"Do they love their families?"

Kerkin looked at the photo with pained face.

"Most men would at least wish for it."

John studied the pain that Kerkin's face expressed.

He decided to take a risky move.

"Your family?"

Kerkin looked away from John, towards a flag on the wall. It was the Armenian tricolor flag of red, blue, and orange that held sway during the brief years of the independent Armenian Republic from 1918 to 1921.

Kerkin looked at the flag distraught.

"I lost my family to that flag."

Kerkin words were reminiscent of the day his wife left him. She had tears in her eyes. His heart was so hard in those days. He was devoted only to the Armenian cause. This, together with the hard economic times of the 30's made him blind to his wife's needs. He could not see that she was in need of his attention too.

John took hold of Kerkin's shoulder.

"It's not too late."

Kerkin looked back to John.

"For your sister?"

John shook his head.

"For my sister and your wife."

Kerkin sat down at the table. He looked over the map then paused at Sasun.

"Our situations are entirely different."

John sat down.

"Those we seek are both lost. They can both be found."

Kerkin could no longer hold back his distraught feelings.

"Your sister was lost not through fault of your own. I lost my wife through my own doing."

John knew he was risking it, but pushed further.

"We both carry the guilt. The only way out of this guilt is to find them and save them."

Kerkin looked back at the flag.

"What if they don't want to be saved?"

"If we rescue them ... they will want to be saved."

John knew Kerkin's wife and son lived in Fresno with her parents.

"Fresno is not so far as Sasun. She can surely be rescued."

A tear ran down Kerkin's face.

"Sasun is not so far either."

Endnotes
1. After 1948 defined as the Armenian Genocide. See Powers, Samantha, "A Problem from Hell": America and the Age of Genocide Harper Perennial (2003) paperback, 656 pages ISBN 0-06-054164-4

CHAPTER THREE

John and Kerkin had decided to get away from Kerkin's house and take a walk along the New York Battery Park waterfront. John had thought this would be good for them both. It was now around 11:00 AM. Boats were moving on the water and they could see the Staten Island Ferry winding it's way past the Statue of Liberty. John paused.

"That statue ... pure American. It's freedom."

Kerkin's thoughts were more immediate. It was a glorious morning, one that made Kerkin hungry. This always was the case for him in New York along the waterfront, usually in the early morning. He could never say exactly what it was, perhaps it was the delicious smells of the delicatessen, but something about the place just made him feel good and hungry.

"What do you feel like eating?"

John looked at his watch to see that it was still well before noon. Having had breakfast just a few hours earlier he would have preferred to just talk. It was evident though that Kerkin was hungry.

"How about fish?"

"I like it. There's a good place just down from here."

Sitting down to eat, John and Kerkin could see the Statue of Liberty in the distance.

Kerkin looked out to the open sea.

"Traveling to Istanbul ... these days it will be difficult."

John knew that Kerkin was referring to Turkey's political position in playing both sides between the Allies and the Axis powers during the war. With a possible landing of allied troops into Europe expected this year, Turkey had shifted its wavering allegiance to the Allies. Of great impact however, was the Russian advance against the Germans on the Eastern front.

There were also rumors of Soviet soldiers amassing on the border between Turkey and Soviet Armenia. Stalin has made it intentionally clear that he was not pleased by Turkey's claimed political neutrality while aiding the Germans with such exports as chromite for German tanks. Germany's war machine would have stopped dead if Turkey had stopped selling the chromite.

Little pretext would be needed for the Soviet army to invade eastern Turkey. They would simply claim it a right to extend Soviet Armenia's borders that were lost during the First World War due to the massacres of the Armenians.[1] Still, Stalin certainly had no special fondness of Armenians. His aim would be a blend of real politic with a taste of revenge.

John looked apprehensive.

"Istanbul these days ... can you make it there?"

Kerkin sighed.

"That's the easiest part of the journey."

John knew all too well that Turks were accustomed to foreigners in Istanbul. When however, they saw them in their heartland, suspicions arose.

Kerkin took out a small map and traced a path from Istanbul to Sasun via Adana. John pointed to the Sasun region.

"But how will you get there?"

Kerkin pulled out a photo that John had seen before. It was of a fierce looking Kurdish Peshmerga fighter.

"A Kurdish Peshmerga ... the best scout and warrior you will ever meet. He will get me to Sasun on horseback."

John became excited. Kerkin noticed this apprehensively.

"Look John, I make no promises. Making it to Sasun will be difficult enough. Finding your sister ... well ... don't expect anything."

John was not deterred.

"Still ... once in Sasun there is a chance."

Kerkin looked at the Statue of Liberty.

"A chance ... that's all I can give you."

Kerkin looked back to John.

"Do you remember your sister ... what she looked like? Can you imagine what she looks like now?"

John didn't know how to answer the question. He wondered if what he remembered about his sister was a trick of his memory. It had been so long. She was just a little girl when he last saw her as she was being pulled back from the fence. He wasn't much older than her. How would she have aged?

"She would be about 34 years old now."

John was trying to figure out how to describe Anna's looks, perhaps something like his mother or father or both? But then, he could hardly remember his parents either. Would someone recognize her as John's sister? The questions gave John no definite answers.

"She had a nickname. We had a friend who used to travel back and forth from Hungary. He used to bring special ribbons from Budapest. One day while playing he recalled a Hungarian poem that referred to a person called Nufi Tuti. He called me Nufi Tuti because I liked that poem. Then he called my sister Dafi Tuti so she wouldn't be left out. Maybe someone may have heard this name. Perhaps it could point you in the right direction. It has to be unusual."

John wondered if his sister could be identified, even with the nickname?

Kerkin saw John's unease but held back the answer. He wanted John to think about the path to finding his sister, that she would not be a little Armenian girl. Rather she would be a woman, most likely looking very much like a Turk or a Kurd. She may not speak any Armenian at all and her culture would not be that of an Armenian.

Kerkin waited a moment longer.

"You can't have any expectations about your sister. Are you really ready for this?"

John hesitated to answer.

"I'm willing."

Kerkin looked back at the Statue of Liberty.

"Good ... now tell me something personal about your sister and your family."

John thought hard for a moment.

"The last words of my mother ... take care of your sister."

Kerkin acknowledged.

"Unfortunately that is not too useful."

"She would perhaps remember our parents owning a bakery. I have tried to find information about her before. Unfortunately the war prevented me from visiting that area. There are orphanages where many children were sent. They may have records."

Kerkin had seen this many times. The look of hope in someone's eyes where they had lost everything. It had been 27 years since John escaped. A lot had happened to the world. The war to end wars had been fought but the world was still plunged into another war. The Allies were fighting back against another tyrant and people had forgotten the massacres[1] of 1915.

John stopped and pulled out a checkbook. He wrote a check, then handed it to Kerkin.

"For you."

Kerkin looked away.

"It's too much money."

Kerkin handed the check back, but John refused.

"No ... this is for you now ... my appreciation for your efforts. Whatever the outcome, I will be grateful."

John hesitated for a moment before speaking again.

"When you decide to go, money will not be the problem. You must let me know what you need. I've also arranged a meeting for you in Fresno ... with your wife and children."

Kerkin was astonished.

"How did you ... ?"

John smiled.

"Fresno is where I live. Everybody knows everybody there."

John pulled out a train ticket.

"Travel and accommodation to Fresno before you leave for Istanbul."

~~~~~~~~~~

Grape vineyards lined with row after row of fruit loaded vines ran along both sides of the train that Kerkin rode. The sight of these vines was both pleasant and bitter for Kerkin.

The vines reminded him of his early days in America. The United States was for him as a young immigrant boy, a chance for untold opportunities. Stories were told in the Old Country of men making fortunes in the raisin business. For Kerkin, having survived with his parents but also loosing the rest of his family in the Armenian massacres[1], it was a fresh start at life, a way to forget the terrible calamity from where he came. This was the pleasant memory.

The bitter memory for Kerkin came some 15 years later when the great depression hit the agricultural center of Fresno hard. His parents had originally owned a 40 acre farm for growing Thompson grapes, the kind used to make a golden raisin that was becoming ever more popular. Kerkin had taken over the farm after his parents had died. It was hard work running the farm but Kerkin did not mind because he knew his hard work was not just for himself but also for his dear wife Karina and their son Mark.

Especially after serving in espionage activities in the Near East during his early years as a citizen of the United States, Kerkin had been grateful for the relatively peaceful life of farming. However, economics dictated something else. Events were at hand which even a hard working and clever man such as Kerkin could not surmount. The good times of the 20's were quickly giving way to the hard economic realities of the 30's. Even before the great stock market crash of 1929, farmers throughout the country were feeling the pinch.

Kerkin's father used to say that if you don't like gambling then don't plan on being a farmer. There are far too many situations that can't be seen ahead of time for the farmer. All he can do is plant his crop, hope that favorable weather prevails, and that he gets a good price for his crop at harvest time. It's all a big gamble.

Unfortunately for Kerkin and the other Fresno farmers, the declining economy had driven down the price of harvested crops so much that not even the expenses could be met. A year or two of this could be managed but year after year leads to catastrophe.

Such catastrophe is just what happened to Kerkin's farm. Unable to pay off the loans he had taken out, not only for the mortgage payment on the farm but also for basic necessities of food and clothing for his family, Kerkin was forced into bankruptcy. He lost not only the farm in foreclosure but also had to suffer the humiliation of going bankrupt. It was not that he was alone in this. Just about all his friends who were farmers were going through the same kind of tragedy. Still, especially for an Armenian, economic failures hit a man hard, to the very core of what he believed about himself.

Except for the rare individual who somehow possessed a deep inner strength, the stress that went along with such catastrophe inevitably oppressed the farmer's family. During the first year Karina, despite having to cut back on basic necessities of life, was able to hold up well. She supported Kerkin through his ever increasing worry about the price of raisins that season. If it were only for that season then Karina's devotion would likely have gotten Kerkin through the worst of it. But the worst was yet too come.

By harvest time of the second season, with the price of raisins at an all time low, Kerkin had fallen into a deep melancholy. It was so bad that he would stay in bed for days, not eating and hardly talking at all. At first Karina was in tears but when her efforts seemed to have no effect on the man she deeply loved, frustration began to take her. She could not understand how this strong man of hers could be battered down by events that he had no control over. She did not think any less of him and told this to Kerkin often. What more could she do?

By the end of the third season, the worst that Kerkin had feared was upon them. The price of raisins was so bad that even harvesting made no sense. Kerkin felt completely hopeless and wanted to just give up. Karina was not of the same mind. Trying not to give up hope herself, and by now completely distressed by her husband, she begged Kerkin to go to the bank and ask for another extension of the mortgage loan payment. Kerkin however was so debilitated in spirit that he could not even manage to leave the house. He had lost all confidence in himself. The thought of going to the bank for another mortgage loan extension seemed to him, entirely useless.

Kerkin's only thought then was to go see the local bankruptcy lawyer to just quit as cleanly as possible. Then, at least he thought, his family could make some kind of fresh start. Some of his friends had done this and it seemed the only course of action. Karina was against the idea. She knew her husband, what he as a man could handle. Bankruptcy did not seem the way out for him.

As Kerkin was on his way out the door to go see the lawyer, Karina pleaded with Kerkin.

"Don't do it. You can still fight."

Kerkin was a completely broken man by then. He could barely say the words "My fighting days are over."

As the train pulled into the Fresno station Kerkin thought of those last words he had spoken to Karina before giving up on the farm. It was a dream lost, not because it had to be lost but because Kerkin lost confidence in himself. Karina had begged him not to give up on himself.

Looking back, Kerkin realized that it was at that very moment when the dreams shared between he and Karina died. Nothing was the same after that. Had she lost respect for him he wondered, or was it something more, something not expressible in words? Whatever the elusive quality was, Kerkin had been trying to get it back for a long time, without success.

The few attempts to bring their marriage back to life had led only to frustration and bitterness. Certainly a tragedy made even more tragic by the estrangement of Kerkin's son Mark. This was no fault of Karina. Despite her estrangement from Kerkin, she always spoke highly of her husband, especially describing him as an espionage agent for the United States.

No words could make a difference with Mark however. He hated his father for leaving his mother and for leaving him. Mark saw himself as different from the other boys at school. They had fathers, why couldn't he have one as well?

Stepping off the train, Kerkin saw her. Karina was still so beautiful, just the way he remembered. It was not so much her physical appearance, although she still did possess a physical charm. No, it was a kind of brightness about her, that inviting quality which he used to partake of freely, to give him strength and balance in life. Now he could only look at that brightness from afar.

Kerkin tried not to be anxious as he approached Karina. She smiled and fought back tears as Kerkin came closer. There was a moment of awkward hesitation as they decided if it was appropriate to embrace. Karina initiated the situation by carefully holding open her arms. As Kerkin and Karina embraced, both could still feel that energy which bound them in times past. They both knew it was still there and yet to act further on it remained just out of reach, as if they couldn't bring themselves to fully comprehend the love that still existed between them.

Kerkin was surprised when he heard the words of Karina.

"I'm glad you came."

Karina broke the embrace while looking directly at Kerkin.

"Are you going to the usual places?"

Kerkin stepped back a bit in a kind of awkward fashion that took the moment from a chance at reproach to the facts as they were.

"I'm going to Armenia, the Western provinces."

Karina was surprised.

"Why would America care about those places now?"

Kerkin hesitated to say but then realized, it not being an issue of national security, he was free to talk.

"I've been hired by John Avedisian ... to find his lost sister."

Karina was again surprised.

"Thee John Avedisian, the agricultural financier?"

"Yes ... it's him. The trip is a long shot. There's not much chance of finding her and even if I do, her memory of things Armenian is likely completely gone."

There was a kind of expression on Karina's face that Kerkin had not seen in a long time, an expression that said she was proud of him. Kerkin followed Karina out of the train station. Suddenly Karina stopped.

She asked the question.

"Why are you looking for his sister?"

Kerkin hesitated to answer. His first thought was to give a standard line of a rich man hiring a man of expertise to do a dangerous job. Instead he thought about the expression on Karina's face a moment ago, one of admiration.

"It's the right thing to do."

Hearing these words melted Karina's expression into something that only two people in love, or at least that had been in love, could express.

Endnotes

1. After 1948 defined as the Armenian Genocide. See Powers, Samantha, "A Problem from Hell": America and the Age of Genocide Harper Perennial (2003) paperback, 656 pages ISBN 0-06-054164-4

CHAPTER FOUR

Kerkin had spent four days with his wife and son. It gave them the chance to know one another again and the resolve to try to make their marriage work. Karina could see that Kerkin was a different person now, or at the very least was trying to be.

On arriving back in New York, Kerkin went to his home and started thinking of what needed to be done. He called John.

"Thank you for what you did. I'm ready to try and find your sister now."

Encouraged by what seemed to him a revival of Kerkin's spirit, John spoke confidently.

"We need to talk about the plans that have been made for you. I am still in New York. Please ... come to my hotel ... say at 6:00 pm."

At last a decision had been made. Now it was the time of details, how the plan would be worked out. That was the question. Those details meant for Kerkin to go by ship to Britain, followed by a plane from London to Spain, and then to Istanbul, Turkey. The Allies were still losing ships in the Atlantic, but given that they were traveling in convoy with protection from the navy, it seemed the best and safest way to start his journey. Kerkin really did not care for planes anyway.

Kerkin looked at his watch, 6:00 pm, right on time as he knocked on Johns door at the hotel. The door opened. Kerkin knew that the journey had begun.

"Please ... come in."

Kerkin followed John into the hotel room, a lavish suite by any standards.

"Can I get you a drink?"

"A drink would be good."

"What do you like?"

"Do you have Vodka?"

John produced a bottle then filled two shot glasses with Vodka.

"I've made arrangements with a friend of mine who works in the British government. You will be attached to the British embassy as a translator for the Spanish part of the journey. Kerkin drank the shot of Vodka that John had poured.

"Good enough until I leave for Spain."

"Exactly."

John handed Kerkin what at first glance was an official document of some sort.

"Here are the details."

Kerkin scanned the official looking document as John continued.

"In Turkey, you will be an archaeologist working for Professor Senchalli. You must pay him a visit before you leave London ... to cover your story ... to keep it straight."

John poured two more shots of Vodka for himself and Kerkin.

"Although Professor Senchalli has not been in Turkey for some time, he can give you an idea of the politics. He has committed to support you in any way he can."

"Are you sure he can be trusted?"

John took the shot glass in hand.

"My donation to his research was appreciated."

Kerkin lifted his glass to toast.

"A condition of trust."

Kerkin's stay in Britain would be of short duration, only one week. It was just enough time to organize the journey from Spain to Istanbul and then into the heartland of eastern Turkey, or what Armenians like to call, Western Armenia. John's connections at the war office of the British government had helped. Passports and bank accounts were obtained. ID for both Spain and Turkey was also provided.

It took Kerkin another two days to make final arrangements. Maps were studied. He checked with his colleagues in the Office of Strategic Services, the OSS, on special equipment he should take with him. Kerkin reminded himself that all of this was critical at best for the success of the mission and at worst, to keep him alive. He knew all too well that if the Turkish police picked him up and began to ask questions then in very short order he would be classified as a spy. It was not an option Kerkin wanted to consider.

Kerkin called John for the last time about an hour before boarding the ship. John had arranged for the transport in a cargo boat along with many other ships taking food and arms from the United States to Britain. It was now July and the Allies had successfully landed in Europe. Once again France, at least a part of it, was free, a consequence of the D-Day invasion at Normandy. Although the trip would be relatively short in duration, about one week total, Kerkin knew that it could be eventful given the German U-boats circulating the Atlantic Ocean in search of just the kind of ship that Kerkin was on.

It was with thoughts of danger, both in the immediate sense of being on a ship targeted by the enemy, and of potential consequences of the mission he was on, that Kerkin's attention was caught by a woman that was seemingly in distress. The woman, who was leaning on the port rails, looked up at Kerkin.

"Lets hope it stays calm."

Kerkin noted a wedding ring on the woman.

"Lets hope."

A brief moment of awkward silence ensued, enough time for Kerkin to consider responding carefully.

"May I ask your reason for making this voyage in such dangerous times?"

As he asked the question Kerkin realized that he may have over stepped.

"Please ... excuse me ... I did not mean to pry."

The woman smiled.

"It's okay ... it's nice to know someone cares enough to ask. I'm going to visit my husband ... in the hospital."

She started to choke up a bit then composed herself before continuing.

"My husband was badly injured at Normandy."

Kerkin expressed sympathy.

"I hope he gets better soon."

The woman, again fighting back tears, looked out to sea.

"It is life I suppose ... I can only accept what God brings."

The woman's last statement brought Kerkin to a moment of contemplation about his own family, why life had not worked out the way he had planned with his wife. He had tried to be a good husband but could not seem to get it right. It would be easy to blame his marriage problems on the collective trauma of Armenians. Perhaps that would be justified. Deep down though, Kerkin knew. More to the point, he feared the problem lay within him. If only he could know what that problem was.

Five days later Kerkin was relieved to be stepping off the ship in Southampton, England. Catching a train for London's Waterloo station, he could feel the brisk air that was for him, Britain. Although summer, the weather felt like winter. It was the kind of damp cold that goes right through a man's bones. Still, Kerkin liked the feeling, a reminder that he was alive and well, at least in the physical sense.

Kerkin knew he needed to get out of this brisk air quickly due to the change in climate from California. Such changes could cause a quick flu to develop, something Kerkin could ill afford these days. Quickly he hailed a taxi. The driver rolled down the window as he approached to a stop.

"Where to guvner?"

Kerkin entered the cab.

"The Sussex hotel please."

As the cab approached the Sussex Hotel, Kerkin couldn't help but admire the classic Victorian style of the building. Built over 100 years ago, the hotel was still charming in décor, both inside and out. Kerkin particularly liked the exquisite garden that the British are known for. Getting out from the cab, Kerkin paid the fare, about double the actual charge. The driver offered change but Kerkin refused.

"No please ... I'm a guest in your country."

The driver smiled in appreciation.

"We Brits and Yanks ... all of us together these days."

"Agreed."

An attendant from the hotel quickly took hold of Kerkin's bag.

"This way please, sir."

Kerkin followed the young man just as air-raid sirens sounded off. In the distance the characteristic buzz droning sound of the VI buzz bomb could be heard.

"This way sir. The shelter is through the back. Please hurry."

As long as the sound of the V1 could be heard, all was well. It was when the sound stopped that destruction was imminent. Kerkin waited then prepared for the inevitable explosion. Just as anticipated the buzzing thump sound stopped and then some seconds later, KA-BOOM.

Twenty minutes later the all-clear signal began to sound. Kerkin followed the attendant up to the reception.

"This way sir." were the hotel attendant's words of relief as Kerkin left the shelter.

Kerkin's attention was drawn to the direction of the explosion. Physical evidence of fire and smoke were just a few miles away in the northeast direction of the city. The hotel attendant looked towards where the rocket had come down.

"The Germans are desperate with the V1s. We get them every day now ... not so bad because we can at least see where they are headed, although the sound ... that's the bugger."

Kerkin could see that although the hotel attendant remained outwardly steadfast, the rocket explosion had rattled him. Day after day of this, how could it not be so?

The hotel attendant picked up the pace towards the lobby. Kerkin followed him to the hotel check-in desk, then reached into his pocket for a tip.

"Remember young man ... this war is not forever."

The attendant took the tip appreciatively in a sigh of relief, not so much for the money but that his fear had been acknowledged.

"Thank you sir."

Kerkin pulled out his passport and papers to hand to the check-in agent. A quick glance at Kerkin's papers caused the check-in agent to take special note. In hushed voice "Your suite is ready now. We will notify the appropriate personnel for your meeting."

Hearing the check in clerk's words, in hushed tone, was the proof Kerkin needed that John had not only the intention but also the seriousness to provide what was needed for the mission.

The check-in clerk then motioned for what looked like a special services complement of two men in suits. Looking closely, Kerkin could see faint bulges of pistols along the inside pocket of the suit jackets of both men. He recognized the two men as agents for MI5, further assurance that John was indeed well connected, much more so than Kerkin expected.

The hotel suite was quite large in Kerkin's estimation, evidence of plenty of money spent. More importantly, it was well organized for strategy planning.

Surmising the resources made available thus far, Kerkin pulled out from his briefcase, passports and papers identifying him as a representative of the British government. These were laid out next to a map of the Mediterranean region from Spain to Turkey. He traced out his path of travel. Drawing lines through Turkey, Kerkin sighed at the prospect of that journey. It was going to be tough. On the other hand, he had a purpose in life for the first time in a long while.

The decision for Kerkin to travel to Spain first, before Turkey, was owed to the fact that Spain, like Turkey, was neutral in the war but was nevertheless a fascist regime. Spain offered in effect a kind of masking of intention from an allied country, Britain, to a fascist country, Turkey. The strategy for Kerkin was to first make initial connections in Madrid then set off for Istanbul Turkey.

Arrangements had been made for Kerkin to hitch a ride on a transport plane for British consular personnel traveling from London to Madrid. Kerkin never liked flying very much but knew that this would be the quickest way. Kerkin reminded himself that his papers were adequate, and that his language skills were sufficient, a mixture of Turkish and English to satisfy his role as interpreter for the embassy. This should satisfy the Spanish authorities. Kerkin was counting on it.

The following morning Kerkin boarded the plane in London in route to Madrid. The plane was Spanish, a G-ACYR Dragon Rapide, one of which had flown General Franco from the Canary Islands to Tetuan during the Spanish Civil War in 1936. The flight itself was for the most part uneventful. On leaving Britain, some British fighter planes had swooped over them, tilted their wings, and then flown away. Given his apprehension of flying, it was enough to put Kerkin at some unease but not so much that a good drink of Scotch Whiskey from an accommodating stewardess would not cure.

Upon arriving in Madrid the customs people looked at Kerkin slightly suspicious, but let him through without incident. So far so good Kerkin thought to himself as early afternoon approached. When he finally walked out of the terminal building Kerkin realized that there was someone following him. He quickly turned round to see a familiar face.

"I wanted to see how long it took you to detect me."

With relief to see it was his old friend Tavos Bedrosian, John acknowledged.

"Good work my old friend."

"Good to see you Kerkin."

Tavos had put a lot of weight on since Kerkin had seen him last. Nevertheless, Tavos's smiling face reassured Kerkin that this was indeed his old friend. Tavos had lived in Spain since just after the fall of the Armenian republic in 1921. Managing to survive the Spanish civil war, he held a high position with the Spanish Secret Service. Tavos motioned to a waiting attendant who came out and opened the door of a black government car. Inside the car, there was an acknowledgment between Tavos and the driver that what was being spoken should not be repeated elsewhere.

Kerkin and Tavos had worked together before, with the OSS. They had killed quite a few men deemed problematic. Kerkin preferred to not think about such previous work. This was actually a mild way of putting it. For Kerkin, to kill another man felt somehow hypocritical in the worse sense because after all, he was Armenian. What kind of right does he have to kill another man simply because of orders? How is he any better than the Turkish soldier that killed his family? He supposed that, like all races of men, some of these Turkish soldiers killed without remorse and even enjoyed the act. But many he thought, were like him, simply following orders and then trying hard not to think about what they had done.

Kerkin and Tavos were now away from the airport on the main road to the center of Madrid. Tavos pulled out some photos.

"Many children were taken and their families shot."

Kerkin viewed the photos carefully. They depicted groups of children off to the side of dead bodies, presumably the dead parents.

Tavos continued.

"The more European looking children would sometimes be adopted by German officers. Most though, were taken in by compassionate Turks or Kurds."

Kerkin continued to study the photos, paying particular attention to one little girl. He imagined that this could be John's sister Anna. Of course he knew it was not her, but the little girl in the photo, crying and looking very scared, provided an image of what Anna may have gone through. Kerkin knew that such an experience could make a child want to forget the pain. This in turn made them forget other parts of their past so that even if found, the child years later may have a kind of self imposed amnesia that prohibited them from remembering their Armenian origins. Kerkin considered that this was likely the case of Anna.

The car pulled up to a large hotel in downtown Madrid, the Hotel Del Mar. Tavos motioned to Kerkin.

"It's a nice place. After you have cleaned up, join me for dinner in the restaurant."

As the two men entered the hotel, Tavos also noticed that they were being watched.

Tavos smiled.

"Friends just keeping an eye out."

Tavos motioned to the hotel registrant to acknowledge that there would be no need for Kerkin to formerly check into the hotel.

As Kerkin entered the hotel elevator Tavos mentioned "We will talk some more ... about Turkey."

A half-hour later Kerkin entered the dining room. Like the rest of the hotel it was a very elegant place. The attire of everyone, both attendants and guests, was formal. Kerkin saw Tavos at a corner of the room and proceeded to his table. The men he had seen previously were still watching. They reappeared in what looked to Kerkin as wanting to be explicitly noticeable. These men wanted Kerkin to know that they, being some kind of agents, were aware of him.

From the look of them Kerkin surmised that they might have been Germans. This was not surprising given the large German consulate stationed in Madrid. The whole business was of no surprise to Kerkin and Tavos. Rather it was a kind of standard protocol between spies of this wartime era. They would want to know everything about foreigners who might be a potential threat.

"Let's order first. Allow me to recommend the Paella con Molluscs. It's a wonderful dish of rice and shellfish."

Kerkin knew well from experience to accept Tavos's advice on food. His old friend had never been wrong when it came to native cuisine.

The two men ate their dinner as a prelude to discussion about Kerkin's departure for Istanbul. Tavos lifted his glass to toast.

"To our families."

Kerkin hesitated for a moment to lift his glass, fighting back memories of his wife. Tavos took note then added on to the toast.

"May our dear families be strong through these difficult times. We will, God willing, get through even this pain. You will be leaving tomorrow morning. All the necessary arrangements have been made."

"Everything you have done ... seems that I owe you a big favor here."

Tavos took hold of his glass of wine.

"What is a favor between old friends?"

The two men clanked their glasses together.

"Come back safe Kerkin."

The next morning Kerkin arrived by car alone at the airport. He was shuffled out rather quickly then boarded the plane. Tavos watched at a distance as the plane took off then headed east, to Istanbul.

"Good luck my friend."

Tavos did not know that even as he thought to himself these departing words to his friend, a message was being sent to Istanbul that the man arriving by plane from Madrid, was a person to watch.

CHAPTER FIVE

Kerkin's plane touched down in Istanbul. As the plane taxied along the runway of Istanbul airport, Kerkin saw security guards posted along all of the entry ports, a reminder that Turks were distinctly aware of their place in the war.

Through consequence of a unique kind of fascism built on the principles of their national hero, Mustapha Kemal, known affectionately among Turks as Kemal Ataturk, Turkey was a place that had natural fascist tendencies towards Nazi Germany. The Turks however were extremely keen in diplomacy, owing to years of negotiating the decline of the Ottoman Empire.

A message from the air hostess came over the speaker system. In Spanish and Turkish she said, "Please have your passports ready. Identification and visas must be presented with your passport."

The passengers started to shuffle about, getting up from their seats, stretching their legs, and reaching for their luggage. Since Kerkin had sat in a window seat he couldn't get up until the man next to him did.

As the man began getting out of his seat Kerkin said, "Long flight huh?"

The man yawned and then stretched a bit before answering.

"Too long I think. But it's better than the train."

Kerkin and the man laughed a bit which opened up the conversation. Reaching for his luggage in the overhead compartment, the man asked Kerkin, "Are you Turkish?"

Kerkin tried not to look startled from the question then composed himself. Remembering the name on his Turkish

Passport he calmly reached out his hand to the man "Mustapha Jendaglu."

The man shook Kerkin's hand.

"Michael Ramirez."

Kerkin calmed down when he heard the Spanish name.

"Pleased to meet you. Is your trip business or pleasure."

Michael pulled down another piece of luggage.

"A little of both on this trip. I want to bring out some Tufa rock from eastern Turkey back to Europe. It's a marvelous stone. Do you know of it?"

Knowing that Tufa was a distinct stone from the regions of Western Armenia, Kerkin realized that he had engaged the conversation too much. For all he knew, Michael Ramirez could be an agent of the Turkish Secret Service, known as the National Security Service.

"I've heard of the stone. It's pink and gray, isn't it?"

"Yes that's right ... beautiful pink and gray tones."

Kerkin was now out of his seat. He motioned goodbye to Michael Ramirez, wondering if that was the man's real name.

Kerkin exited the plane in route to the international entry terminal. He sensed that someone was watching him, perhaps the Turkish National Security Service, alerted by Spanish sources. It would be difficult to know for sure as the Turkish National Security Service was probably mixed in with the regular airport security guards.

Given the war, the Turkish National Security Service was keenly aware that spies, both on the side of the Allies and the Axis Powers, were lurking about, especially since there was an imminent threat from Stalin. Russia had their attention on eastern Turkey all the way to the Mediterranean Sea. This was the former homeland of the Armenians before the massacres.[1] For this reason, it gave the Turkish National Security Service real concern.

The Turks were all too aware that Stalin had the perfect pretense for war. The massacres of the Armenians in 1915 were a blight on human existence and should therefore be brought to justice.[1] What better way for justice to be served than for the lands of eastern Turkey, that had been the Armenian homeland for some 3000 years, to be reunited with the Soviet Armenian republic. Of course for Stalin this was merely a pretense to gain access to the Mediterranean Sea.

Kerkin approached the passport control. Behind the counter was a customs agent that looked quite fierce with stern features accentuated by a thick mustache.

"Business or Pleasure" the customs agent asked.

"Business actually."

The customs agent looked at Kerkin with suspicion.

"What kind of business?"

"I am doing research for a Professor Senchalli."

"What kind of research?"

"On the Armenians ... their history."

"Wait here."

It's not the response Kerkin wanted to hear.

Did I say too much?

The customs agent returned with another man. Kerkin surmised that he was brought in for problem cases, a manager of sort. This was confirmed with his question.

"Why are you studying Armenian history?"

Here it is, Kerkin contemplated before answering the question. A suspicion has been raised. He had better cut off the curiosity in short order. Otherwise the mission to find John's sister would end right here. That was the good part. The bad part could land him in prison. Kerkin knew all too well that Turkish government officials get very nervous about anything Armenian, especially the history.

It was at this point that Kerkin wondered why on earth he had even brought up that he was in Turkey to do research on Armenian history.

Am I crazy?

At that very moment, Kerkin resolved to face the problem head on, now. Better he thought, to throw the worst at them. This way any further investigation will offer no further suspicion.

"Professor Senchalli is my research advisor."

Kerkin hoped that would cut off further questions. He was wrong.

"Are you in graduate school?"

"Yes ... Cambridge. I'm working on my PhD."

"Why is Professor Senchalli concerned about Armenian history?"

Kerkin forced himself to maintain an even demeanor.

Don't break.

"Do you know of the Professor's work?"

The question turned then on the manager. It was a strategy that Kerkin hoped would mitigate the situation. He tensely waited for the answer.

"Vaguely. His work on the decline of the Ottoman Empire was, in my opinion, a bit too far."

"Far?"

"Meaning that the empire fell solely to the complexity of race relations. It's too simplistic."

Kerkin found the manager's answer interesting, so much so that he reminded himself that he was being investigated. Still, he needed to follow up on the manager's question.

"Certainly ... though you must agree that race relations ... say between Muslims and Christians ... did play a significant role in the empire's decline."

"Significant yes ... I will give you that. Solely no. But ... you still have not answered my question. Why are you studying Armenian history."

Kerkin was brought back to reality with the manager's reminder of his original question.

"It's very much for the position you take ... or should I say ... that Professor Senchalli challenges you on."

The manager smiled at Kerkin.

"A very diplomatic ... I could say ... intellectual answer. I suspect you will do well in your studies."

"Well thank you."

The manager reached to shake Kerkin's hand.

"I am Dr. Bedros Safarglu."

Hearing the manager's first name, Bedros, was a dead give away to Kerkin that this man had Armenian origins. His surname was likely Safarian originally. Kerkin wondered if the manager knew that he was Armenian. It turned out not to matter except for curiosity sake as the manager gave the custom agent the okay to give Kerkin his passport back. As he left passport control, Kerkin paused with a glance to the manager.

"A pleasure to meet you."

"The pleasure is mutual. Good luck on your PhD."

Kerkin went outside and hailed a taxi. In perfect Turkish he asked the driver to take him to the Savoy hotel in Taksim Square. After the taxi began moving, Kerkin looked back and saw a black Mercedes sedan following his taxi.

The taxi curved around the ancient walls of Istanbul built by the Byzantine Empire in the days when it was called Constantinople. The Sea of Marmara ran just along the edge of the walls. Despite Kerkin's hatred for what the Turks did to the Armenians, he still admired the beauty of Istanbul, said to be the city set on seven hills. From a distance the great Mosque of Hagia Sophia, at one time a Byzantine church, could be seen. As they entered Taksim Square, the sound of the Muslim Imam's call to prayer could be heard. Kerkin was reminded that Turkey, despite it's call to secularism, was still at its heart an Islamic land.

The taxi stopped in front of the Savoy hotel. It was an old place but very elegant, and it was in the heart of Taksim Square.

As he got out of the taxi, Kerkin looked around to see the hustle and bustle of his surroundings.

Having spent time in Istanbul on a previous OSS mission, Kerkin especially liked Taksim Square. There was an energy here that could hardly be found elsewhere. Merchants lined the streets selling all kinds of wares from musical instruments such as an hour glass shaped drum known as the Dumbeg, to curved Turkish knives ornately inscribed with beautiful gemstones. There was also the savory shashlik meat being sliced thinly then wrapped in paper-thin bread that to Armenians was known as lavash.

Kerkin was determined that his first priority after checking into the hotel was to have a shashlik sandwich with a glass of fresh squeezed orange juice. The thought was pure pleasure for Kerkin until he noticed the black Mercedes sedan again. Kerkin made an effort not to notice as he paid and then thanked the driver. Walking up to the hotel entrance, Kerkin deliberately turned toward the black Mercedes sedan and smiled, his way of letting the Turkish National Security Service know that the game was on.

The next morning Kerkin headed off in the direction away from Taksim Square. He had decided that his first visit should be to the Historical Archives. Again, two men followed him from a distance. Approaching the Historical Archives Kerkin glanced back at the two men following him. He wondered if there would be a confrontation soon coming.

Kerkin entered the building. It was a dignified place, looking to be a couple of hundred years old. He took out papers as he approached a clerk. The clerk examined the papers then looked up at Kerkin,

"Doing research huh ... for Professor Senchalli? That man's interest in Armenians is dangerous these days."

Kerkin joshed "Indeed ... but what can a junior researcher do. The old man keeps me busy."

The clerk pointed Kerkin in the direction of tall doubled book stacks.

"You will find the old records back there."

Kerkin headed in the direction of the book stacks. The two men from the Black Mercedes were following him and had now come into the Archives. He could see them talking to the clerk. Kerkin knew he must move fast to get the information he needed. As he was able to read the old Turkish script, Kerkin quickly retrieved a catalog labeled 'Sasun Province, 1915'.

Having pulled the book from the stacks, Kerkin then disappeared into the recesses of the Archives. Finding a secluded spot he opened up the catalog. It was mostly a description of property collected from Armenians during the time, circa 1915. He looked specifically for anything associated with the name Avedisian.

Kerkin knew he only had minutes until he would be pulled away from the Archives. Quickly, he needed to find something, anything about the Avedisians. Then he saw their names, John and Anna Avedisian, children of Bedros and Elisabeth Avedisian.

For a moment Kerkin was reminded of his own family, that his brother and two sisters were killed, including most of his uncles, aunts, and cousins. Fortunately for him, his parents had seen what was coming and had made their way to America. Hardly anyone from his family had survived.

Kerkin purposely stopped his reminiscing to find out what he needed to know. He sifted through the information of property records involving a farm and meat packing business. Then he found something, the name of a Kurd employed by the Avedisians. The Kurd was responsible for helping in the bakery owned by Bedros Avedisian. His name was Kashan.

Kerkin continued to scan the Avedisian records but was abruptly stopped by the two men who had followed him. One man took the book from Kerkin's hand. The other put a German Mauser pistol to Kerkin's back.

"Follow us."

As they left the building, the clerk shook his head at Kerkin, confirming his earlier warning that information about Armenians was dangerous these days.

Endnotes
1. After 1948 defined as the Armenian Genocide. See Powers, Samantha, "A Problem from Hell": America and the Age of Genocide Harper Perennial (2003) paperback, 656 pages ISBN 0-06-054164-4

CHAPTER SIX

"How many times can I tell you? I'm doing research for Professor Senchalli."

Kerkin shouted to the Interrogator at the Turkish National Security Service station.

The interrogator slammed his fist on the desk where Kerkin was sitting. A harsh bright light swung overhead.

"Why send you to the eastern provinces? This is war time. Why now?"

The interrogator demanded an answer. Kerkin defiantly remarked back.

"You know his work. He wants to know what happened to the Armenians."

"What were you doing in Spain? We have a report that you met a man by the name of Tavos Bedrosian there. Are you also working for the Spanish Secret Service?"

Kerkin was impressed. Or was it fearful? At that moment he could not decide which. He had remembered the two German foreigners at the hotel in Spain. The fact that they had put a request for him to be apprehended in Turkey meant that he had to be extra careful now.

"No ... I don't work for anybody other than for the Professor. Tavos and I met in Madrid because as a child we grew up together. I was just trying to get information from him for my research."

"Where did you and this Tavos Bedrosian grow up?"

Kerkin knew this was a loaded question, intended to provoke him. He was determined not to allow it. No, he had been through rougher spots than this before. Kerkin told himself, they were just playing the game.

Hold on, to the end.

The interrogator considered why the man in front of him was there. They had received information from the German consulate in Spain that Kerkin had spent time with a high level official in the Spanish Intelligence Service. This was suspicious in itself, but the fact that the intelligence official also had an Armenian name made it even more suspicious.

"Why does the Professor persist in his lies about Armenians? Why doesn't he tell the truth ... that many people died and that the Armenians helped the Russians?"

Kerkin realized that he must be careful here not to reveal his sentiments about the Armenian people while at the same time not backing down from stating historical truths, as this would be expected of him from the interrogator.

"You know as well as I that the good Professor is not concerned with the party line of the Turkish government. He is an intellectual and by requirements of his job he must look at history, not from the position of what is convenient to hear, but what the facts speak and what they imply. It's as simple as that."

Though not ready to admit it to Kerkin, the interrogator was becoming intrigued with the conversation.

"What are you implying?"

Kerkin hesitated for a brief moment, knowing that his next collection of answers could well determine his fate of being put into jail or not.

He looked up at the interrogator through the swinging light.

"It's a well known fact that approximately three million Armenians existed in the eastern provinces, the Armenian villets as they were called, prior to 1915. What happened to all those people?"

The interrogator was quick to answer.

"Many people died, Turks and Kurds, as well as Armenians. It was war."

Kerkin was almost enjoying this makeshift debate of sorts.

"Why then are there Turks and Kurds still in these lands while Armenians are essentially negligible in these regions?"

The interrogator was a bit frustrated trying to search himself for an answer.

"It proves nothing."

Kerkin knew that his next statement would be provocative but couldn't resist.

"Then there is the matter of the eyewitness accounts and photographs of deportation and outright slaughter."

The interrogator knew he couldn't respond to these facts and so responded with a different argument.

"Why not just let the history go. Of course it's tragic what happened to the Armenians. I had many good friends of that race in the old days. But the old days are gone now. This is a new Turkey ... a Turkey of only Turks."

The interrogator had a worried look on his face.

"There is no room for other races as in the days of the heterogeneous Ottoman Empire. It's not necessary for the case of the Armenians. There are officially only about 70,000 of them left. Mostly now they live in Istanbul. No, it's the Kurds that are the trouble. They took over where the Armenians used to live and are constantly demanding for some kind of autonomy."

Kerkin could not stop himself from asking the obvious question.

"Why such fear ... of the Kurds ... their culture?"

"What is your business with the Kurdish rebels?" demanded the interrogator.

Kerkin looked at the interrogator through the glare of overhead light.

"I have nothing to do with the Kurdish rebels. It's like I already told you. I'm only going to the region of Sasun for research."

The interrogator fought back to restrain his agitation.

"Kurdish culture would eventually lead to a divided Turkey. It must not be allowed."

Although he didn't agree with the interrogator's conviction that Turkey should only be a place for Turks, Kerkin could understand the concern of the interrogator, that a divided Turkey based upon ethnic lines implied an eventual dividing up of the Turkish state. Once again though, Kerkin reminded himself that the situation, in which he currently found himself, was not an intellectual debate. What he said would determine whether or not he went to a Turkish jail.

Bite your tongue.

"I will not disagree with you that Turkey has a right to a sovereign state."

Kerkin hesitated before uttering the next phrase that he well knew could be his demise.

"However, that should not stop researchers such as Professor Senchalli from rightly doing what they know to do ... to find the truth as best it presents itself."

Kerkin knew the research angle was a weak one in the mind of the interrogator but it was all he could play at that moment. The interrogator obviously had already checked out Kerkin's connection to Professor Senchalli. That was a given. Otherwise Kerkin would already be behind bars instead of being interrogated. No, the interrogator must have suspected a Kurdish connection, that Kerkin was some kind of spy for the latest of the Kurdish rebellions. At least he didn't yet suspect his Armenian roots, Kerkin mused. That would surely bring trouble.

Pushing for a connection to the Kurds, the interrogator became more aggressive. He slapped Kerkin on the chin to rile him up. It worked. Kerkin did get riled up.

"Is that really necessary? I've told you what I know and what I'm doing here. Look, I'm not here to be part of yet another

Kurdish rebellion. My concern is that of Professor Senchalli. He is my adviser and therefore the one person I must satisfy."

The interrogator paced the floor a few times.

"Yes ... yes ... I know you work for Professor Senchalli. That's all fine and good. Go and flourish in your research. That means nothing to me."

The interrogator went silent. Now he chose his next words carefully, not because he had any immediate fear of the young would be researcher before him but rather because of the potentially far reaching fear that such intellectual inquiry brought. Deep down he did not really believe that this was a Kurdish conspirator. It was all he had though, at the moment. The other, more real conclusion, brought that inevitable fear, even though momentary, that comes with the truth revealed.

"I don't believe you ... that your intentions are purely intellectual. Are they purely intellectual?"

Kerkin now realized he was very close to being found out. He had to figure a way out of this or else end up in jail for who knows how long. So that was it. Kerkin stood up in a bold move to assert his conviction concerning what he was about to say.

"Very well then ... here is what you want to hear. I do believe in Professor Senchalli's work because as a Turk it's essential that you know your history, the good and the bad. If not then you are doomed to live a lie, something that will eventually come to haunt you in a terrible way. So many of our leaders are obsessed with covering up what happened to the Armenians. Why so much trouble over the truth? What are they so afraid of? I tell you this, if the cover up succeeds in the short term, it will come back to you with an unrelenting persistence in times to come. That you can be sure of."

"I think your dear Professor deludes himself with the work on Armenians. Why does he bother with a race that is long since gone?"

Kerkin joshed.

"Intellectual necessity I suppose."

Careful here.

Kerkin pinched himself; do not under any circumstances remind the interrogator that the professor was also Armenian.

The interrogator motioned at the door to the room.

"I need not have to warn you that these are troubled times in the eastern provinces."

The interrogator impatiently waited for a response to his question but Kerkin decided not to answer.

"Very well then ... go to Sasun for your research. But be aware ... any covert actions will be taken with utmost seriousness."

The interrogator opened the door to the room and motioned for Kerkin to be escorted out.

He gave Kerkin a last parting glance.

"Be aware."

The words of the interrogator rang clear for Kerkin, not only in the sense of a warning about paying too much attention to what is Armenian, but also to what drove Kerkin internally. Was he 'aware' in days gone by, back on the farm in Fresno? How was it that in the midst of such important decisions to be made, that he would greatly affect himself and his family, losing all confidence in himself? Was it fear that overpowered him, or just being so beaten down that he could not try any longer? Or was it something else entirely?

Kerkin knew that these questions could no longer be ignored if he wanted to move forward in the life that he wanted to accomplish.

CHAPTER SEVEN

The previous day had been torturous. Kerkin understood that the interrogator was just doing his job but the relentless questioning, that he did not appreciate. The agents that had originally apprehended him drove Kerkin back to the hotel about midnight. From their behavior, it was clear to Kerkin that they didn't want to be seen. At this point, Kerkin did not really care what their motivations were. He simply wanted to get out of the car, into his room, then to bed.

"Just let me off here."

The agent sitting next to Kerkin laughed.

"We're all tired these days."

Given that the only words of this man, besides what he just spoke, were at the point of a gun, Kerkin found the situation amusing.

"All in a day's job I suppose."

There was a kind of relief in the expression of the agent when he heard Kerkin's words, as if to acknowledge that his treatment of Kerkin was nothing personal.

Kerkin slipped into the hotel then through the lobby to the reception desk. He was grateful for the late hour, as he did not want to attract attention to his disheveled appearance. Approaching the clerk at the desk, Kerkin tried to seem nonchalant.

"My key please."

"Your room?"

"428."

The clerk handed Kerkin a key.

"Long day?"

In tired voice "Yes."

Entering the room, it hit Kerkin, as if the entire day collapsed into that moment. It wasn't that he was necessarily scared or even severely exhausted. Except for the slap in the face, he was not in the least physically hurt. There was something else, and it had to do, Kerkin suspected, with identity.

The entire day Kerkin had been under scrutiny to uncover some veiled identity. He was not even sure if the interrogator realized that. But Kerkin knew. He was living a life of someone else, a graduate student in this case, that was the student of an infamous professor, himself a kind of illusion of Turkish or was it Armenian identity. The whole experience in total, of defending an identity not his own, that was his collapse.

Early next morning Kerkin boarded a train in route to Adana. The distance from Istanbul was about 800 miles. Being a reasonably fast train, the total journey time was about a day's travel. It would be an all day all night trip.

As the train left the station, Kerkin glanced to the rear of the cabin to notice two men in business attire that gave away their trade. They obviously worked for the Turkish National Security Service. Kerkin was an expert at identifying these types of people. Given his recent interrogation, it was not unexpected to see them on the train.

What Kerkin was not prepared for was to see the numerous German businessmen as well. Although it was common knowledge that Germany and Turkey, while not being official allies, did work together exporting various minerals such as chromite from Turkey to Germany.

Kerkin was surprised to see this many Germans on the train, this late in the war. It gave Kerkin reason to wonder why this was happening. He supposed that it shouldn't be too much of a surprise that they worked together, given what had happened on his arrival in Turkey. The police here had certainly been asked by the Germans in Spain to interrogate him. That much was for certain.

As the trip dragged on, Kerkin became increasingly anxious about the Turkish National Security Service on the train, especially that they were talking with the German businessmen. What were they talking about he wondered? Could it be that these Germans were some kind of Turkish collaborators?

Kerkin had learned on his many missions to the Middle East that people and situations are not always, or even likely, the way they appear. For his part he could simply sit in his seat, waiting to see what, if anything would result from these conversations that might affect him.

The other alternative was to take the bold approach and introduce himself to the Turkish National Security Service agents and the Germans. Perhaps this would lead to some useful information. At the very least, it would get everything into the open, albeit with pretense.

Kerkin turned around and saw the Turkish National Security Service agents looking at him through the side of their eyes. He gave them a wave and they nodded back. The game was on. Boldly Kerkin stood up from his seat and walked in the direction of the Turkish National Security Service. He smiled slightly as he walked towards the two Turks. It was a tense moment as they acknowledge him with slight return smiles. Their smiles feigned as Kerkin reached out his hand and introduced himself. Trying to not give away their shock, the two agents reached out their hands in friendly gesture.

"I'm headed east ... for some research. But of course ... you know that."

Am I really doing this? Careful.

Kerkin could hardly believe what he was doing. It was not his usual style. Had he lost his senses due to the previous day's interrogation? Or, was he just bored? Whatever the case, he was living it now, this new identity of his.

One agent motioned for Kerkin to sit down beside them. The German businessmen observed the situation in apprehension. The agent spoke directly to Kerkin.

"What kind or research exactly are you doing?"

Kerkin braced himself.

"It's about the Armenians ... what happened to them."

There was dead silence for a few moments. Then, when the situation demanded some kind of break in the tension, Kerkin again spoke.

"Of course such a popular topic pays very well."

All present couldn't resist the obvious joke and so laughed at the absurdity of the situation. Everyone knew they were all playing a game here.

The train made it's way initially through the central part of Anatolia. This was the land west of Armenia, the land of the Hittites, a place from a history book he read what seemed to him, long ago. Then again, long ago was a relative term, exemplified by the history of the very terrain he now traversed. How many different kinds of people went through this place he wondered? No one knows their schemes and planning. They are all forgotten now.

Kerkin pondered the moment, that just as those ancient peoples of Anatolia schemed and planned and are now long forgotten, he sits here now, an Anatolian of Armenian origin sitting next to an Anatolian of Turkish origin, each one planning and scheming. Like those ancient ones, they too will be long forgotten.

Thoughts drifted into the very mountains of Cilicia. The train was now alongside the Ceyhan River of which Adana runs near. For Kerkin, Cilicia brought feelings of displaced patriotism because he knew that this was once part of Armenia with a centuries old flourishing Armenian culture.

Approaching the train station at Adana, Kerkin glanced at the two Turkish National Security Service agents. He decided to test them once more before getting off the train.

"This is where I get off."

The two agents tried not to look anxious but they knew all too well from the business they are in, that Kerkin was on to them. They played along nevertheless. The agent sitting next to Kerkin reached out his hand to shake.

"My best to you ... on your research then."

Kerkin shook the man's hand.

"Thank you."

A pleasant enough farewell Kerkin thought to himself as he made his way off the train. He of course knew that this was only a facade. The agents, whether themselves or others of their type, would be with him for a very long while.

Kerkin made his way off the train then hailed a taxi to take him to a hotel along the Ceyhan River. It was a beautiful drive along the river, simply gorgeous. The hotel Ceyhan, named appropriately from it's shoreline position on the river, at first sight was modest in appearance, but it did have an exotic oriental tradition of old Ottoman Empire days. This was what Kerkin wanted to experience. It had been too long since he felt that sense of appreciation for his culture. Now he had it back.

The hotel dining room was all too inviting as Kerkin entered. He was famished from the long train ride. A buffet table had been set to the far right side of the room. Kerkin did not have to question whether the food would be good. It was Turkish cuisine sure enough but really it was the food of Anatolia, the food of Armenians as well as Turks, a treasure both peoples held in common.

Kerkin was dishing up some rice pilaf onto his plate when he heard his name being called.

"It's Cemal."

Kerkin looked around to see a familiar face, a man he had not seen in five years, since the days just before the start of the Second World War. They worked together in northern Iraq, Kerkuk and Mosul to be specific, organizing Kurdish forces there in the event that Turkey would side with the Axis Powers in the war. Often they would cross the border into Turkey, the idea being to unite the Kurds of there with those of Iraq into a unified force that could hinder Axis advances into the Middle East.

Cemal diverted Kerkin's attention to a table across the room where a man sat alone eating.

"Abdul is over there."

Abdul and Memet were actually Kurds posing as Turkish intellectuals, a necessary ploy to divert the attention of the Turkish National Security Service. The meeting had been preplanned by friends of Kerkin with the specific aim to get information about John's sister Anna. Knowing that the Turkish National Security Service agents were watching, the three men specifically began speaking Turkish in a loud voice. They did not want to give away that they were not Turkish.

Once they had established their presumed identity, they huddled up for real discussion. Kerkin explained "I need to visit the old orphanage in Sasun. It's the one ... I can't remember the name."

Abdul interrupted.

"Heritish orphanage. Its now virtually abandoned. There may still be some attendants available that keep records."

Kerkin glanced at the Turkish National Security Service agents who were trying to overhear anything they could from the conversation. He spoke in a quiet voice back to Abdul.

"Are the people there vulnerable in any way ... that is for money?"

Memet came into the conversation.

"Likely not. You can expect some old faithful bureaucrats these days. Your best approach is to be concerned about children. This will get you further than bribes."

At sunrise the next day Kerkin headed off with Abdul and Memet on horseback northeast through Cilicia into the Western Armenia highlands. Their destination was the Heritish Orphanage in the Sasun province. If there was any chance for information about Anna, it could be at this orphanage.

The trek on horseback was arduous and yet for Kerkin deeply moving. He was now back in his beloved homeland. It took them three days traveling east to make the journey, finding camping places near rivers. On the third day they found themselves in the Sasun province, a very mountainous region. They had enjoyed camping out both nights. Kerkin in particular liked waking in the early mornings to see the rising sun.

Abdul had mentioned that local Kurds were restless in what seemed to be the makings of a rebellion against the Turks. Such rebellions had been going on ever since the Armenian massacres.[1] For their help in the massacres[1], the Kurds were promised the land of the Armenians. Once the Armenians were gone however, the Turkish government betrayed its promise, bringing to the Kurds a bitter resentment of the Turks.

The Turkish government constantly worked to suppress Kurdish culture as it once did to the Armenian culture. Ironically it was this repression of cultures that united Armenians and Kurds against the Turks. The Kurds were in the open while the Armenians remained hidden, posing as Kurds, and sometimes Turks.

Trekking up what seemed a long upward climb through a mountainous region of Sasun, Kerkin saw at a distance, on top of a ridge, a large building. Continuing closer he realized that they had found the orphanage. The building itself was old and clearly in disrepair. Surrounding the building were old vineyards that still appeared to be producing grapes.

Kerkin was surprised by strong emotions of his childhood. He had known many orphans, owing to the massacres.[1] Lonely memories came to mind. The place was almost deserted as Kerkin and his two comrades rode up. They dismounted their horses and entered through an old entryway. Kerkin could almost hear the voices of lost Armenian children. In fact now, there were no children at the orphanage, just a few clerks that managed records.

Kerkin approached one of the clerks. She was an elderly woman with a seemingly gentle disposition. Even though she appeared to be Turkish, Kerkin couldn't help but like this woman because of her natural kindness. He had seen women like this before, from his days at an orphanage.

The Turkish matrons usually did not care if any child was Armenian or Turkish, only that the child was a little boy or girl who had lost their parents. Kerkin understood even at a young age that such kindness went far beyond any kind of racial hatred.

"We are looking for a young Armenian girl."

The clerk smiled.

"Oh my boy ... they are all gone now."

The clerk explained how all the children were gone. During the period they were talking about, there were many girls and boys who were brought to the orphanage. These were the lucky ones because the orphanage was able, at least some of the time, to place children with people of their own culture. Most children though, were unlucky. They went straight to families that bought them. In the case of Armenian children, they were more often than not, sold to Kurds or Turks.

"There were so many little Armenian girls in those days. Can you tell me anything personal about her?"

Kerkin pointed to the side of his left wrist.

"She had a small egg shaped birthmark here."

The clerk looked at Kerkin's wrist apprehensively.

"I do remember such a mark. It was very unique. I remember thinking that the mark was for good luck. But I must tell you that there were a few children with such marks."

Kerkin became slightly encouraged that at least the clerk had seen some children with marks."

Do you know where those children might be ... anything about them?"

The clerk shook her head sadly.

"I'm so sorry ... in those days children were taken to all parts of the country ... even to other countries."

Kerkin's enthusiasm subsided dramatically.   Still the clerk continued.

"Many of the children did remain here in Sasun.   Perhaps there is a chance you will find her."

The clerk motioned to Kerkin to come close so she could whisper.

"There is someone that maybe can help you.   Come back tonight ... just outside.   I will introduce you."

Endnotes

1. After 1948 defined as the Armenian Genocide. See Powers, Samantha, "A Problem from Hell": America and the Age of Genocide Harper Perennial (2003) paperback, 656 pages ISBN 0-06-054164-4

Chapter eight

A full moon illuminated the orphanage from a distance as Kerkin approached the place where the woman had told him to be. She had told him a little about herself, that she was actually Turkish but didn't care what politics had happened. When little children came to her or soldiers found them, they were just children. Sometimes starving, many had watched their families die. It did not matter to her. She took them in and tried to care for them. Kerkin could plainly see that what the woman had tried to do was very hard. Maybe with someone like her, Anna had stood a chance.

Kerkin saw the orphanage clerk standing next to a man dressed in Kurdish Peshmerga attire. Owing to the Kurdish look of the man, Kerkin approached cautiously. The clerk smiled as Kerkin came close.

"It is safe here. This is Agha Bey, the Kurdish Sheik of Sasun."

Kerkin cautiously reached for Agha Bey's hand. He thought back to the days of the massacres when Kurds could not be trusted for good or bad.[1] Some would help the Armenians while others would take advantage. Kerkin couldn't help but be very cautious.

Noting Kerkin's caution, Agha Bey reached out his hand to Kerkin.

"In the past we may have been foes but now please ... consider me a friend."

Agha Bey looked past Kerkin at the two men standing behind him.

"To prove it I sent my two trusted friends to help you. Abdul and Memet have been with me since I was a boy. I wanted to make sure that you arrived safe."

Agha Bey looked over to the clerk.

"I have been told of your search for the Armenian girl. It would be an honor to help you try to find her."

Kerkin was taken aback. Abdul and Memet could have harmed him anywhere on the journey but hadn't. With the suspicion beginning to ease now, he became more confident with Agha Bey.

"Why would you help me to find her?"

Agha Bey knew the question all too well. How Kurds raped and massacred[1] Armenians. Even now he felt ashamed of the acts committed by his fellow countrymen. Was it for promises by the Turkish government that were never meant to be kept, or just rape and plunder? Agha Bey hoped at least it was the former. If not, then what can be said of the character of the Kurdish people?

Agha Bey came back to Kerkin's question.

"I will help you because it is right and honorable. If this girl, now a woman, is in Sasun or any other place we will find her. I assure you. Meet me tomorrow where the two rivers, the Tashan and Kerda, meet."

Agha Bey pointed in the direction of a ridge outlined by the moonlight.

"Just over that ridge."

As Agha Bey walked away from the Armenian he had just met, he thought back to his days as a boy, during the times of the Armenian massacres.[1] Those days still haunted Agha Bey. He had seen how his own people, the Kurds, participated in the massacres.[1] How he wondered, was it possible for what seemed a good man, to commit bad acts?

There was one incident in particular that he remembered from an Armenian village near the Kurdish camp where he lived. His parents told him not to go outside the camp because it was dangerous. That even though he was Kurdish, he could get hurt. Later he realized that his parents were not so concerned for his physical safety as they were for saving him from terrible sights that later would haunt him.

However, as children are, Agha Bey, simply Agha in those days, had to see what was happening. In the late hour he left the camp and quickly scurried down towards the Armenian village.

A boy should never have to see what Agha saw that day. Houses were on fire. People were running and screaming. Then he saw something that horrified him. His older cousin Jermak was leaning over a woman. She was crying. He did not understand in those days exactly what was happening, only that Jermak was somehow hurting the woman.

Knowing instinctively that what Jermak was doing was wrong, Agha ran over to try and stop him. Jermak's eyes were glazed over. He would not listen. He just told Agha "Get out of here ... its no place for a young boy ... get out of here."

Agha would not listen. He just kept watching. The rape that ensued was terrible.

~~~~~~~~~

The next morning Kerkin started the trek up to the ridge mentioned by Agha Bey the night before. It was an arduous climb with steep cliffs that had to be traversed carefully. Coming up to the top of the ridge Kerkin saw the two rivers. It was a beautiful sight looking down at the rivers in the early morning.

Kerkin saw Agha Bey at a distance with two other men dressed as Kurdish Peshmerga. They had three horses with them. Kerkin made his way towards the three Kurds. Agha Bey yelled out as Kerkin approached.

"These are two of my best men, Jamal and Sadik. Abdul and Memet will leave us here. Jamal and Sadik will accompany us in the search."

Both men, although tough in appearance, had a friendly approach to Kerkin as they shook his hand. Agha Bey motioned to a brown horse.

"This one is for you ... a strong horse for these mountains."

Kerkin walked over to the horse and stroked it's mane.

"A good horse indeed. Thank you."

Agha Bey acknowledged a welcome then motioned to Jamal and Sadik.

"We ride north."

The four men mounted the horses then followed Agha Bey along a trail that pointed north towards rugged looking mountains.

It was a fairly steep climb into the mountains. The air was getting cold. Soon they began riding over snow on the ground. More than once Kerkin's horse had to be coaxed to continue moving.

Agha Bey motioned to Kerkin.

"Do you remember the cold air?"

Kerkin joshed.

"Good memories of the clear Armenian air."

Agha Bey joshed back.

"Or is it the clear Kurdish air?"

Both men acknowledged the teasing yet serious nature of the remark since both Armenians and Kurds considered that it was their land. Armenians could mostly be found in the settled villages whereas the Kurds would live in the mountains. It has been said that at one time the Kurds and Armenians were the same people. Riding with Agha Bey, Jamal and Sadik, Kerkin wondered if perhaps this could be true. So much time had passed through history, who could say?

There had been discussions in years previous to the Armenian massacres of a rapprochement between Kurds and Armenians.[1] Political leaders on the part of Armenians and tribal leaders of the Kurds had held meetings to discuss some kind of mutual arrangement where Kurds and Armenians could live in peace.

The Ottoman Turkish government was of course always against such talks and would use any opportunity they could to thwart Kurdish – Armenian alliances.

Following World War I there were serious discussions, not only amongst the Armenians and Kurds, but also between the Allied powers as to how the regions occupied by Kurds and Armenians would be divided up equitably. A map was even drawn up which roughly placed the Armenians in the northern part of eastern Turkey and the Kurds in the southern parts. Lake Van would roughly be the dividing line for the two peoples. However, with the rise of Turkish nationalism and the retreat of the Allied powers in the region, such an arrangement never happened. Instead, the Armenians, what was left of them, were completely driven from the land and the Kurds were forced into a kind of ongoing rebellion.

The four men were just reaching the top of the mountain when they came to a snow-capped peak. Below were a valley and a small village. Agha Bey motioned down to the village.

"The first of many places we must check."

With reluctant agreement Kerkin acknowledged that it would not be an easy search and remembered what he had said to John back in New York, that there is only a chance Anna will ever be found.

How is it that I'm on this journey?

Was it a hopeless quest or was there something more, about himself that drove Kerkin forward on this journey? Whatever the answer, he was on the journey now and must inevitably see for himself where it would take him.

Endnotes
1. After 1948 defined as the Armenian Genocide. See Powers, Samantha, "A Problem from Hell": America and the Age of Genocide Harper Perennial (2003) paperback, 656 pages ISBN 0-06-054164-4

CHAPTER NINE

As they rode into the small village Kerkin noticed a tiny Armenian church, so tiny that it was actually more of a chapel. Sadly, it was terribly run down which indicated to Kerkin that there were either no Armenians left here or they were 'hidden Armenians'. That is, they reveal their Armenian identity only to each other. To do anything else was certain danger these days, not so much with the Kurds but with the Turkish government, that wanted to eradicate any evidence of Armenians on their ancient soil.

Kerkin reflected on why the Turkish government would have let him come here at all. His stated reason for coming was to research the Armenian past. He could only assume that the Turks wanted the history to come out their way and had granted him the search rights under pressure from the British and American governments. This could especially be the case since there was a chance of a Russian invasion on its boarders. The Turks didn't need to love the idea of the research but it kept the friction down for them.

"They call this place Tashen." remarked Agha Bey as they rode through a roughly paved road of sorts that ran through the middle of the village. Curious children ran up to the visitors as they rode their horses slowly through the town. Two women who were washing clothes were more cautious.

Two Kurdish men of the village seemed to acknowledge Agha Bey. They walked up to him as he dismounted from his horse. Agha Bey looked to Kerkin then to the two men of the village.

"We are looking for a woman ... an Armenian. She would have come here as a child and been adopted into one of our families."

The two men became distant when hearing the word Armenian as if to say "Do not say that word here. It only brings trouble."

Agha Bey persisted.

"She would have been brought here in 1915 as a young girl."

Agha Bey looked towards Kerkin.

"She is related to a friend of this man. It's important to him to find her."

Agha Bey allowed purposeful silence for just a moment, then pointed to Kerkin.

"This man will pay a reward for finding her."

Again Agha Bey allowed for a moment of silence so that the men could consider their options. He then spoke.

"Do you know of such a girl?"

One of the men spoke out forcefully.

"There is nothing to know. Many children were taken in those days. You are talking about a long time ago."

Agha Bey understood that there was no chance with these men for information. Still he thought they might know something but were not saying so he left them with a message.

"You have friends, people you know ... ask around. We would be most grateful."

Kerkin was starting to get a bit anxious now. Anyone could be a spy for the Turks.

Be more careful man.

Still, without asking questions, could there be any hope of finding Anna? Kerkin had to trust Agha Bey. He knew the Kurds, his people. With such thoughts in mind, Kerkin and Agha Bey approached two other men whom Kerkin believed could be hidden Armenians. Feeling bold and also frustrated, Kerkin came right out and asked the two men, "Are there any Armenians in this town?"

The two men looked at each other in a way that suggested they do not want to answer but they must. "There are no Armenians here."

Kerkin could tell by the man's accent that he was Armenian. Kerkin spoke to the man in Armenian.

"Tune Hyes?" which translated meant, "Do you speak Armenian?"

The man knew he was caught but tried not to act it out. Kerkin laughed out loud then put his hand on the man's shoulder as a friend.

"It's okay brother."

The man breathed a sigh of relief.

Seeing that the visitors were friendly and that at least one of them was Armenian, others from the village came forward.

Agha Bey again stated "We are looking for an Armenian woman."

Laughter came from the two women washing clothes.

"Which Armenian woman are you talking about?"

It now became obvious that this village was one of hidden Armenians. Jamal and Sadik were not surprised but only grinned at Kerkin's amazement to see all these Armenians posing as Kurds.

"We see it often."

Agha Bey shook hands with what seemed to be a village leader curious to know about the woman they were seeking.

"Tell us more about this Armenian woman."

Kerkin stepped forward.

"Her birth name was Anna. She would be about 35 years old now. On her left wrist there is an egg shaped birth mark."

The village leader looked with a questioned expression.

"I don't know of such a woman here. But, there are many villages like ours in Sasun."

Not really expecting to find Anna on the first try, Kerkin was not disappointed, especially when he saw that the villagers were bringing food. The village leaders motioned for the visitors to sit down with them to enjoy a meal together. These people had to be Armenian. The food and hospitality was all too familiar to Kerkin.

Fresh Armenian flat bread known as lavash was placed on the table. The men broke the bread together and ate. It was as delicious as Kerkin ever had remembered. Then appetizers called mezze of all kinds were brought to the table. Kerkin enjoyed a stuffed grape leaf dish, called sarma in the Sasun region, just as kebab was being brought to the table. Agha Bey took a skewer of kebab with some lavash. He put the meat on Kerkin's plate. The eating of the kebab commenced when all at the table clanked glasses of fresh tahn, a drink made from yogurt.

Although they had not found Anna, not even a clue, the day had been a good one for Kerkin and his new Kurdish friends. They had enjoyed a wonderful meal and the company of good people. For Kerkin it was a day to consider the fate of these hidden Armenians. He wondered if their grandchildren or even children would speak the Armenian language or even know that they were Armenian? Although he hoped they would, sadly he knew that this village would loose its Armenian identity, likely becoming known as Kurdish. It was the natural way of things when a people are not allowed to claim their identity.

The party went on late into the night. Kerkin pondered the good food and music, but to what purpose was this visit to this village?

Am I any closer to finding her?

The answer for Kerkin was NO. It was a reflection of his life somehow, at least that was what he thought. Simply a series of mistakes that had no meaning or connection, just random events that had directed his life to nowhere.

Kerkin now couldn't help obsessing about his failed life in Fresno.

How did it all go wrong?

Simply the randomness of life or was God somehow involved? Trying to find an answer to this question was maddening to Kerkin. There was simply no answer.

CHAPTER TEN

After four weeks of not having found any trace of Anna, the only course of action for Kerkin, however reluctant, was to press forward, deeper into the region of Sasun. It was not so much that he had expected to find Anna on the first try but at least had hoped for some kind of direction. His fears, mentioned to John in New York, again came to the surface of his mind.

Why not just give up now?

Should he deal with this question of continuing the search? He was tempted because of the more practical question, was this a course that Agha Bey and his Kurdish comrades were willing to take with him? After all Kerkin reasoned, why should they care about a lost Armenian girl? Before continuing he felt an obligation to find the answer.

Speaking directly to Agha Bey, Kerkin asked, "I do not have a right to ask you to go further. If you choose to continue with me then I shall be grateful but if you choose not, then I shall still be grateful to you for going this far."

Kerkin knew that he only had to ask Agha Bey this question. Jamal and Sadik would follow their tribal Sheik in whatever direction he chose. It was the Kurdish way.

Not getting an answer to his question, Kerkin followed Agha Bey and his comrades into another Kurdish town. It seemed to Kerkin that Agha Bey knew everybody. The village chief was met with the purpose of getting the word out about John's sister. Kerkin pointed out that he had come to talk with the sister of his friend, to know that she was alive. It was a promise to a dying mother. The village chief seemed to understand but still looked at Kerkin with suspicion.

The next day Agha Bey looked to the mountains.

"They say the mountains are the only friend of the Kurds. But now I must ask what it means to be a friend?"

Agha Bey looked directly at Kerkin.

"But now I see before me a friend. Can a Kurd leave the mountains? In the same way, I must press forward with you in this search."

Agha Bey pointed his horse in the direction of the mountains. "We go to the mountains of Sasun."

As they rode into the mountains Kerkin asked Agha Bey, "Why have we not yet seen any Turks?"

Agha Bey glanced back to what looked to Kerkin as nothing more that rough terrain.

"Be sure ... Turkish National Security Service agents are not far from us. They know these mountains well and unfortunately there are Kurds who would spy for money and will use them to hide from us as long as it suits them."

Kerkin glanced back.

"When it no longer suits them?"

Agha Bey picked up the pace. Kerkin picked up the pace with him while Jamal and Sadik stayed back. Agha Bey rode faster and faster. Kerkin followed in pursuit.

"What will happen?"

Agha Bey turned.

"You are Armenian. You know the answer."

Kerkin indeed knew the answer, one that he feared to face. Turks treat the Kurds with a certain kind of disdained respect. Perhaps it's that they both shared the same religion of Islam, but Kerkin suspected it was more about Kurds always fighting back, never giving in to the Turks.

For Armenians it was different. They did not fight back until it was too late, too late to stop the massacres.[1] The Armenians were tricked. They had helped the Turks put a new government in power and had a certain amount of trust for the Turks. It was a thought that Kerkin could not bare to face.

Why did we trust them?

True, there were always some, they called them Armenian Fedeyeen, the freedom fighters that would face off the Turks no matter the odds. But there were never enough of them to drive the Turks from the land. The result was eventual massacre with remnants hiding amongst the Kurds.[1]

The question of the fate of the Armenians started to burn in Kerkin's mind. Finally he stopped Agha Bey.

"Have you not heard of David of Sasun?"

Agha Bey smiled at Kerkin.

"At last you answer your own question."

Kerkin realized what Agha Bey had not been saying, that just as David of Sasun was an Armenian legendary hero who had single handedly fought back the Arab advance into Sasun back in the 9th century, so too there was an Armenian spirit that will fight back those who advance against them. Then he realized, that this journey is part of that spirit, of not giving up and not backing down to the Turks if and when they are confronted by them. Somehow, like David of Sasun, they would prevail.

The search for Anna continued for the next three months. Visiting different towns, talking to different people. In one town they thought they might be lucky. There was a woman who had a mark on her wrist. It was close but it wasn't where it should have been. Even then they thought of taking a chance but the woman didn't know the nickname. The journey took its toll on Kerkin.

How much longer?

Kerkin decided that he would give it just one more week and then the search would have to end. The mountain passes would be impossible to go through and he had no right to ask Agha Bey to continue.

It was a frustrating time going from village to village with no real clues as to Anna's whereabouts. Kerkin considered the real possibility that she was taken to another part of Turkey or even somewhere in Europe, Germany for example. Perhaps it was far worse, that she was killed early on. Certainly that was the fate of so many Armenian children.

Kerkin knew the Turkish National Security Service agents were biding their time. What were they thinking, he wondered, about this Armenian and three Kurds going deeper into the hinterland of Sasun. Would he be able to convince them that he was doing his research? Most likely they would consider the group as part of a new uprising. They would strike when ready.

So why this journey? Again Kerkin came back to John, the desperate young Armenian man that would not give up on his sister. Kerkin was finding his resolve to continue John's quest increasingly difficult.

How long can I possibly continue?

Endnotes
1. After 1948 defined as the Armenian Genocide. See Powers, Samantha, "A Problem from Hell": America and the Age of Genocide Harper Perennial (2003) paperback, 656 pages ISBN 0-06-054164-4

CHAPTER ELEVEN

Now deep into the interior of Sasun, Kerkin looked at Agha Bey.

"It seems that we may be running out of villages to search."

For Agha Bey this was a clear message that Kerkin was becoming disillusioned with the search and was about to give up. Ironically it was Agha Bey who, despite not having a vested interest in finding Anna, was nevertheless the most committed to the search. Something inside himself insisted that he must not let Kerkin give up, especially now. He felt some kind of intuition that Anna was close.

"We will give it another week then. Let us go to the village of Pezme."

Agha Bey was sure that any soldier wanting to sell a child during the massacres would not have dragged the child over great distances.[1] It was certainly possible that the child was sold to a Kurd. Unfortunately there was also the possibility that the child at some point was sold to a German or out of the Turkish area. If that happened, they were never going to find John's sister.

Agha Bey knew Pezme well. As a boy his father would take him to the nearby woods to hunt, there being an abundance and diversity of wildlife. It was a wild place. Agha Bey remembered one day when his father took him to hunt deer.

Agha Bey and his father were positioned for a kill when out of nowhere they heard a scowling growl. Agha Bey was completely caught off guard when he realized that the growl was coming directly from behind him. It was a leopard, ready for a kill. Too close to take aim with his gun, Agha Bey could do nothing but stand still, hoping that he would not become prey, or perhaps too frightened to do anything else. Amazingly the leopard stopped in its tracks, as if to give young Agha a fair warning that this place was for leopards to hunt. Acknowledging the moment, the leopard walked away with a growl. It was a defining moment for the young boy.

Agha Bey pointed to his right.

"The gathering place of Pezme is over there. Follow me."

Kerkin, Jamal, and Sadik followed Agha Bey to what seemed to be a heavily wooded area, nothing at all that could be expected of a settled village. It was only when they rode deep into the woods that the situation became clear. There, in the middle of a thick wooded forest, was a small lake. Kerkin took notice of the beauty of the place, owing in large part to the quaint village that followed the lake perimeter. They had arrived at the village of Pezme.

Kerkin followed Agha Bey to the village apprehensively. There was something about this place.

Could Anna be here?

Probably just a feeling of coincidence, Kerkin thought. On the other hand this entire journey, starting in New York with the first meeting with John, had more than once suggested to Kerkin that there was some kind of meaning beyond just finding Anna, almost a kind of spiritual relevance that would have purpose years later.

A group of villagers from Pezme had gathered to meet the newly arrived visitors, for whom Agha Bey spoke for. One such villager was Kalesh, a skinny young man, 18 years of age, who listened intently about what Agha Bey had to say, especially about the woman for which the reward was being offered. She had a birthmark and a nickname.

Could this be his mother, Kalesh thought? Although she never would tell him about her past, his mother did admit to a nickname and the birthmark, she could not hide. It always bothered Kalesh that his mother would not confide in him.

She always said, "One day I will tell you."

Was it something so terrible that she couldn't even let her son know about it? Kalesh's father did not help either, but that was to be expected from a man that beat his wife regularly. Kalesh hated his father for this.

Kalesh waited until dark to approach Agha Bey. He thought the best time to ask questions would be during festivities in honor of the visitors. The village, like many of the others villages they had been to, was poor. However having visitors, especially Agha Bey, who many remembered and whose father was very admired, was a time for celebration.

The night was cold and crisp. Kalesh approached Agha Bey to ask him about the woman they were seeking. What was her nickname? Who were they looking for? Agha Bey refused to give the nickname. When Kalesh asked why, Kerkin interrupted.

"If we tell the name then certain people could take advantage, just making up a story that they have the woman we are looking for."

Kalesh could readily see that Agha Bey and Kerkin were waiting for an answer. They wanted the nickname, so Kalesh gave it.

"Dafi Tuti."

Even just hearing the nickname after so many months of searching, gave Kerkin reason to laugh a bit. It was funny sounding to him and did not at all remind him of Kurdish or even Turkish. Kalesh did take notice of Agha Bey and Kerkin's reaction to the name. There was some kind of connection here.

Agha Bey stayed poised as he asked Kalesh if they might speak with his mother?

"My mother will never talk about this. Then there is also my father."

"Could some money change their minds?"

Kalesh raised an eyebrow.

"Not likely for her, but my father will make her."

Kalesh cut his answer short, owing to embarrassment of his father's abuse of his mother. Without saying more, Kalesh pointed in a direction, north, along the lake perimeter.

"Follow me."

Kalesh lead the visitors to his house, which was just about a five minute walk from where they started. The house was slightly run down in appearance suggesting to Agha Bey that Kalesh's father was a man of little respect for not only his wife, but also his family's well being. Kerkin thought similarly and saw it as an opportunity to get the information they needed. Kalesh motioned for everyone to wait outside while he asked his parents about the situation.

The door opened with a man, smiling in a way that suggested he intended to take advantage. Kalesh pointed to Agha Bey and Kerkin.

"They want to ask mother some questions ... about her nickname."

Kalesh's father suddenly reacted.

"Go away."

Kalesh took his father's response in stride as if scripted.

"There is a reward. They have come from a long distance."

Kalesh's father suddenly smiled.

"I am Bedosh."

From the crooked smile on Bedosh's face it was clear to Agha Bey that the jig was up.

"My son tells me that you are looking for a woman with a birthmark and a nickname that is my wife's. There is money involved?"

Agha Bey carefully responded.

"There is money if there is information. We must be cautious."

Smiling again as to take advantage.

"Of course ... this is understandable. Please then come into my home for a meal my wife even now has prepared for you."

Agha Bey paid attention to the appearance of the house interior. Even though modest, it had the look of someone who cared about the family. This gave Agha Bey immediate appreciation of the woman bringing food to the table, Kalesh's mother.

Kerkin did not care about the condition of the house. Instead he focused on the appearance of Kalesh's mother. She did not look very much the way John described. But then that was a description of a little girl and this was a grown woman. If Kerkin had to describe her, she was a typical Anatolian woman in her mid thirties, typical here meaning dark brown hair, light to medium complexion, and beautiful almond shaped eyes.

Bedosh motioned for the men.

"Please sit down and enjoy a meal with us."

Hearing these words with deceitful tone increased Agha Bey's irritation of Bedosh. He thought to himself how easy it would be to put a knife in this man's throat.

The meal was simple but delicious. Kalesh's mother had prepared a lamb stew along with a salad of tomatoes and a local cucumber called the Gouta. Kerkin knew this cucumber well from his days as a boy. It was an indication that there may be an Armenian connection. But then he reminded himself that all peoples of Anatolia, be they Kurd, Greek, Armenian, or Turk, eat the same food. Really, except for their religion and language, these peoples were much the same.

Bedosh tore at a piece of bread then asked Kerkin directly, "Is my wife the woman you look for?"

Kerkin purposely did not look at Bedosh. Instead he focused his attention on Kalesh's mother.

"The woman we look for has a brother who also has a nickname. Do you know this nickname?"

Kalesh's mother looked down at her plate in a conscious refusal to answer the question. Bedosh became impatient with his wife.

"Answer the man!"

Scared and almost crying she looked at Kerkin.

"His name was Nufi Tuti. I have never stopped thinking of him."

Kerkin looked intently at Kalesh's mother and wondered in utter amazement just how it came to be that at last he had found John's sister. In cautious speech he addressed her by her Armenian name.

"Anna."

Kalesh watched his mother break down at hearing the name.

"Where is John? Where is my brother?"

Endnotes
1. After 1948 defined as the Armenian Genocide. See Powers, Samantha, "A Problem from Hell": America and the Age of Genocide Harper Perennial (2003) paperback, 656 pages ISBN 0-06-054164-4

CHAPTER TWELVE

Bedosh stared blankly at his crying wife. For him there was no emotion concerning the whereabouts of her brother or even that she had a brother. Of course he knew she was Armenian when he bought her from the Turkish soldiers so many years ago. Thoughts ran through Bedosh's mind. She was just a child then but still useful in the house after his first wife died. How much will they offer was the main question here? But what was it that they wanted?

The only real concern of Bedosh was how to get the most money? Kerkin was the one he must manipulate. He had the money. Agha Bey could be a problem. Bedosh was a bit scared of him. Kerkin seemed to trust him. Could he play off the Armenian and the Kurd? Not likely. Maybe a deal could be made with the Turkish army. Then he would get the money and lose nothing.

Finally Anna had stopped crying. Agha Bey stood up and motioned for Bedosh to go outside with him.

"Kerkin needs to talk with her ... in private."

Bedosh was taken aback by this course of action as he could see that Kerkin controlled the money. He began to think that Agha Bey and Kerkin were maybe playing with him. His wife was of no concern to him. No, he must find a way to get the most money for whatever they wanted from his wife.

For now Bedosh had decided to go along with the request. He smiled at Kerkin and Agha Bey, then motioned for Kalesh to come out of the house with him. Bedosh then looked directly at his wife.

"Careful what you say."

Seeing the crooked smile on his father's face infuriated Kalesh. Agha Bey took note of this. The three of them left the house, leaving only Anna and Kerkin remaining inside.

Kerkin was careful not to make Anna feel uncomfortable. Even though she was originally Armenian he knew that this woman had lived the life of a Kurd. Her Muslim religion prohibited her from any kind of physical contact with a man not part of her family. Kerkin looked directly at Anna.

"How has life been for you here?"

Anna looked away from Kerkin.

"You have seen my husband ... how he is."

Kerkin tried to pull Anna's attention back, but realizing that it would be difficult, accepted the reality that he must ask questions with the limited attention available. Standing up for a moment and walking over to the earth kiln stove, Kerkin again posed a question.

"How long have you been married?"

Anna starred at the ground.

"I have known him since that day ... the day the Turkish soldier took me."

Anna fought back the tears.

"That day they took me from John and I saw my mother die."

Kerkin was hesitant to ask the next question. Anna sensed what was on Kerkin's mind. It prompted her to focus attention on Kerkin before answering.

"I was so little then ... I could not understand the purpose of this man."

Kerkin's thoughts raged over what he assumed Anna would say next.

Anna wiped a tear from her face.

"There were a lot of girls then ... just like me. We had to do what they told us. If you did not ... then you were punished. One girl I knew from before ... her name was Hripsime ... tried to run away but they caught her. They beat her that night. Hripsime was never the same after that night. The things I saw back in those days ... terrible. I have tried to be a good wife. My son Kalesh is a gift for that I think."

Anna hesitated for moment, feeling her self-created tension of the moment.

"Do you think my son is a good man?"

Kerkin looked sympathetically at Anna.

"He is a fine young man. The Armenian spirit runs strong in him."

Anna smiled when she heard Kerkin's words.

Now that he had Anna's attention again, Kerkin went back to the table.

"I have come to take you out of this place."

Kerkin was taken aback when Anna answered.

"I know that John made a promise to our mother ... to look after me. I have prayed that one day he would come for me."

Anna's face became resolute.

"I will go with you ... but only if my son comes too."

Kerkin had not considered such a complication. Of course he knew the son must come too, but until entering Pezme he never imagined to even find Anna, let alone her son. What would John do when he found out that not only was his sister alive but that he also had a nephew? A smile came to Kerkin's face.

"Your brother's happiness will increase all the more when he sees his nephew. Of course your son will come with us to Armenia."

Anna was surprised.

"Armenia ... how is it possible to go there?"

Kerkin thought about the seriousness of the question. Indeed, how will they get to Armenia? He knew that the Turkish army was as close as they wanted to be. They were ready to pounce at any time. Then there was Bedosh to deal with. Kerkin intuitively knew that he would be trouble, one way or another. He was the type that would never be satisfied with the arranged terms and would in the end betray.

For now Kerkin reassured Anna.

"Armenia is not so far from here by horse. Once in Armenia my associates there will take good care of you and Kalesh. Soon, you will see John again. If you then want to go to America, John will be able to arrange everything."

Anna put her hand over her mouth. A tear ran down her face at the thought of seeing John after so many years of never thinking it possible.

Anna's face then turned serious.

"What of Bedosh? How will you get him to let Kalesh and I go with you?"

Kerkin pulled out some money from his pocket.

"This will take care of him."

Anna looked at the money.

"Be careful of him. He is a man that is never satisfied."

Agha Bey looked at the lake. The shine of moonlight gave its surface a perfect stillness. He took in the moment before speaking to Bedosh.

"We want to take Anna back to her family. You are young enough to find a new wife and we will give you money."

Before answering, Bedosh smiled and began thinking how he could manipulate the situation.

"What do you want with her?"

Agha Bey purposely hesitated to answer. He then looked over at Kalesh to give the boy a sense that all would be well.

"We want to take her to Armenia ... to be with her family."

Bedosh continued to smile.

"You wish to take her away from me. How can I as a man allow this?"

Agha Bey could no longer restrain his contempt for Bedosh. For him this was a man that only sought to take advantage of others. Bedosh being Kurdish was particularly disgusting for Agha Bey. Despite these irritations, Agha Bey was still willing to work with Bedosh, if for nothing else out of respect to his son Kalesh. However, Agha Bey determined that if Bedosh made problems then he was also willing to end the man's life. He would gladly do this without hesitation.

Agha Bey became resolute to Bedosh's question.

"We will take her to Armenia and for that you will get money."

Bedosh's smile turned to seriousness.

"How much money?"

Kalesh was incensed at his father's emphasis on the money and obvious lack of love for his mother. It was not that he expected anything different from him. He had long ago lost all respect for his father. Still, a son sees himself as an extension of his father. For Kalesh this was a suffering thought that he could hardly bear. He watched his father respond to Agha Bey's question of how much money. Agha Bey was resolute in his answer.

"Plenty of money. You will not be disappointed."

Bedosh still questioned.

"You do not tell me how much."

Agha Bey was now noticeably irritated at Bedosh.

"Kerkin will tell you how much."

This was enough for Kalesh. Even though he was glad that his mother would be free in Armenia, he was still disgusted that his father would stoop to such a low level as to sell his mother. But then again, he considered just how his mother was brought to his father in the first place, essentially sold to him as a slave.

One of the villagers came running.

"Turkish troops have been spotted by Kurdish Peshmerga just outside of Pezme. All total there are about 100 men, fully equipped for fighting."

The Turkish troops, especially trained for guerrilla war against the Kurdish Peshmerga, had been assembled in response to frequent Kurdish uprisings since the 1920's. Although none of the uprisings had been successful, they had come close to succeeding. This had brought recognition by the Turks that they must fight using the same tactics as the Kurdish Peshmerga fought, that is, guerrilla war.

At sunrise the next morning, Agha Bey loaded up supplies on the horses. The villagers had been very accommodating. Although needing everything for the long winter ahead, they were able to supply vegetables and flour for making bread.   Kerkin glanced over to Agha Bey as he was paying money to Bedosh. He counted 1000, 2000, 3000, 4000, 5000 Turkish Lira.

Kalesh had told his father that he would serve as a guide through the mountains and then return. He did not expect to keep that promise. The previous night and out of range of Bedosh's hearing, he had already agreed with his mother that he would go with her. There was the danger that Bedosh would follow after them to try and bring his son back, but Kalesh had no intention of returning.

Bedosh had put the money in his pocket. He no longer had the fake smile on his face. Bedosh no longer needed to manipulate. He had what he wanted and would simply purchase another wife. There were always young girls available for marrying.

Anna came out of the house, ready for the journey. Kalesh, also ready for the journey, glared at his father. Bedosh sensed the disdain.

"You will see the value of money someday."

Kalesh could not respond to his father. He only continued to glare.

As they rode out of Pezme, Kalesh looked over at his mother.

"How does it feel to be Armenian again?"

She looked at Kerkin and the accompanying Kurds ahead of them.

"I was only an Armenian as a little girl."

The discussion was suddenly cut short when a Kurdish Peshmerga rode up fast to Agha Bey. Pointing to the west, deep into the woods surrounding Pezme, the Kurdish Peshmerga addressed Kerkin and Agha Bey.

"Be careful in that direction. We have spotted about 100 Turkish troops."

Several hours later and 20 miles away, Colonel Tashkent with his Turkish troops were camped on a hill. A rider appeared. He was dressed as a Kurd. The man was told to step down from his horse. Five soldiers surrounded him.

"I want to report Armenian spies in Pezme."

Colonel Tashkent viewed the man suspiciously.

"What is your name?"

"I am Bedosh."

CHAPTER THIRTEEN

It had been a two-week journey on horseback from Sasun. Agha Bey had been pushing the group to a fast pace through the mountains of the historical Armenian provinces.

The stamina of Anna and Kalesh amazed Kerkin. It testified to the feelings of Anna for the world she left. Kerkin alluded to this when he asked Anna "Are you happy to have left that village?"

The question was painful for Anna, her answer even more so. "Yes. My life was miserable there. They all supported my husband and would watch everything I did. There was only one person who helped me. She taught me to read and write in secret. The books were in Turkish but still ... they gave me a view of a world unknown to me. Unfortunately we were caught one day ... reading. Bedosh beat me for it ... for reading. I prayed for a way of leaving that place."

There had been some time to talk about what would be the best place for Anna and Kalesh to live. Soviet Armenia or the United States were the main choices. Kerkin knew that the United States would be John's choice but it was important to consider Anna's welfare. The Soviet government was welcoming Armenians from throughout the Middle East to settle in the Armenian Soviet Socialist Republic. In fact, Anna had heard the stories of the Soviet Union encouraging people to return.

Kerkin had mixed feelings about taking Anna and Kalesh to Armenia, as he was a staunch anti-communist. Nevertheless, Soviet Armenia would be for Anna and Kalesh a place of refuge where they would be with people of their own kind. John had told Kerkin that there were relatives in Yerevan, the capital city of Soviet Armenia, that would help.

Kerkin had not fully thought out the process of relocating Anna. In retrospect, he never really believed Anna would be found. Of course, John had no idea when talking of his relatives, who exactly these relatives would be helping. Anna almost certainly would be acceptable, but Kalesh being half Kurd, could prove to be more of a challenge for convincing the family. Still, knowing John, Kerkin knew that the problem would be solved. Kerkin just had to get them to Armenia.

Thus far they had managed to outrun anybody that might be following, sleeping very little, just enough to let the horses rest. Most nights Agha Bey, Jamal, and Sadik, took turns keeping a lookout on their small camp. They hadn't seen anybody pursuing them but the thought of Turkish troops somewhere near made them nervous.

A few times it was very close. Once they had no choice but to confront two Turkish army scouts who came upon the group. They had found a convenient place to hide but the scouts were well trained and on fast horses. The scouts had their pistols out, telling everybody to halt.

Kerkin moved off to the right. The scout fired his gun at Kerkin, just missing due to the scout's horse moving at a crucial moment. This probably saved Kerkin's life because it allowed Agha Bey to seize the initiative, taking out his knife, and then sending it into the heart of the scout. Jamal and Sadik immediately followed suit, taking the other scout by surprise with their knives. It was all over in less than a minute.

Kerkin had some regret for killing the scouts, but it was the only way. Otherwise the scouts would have alerted the Turkish army to the group's position and that would have meant certain capture.

Anna was in near shock at the sight of the dead Turks.

" I am scared." was all she could say.

Kerkin could see that Anna was badly shaken by the experience. Perhaps he thought, it took her back to the terror of 1915.

For the rest of the day they distanced themselves from where the soldiers had been killed. Coming to a clearing Kerkin halted his horse ahead of the rest of the group. It happened to offer a vantage point to the ancient city of Ani. Tall walls surrounded the city's large perimeter.

Ani was the ancient capital of Armenia during the Bagritid dynasty years of approximately 850 – 1050 AD. It was known in those days as the city of 1001 churches. Since that time it had seen many devastations from conquerors to earthquakes. What remained were the ruins of this once great city. Churches mostly, and a large cathedral built entirely of the pink-grey Tufa rock, were found everywhere in the region.

There was not enough time to go into the city proper, as the Turkish army was sure to be following them since Sasun. They could be coming up fast behind them. Kerkin could only appreciate from a distance what once was Armenia in its days of glory.

Agha Bey and Kerkin began discussing the next course of action. Kerkin wanted to go into the nearby city of Kars to get supplies. Agha Bey did not like the idea because Kars was too close to where the incident with the Turkish scouts had occurred. They needed more distance from the Turks.

Going to Kars also meant taking a detour away from the Armenian border. That the Turkish army was probably so close now, going into Kars indeed risked capture. This was Agha Bey's persistent argument. Better he thought, to continue on towards an achievable entry point into Armenia.

Kerkin argued his position.

"We risk loosing our strength if we don't have proper food. Look at Anna. She needs better … more food. Without supplies we will not be able to go any further. Already our food has nearly run out."

Neither man was able to persuade the other. Acknowledging that it was ultimately Kerkin's decision, Agha Bey relinquished the argument.

"I warn you though. We most certainly risk capture in Kars."

A bustling border town, Kars had a distinctly different culture from other Turkish towns. The difference resulted largely from the years of Russian influence during their occupation from the 1800's through 1920. Turks recaptured the city from a fledging Armenian republic that itself had inherited the town from the defunct Russian Empire.

The destination of interest for Kerkin was the Town Bazaar. There they would buy food and warmer clothing that would be necessary in Armenia's cold mountains.

Making their way through Kars towards the Bazaar, Agha Bey had the feeling that they were being followed. He glanced back, then at Kerkin with alarming thoughts.

Someone is watching us.

Kerkin glanced back to see Agha Bey's concern.

"Look … I know you don't like the idea of being here but the Turkish army is still a ways off. We know that for a fact."

Agha Bey glanced to his left. Someone appeared to have just gone behind a crowd of people. Perhaps it was just his imagination, he couldn't say. Still, there was the lingering suspicion. Kerkin sensed this.

"Who are you looking for?"

The question gave rise to just what was bothering Agha Bey. Glancing again to his left he saw, just for a moment, the face of a man he had seen before. It looked a lot like Bedosh. But how could this be? Agha Bey reluctantly answered Kerkin's question.

"I think it's Bedosh."

Kerkin was dismayed.

"But why would a Kurd side with the Turks?"

Agha Bey sighed.

"His kind only looks to take advantage."

CHAPTER FOURTEEN

Making their way through the Bazaar, Kerkin told everyone to stay close. It was a tense situation for Kerkin as he pushed to enter the city of Kars. If anything happened here then the responsibility was entirely on him.

Agha Bey was preoccupied with the possibility that Bedosh was somewhere close. Kerkin lead the group and Agha Bey guarded the rear. The two men had agreed that if any danger presented itself they would immediately close ranks and get out fast.

Under different circumstances the Bazaar would have been a welcomed sight to Kerkin. People were crowded tightly in the Bazaar. All sorts of food and wares were available: fruits and vegetables, knives, guns, jewelry.

The bazaar was really a very long street with shops on all sides. Shopkeepers were coming out all the time to ask them to test their wares. It was a scene that Kerkin had seen many times throughout his life. Even though hectic and stressful, the ambiance of the place was reassuring for him. It was what he knew.

So far so good as they made their way to the first of the supplies they needed, dried fruits. Because Kerkin and Agha Bey were watching over the security of the group, it was left to Jamal and Sadik to take on the job of making the deals for the supplies. They bought lavash, a kind of flat bread from the region that was hearty and would last a long time, qualities in a food that were especially necessary for the rest of the trip.

Kerkin had told Jamal and Sadik not to worry too much about bargaining. He had plenty of money. Time was more of the essence now. Despite this, it was accepted practice that a deal should be made for anything bought. The traders might have been suspicious if they didn't bargain for the products a little bit. Fixed prices at the Bazaar were simply not imaginable.

Sadik went to one merchant while Jamal approached another. The merchants were well aware of this collusion between Sadik and Jamal. They prepared accordingly. It was likely that all the merchants themselves were colluding, a common practice at the Bazaar.

Jamal tasted a dried fig.

"Is it grown in Kars?"

The merchant smiled.

"All wonderful fruits come from Kars."

Jamal acknowledged the friendly attitude of the merchant respectfully but knew that this was probably just a ploy to sell figs. He could not show too much enthusiasm, otherwise he would not get the best deal. Jamal looked aside to another table to put the merchant on notice that there will be no advantage taken of him today. Glancing back at the figs in front of him, he asked in the most unenthusiastic way he could.

"How much?"

The merchant knew the game was on, so he bid a high figure. He took a bag and began filling it with figs.

"A full bag … 15 Lira."

Jamal tasted another fig.

"Not so sweet. I will give you 5 Lira."

The merchant's disposition became disappointed.

"How can I feed my family for such a low price?"

Jamal had seen this ploy so many times he fought back not to laugh. Even in this game such a reaction would be disrespectful. Instead his face became solemn.

"May Allah bless your family ... but I too must feed my family. At 15 Lira my family will starve."

The merchant glanced over at Sadik, making sure Jamal noticed.

"Yes ... I see your poor starving brother over there."

Jamal again fought back a laugh.

"My family can still eat for 8 Lira."

The merchant, shaking his head, started to pour out the figs from the bag.

"May neither of our family's starve ... 12 Lira for a full bag of figs."

Jamal now posed a sincere look.

"May both our families prosper ... 10 Lira."

The merchant started to pour some figs out of the bag. Jamal wondered if his price would have to go to 11 Lira? His disposition was one of stillness. The merchant watched Jamal, looking for any sign that Jamal would go to 11 Lira. He then considered Jamal's friend or brother or whomever, just down from him. Likely he was striking a similar deal. The point in the merchant's mind was that these two were working for the best deal. Maybe even now the price at the other table was being negotiated to less than 11 Lira.

The merchant told himself that he must close the deal now before the price at the other table was revealed. He stopped pouring figs from the bag then smiled at Jamal.

"We both must provide for our families. By the mercy of Allah, I will sell you a full bag of figs for 10 Lira."

Jamal could now let down his guard but still not too much, as the game was not yet over. Still, he smiled at the merchant.

"By Allah's benevolence I will pay 10 Lira. Do you have enough for 5 bags? "

The merchant glanced back to a big basket.

"Plenty of figs in there."

The merchant started to fill bags with figs.

"So tell me ... how does your brother know the price you have?"

Jamal laughed.

"Ah ... a family secret."

The merchant laughed as he set a bag of figs on the table. Of course the truth of the matter was that both Jamal and Sadik knew the going rate for the price of figs. They agreed ahead of time that if a better price could be arranged then a sign would be given. Since the merchant likely knew this himself, both he and Jamal were satisfied with a mutual laugh about the matter.

Jamal walked back to where the others were, bringing with him a big bag containing the 5 smaller bags of figs. Agha Bey took a fig from one of the bags. His manner was highly agitated as he ate the fig. He motioned for Jamal to glance left.

"They are here."

Jamal glanced into the crowd to notice suspicious looking men, suspicious because even though dressed as Kurds they had the look of Turks.

To notice such a difference was a trait that a Kurdish Peshmerga had to possess if he was to survive and ultimately prevail against the Turks. There were just too many Turkish soldiers and not enough Kurds to fight them. The only way for the Kurds was to fight smarter. But the Turks were smart too.

Jamal estimated there were about 10 Turkish soldiers in the crowd. The rest he figured must be outside the Bazaar in full uniform. Otherwise, too many soldiers in a crowded place like the Bazaar would create notice and with that, certain danger from the many Kurds around them. The Turks knew that even 100 Turkish soldiers were no match for all the Kurds in Kars.

Kerkin walked up to Jamal and Agha Bey in the most unassuming way he could. He took a fig then glanced into the crowd.

"Are they ready?"

Jamal handed a fig to Kerkin.

"Peshmerga match them about evenly in strength."

Kerkin then noticed what he thought were Kurdish Peshmerga in the crowd. But then he couldn't tell if they were Kurds or Turkish National Security Service agents posing as Kurds. All total he counted about 20 fighting men. He figured it was about 10 on each side.

Kerkin started to eat the fig.

"What about Bedosh?"

Agha Bey glanced forward. There before Kerkin's own eyes was Bedosh, standing so all could see him. It was an open invitation for Agha Bey, a matter of honor to him, to take Bedosh down. Grasping his knife then repositioning it in his belt, Agha Bey made sure everyone, especially Bedosh, saw.

Taking his cue from Agha Bey, Kerkin let the others know that now was the time to get out of this place, and fast. In concealed fashion he took Anna by the arm. Kalesh saw this and prepared to follow Kerkin. They moved down a street going with the flow of shoppers so as to avoid being noticed. Given the distraction of the showdown between the Kurdish Peshmerga and the Turkish soldiers, this normally very noticeable act seemed to work, at least for the present moment.

Kerkin knew though that if he did not get Anna and Kalesh out of harms way very soon then it most certainly would be too late. They must act fast to conceal themselves.

As providence would have it, there was a Mosque just in front of them. Kerkin had to decide quickly if this would be a friendly place with someone he could confide in. It would depend on the Muslim Imam's feeling about Christians. Throughout Kerkin's days in the Old Country he had heard of some Imam's that were against Christians simply because they were not Muslims. This however was almost never the case in Kerkin's experience. Be they Muslim or Christian, they were still, 'Men of God', and most realized that their calling was to help any in need. So Kerkin thought, hiding in the Mosque was a chance that they must take. There really was no alternative.

Kerkin walked in front of Anna and Kalesh to greet the Imam of the Mosque. Jamal and Sadik followed close behind. Thankfully, the time was between Muslim prayers for the day so the Mosque was empty of other people. It was apparent to the Imam that the three people he saw in front of him were in some kind of trouble. What was also apparent was that they were good people. Especially Anna's presence, it was a sign to the Imam that

he should help. Kerkin quickly explained their circumstance.
The Imam could see that Kerkin was telling the truth.

"Come in ... quickly."

Kerkin honored Muslim tradition by taking his shoes off
before entering the Mosque. He was apprehensive as to how this
Imam could be so helpful without knowing them until this very
moment. The Imam noticed Kerkin's apprehension.

"Allah is benevolent ... and I too must be benevolent to follow
his example."

Kerkin was grateful to the Imam for helping them despite
religious beliefs. It was a moment of understanding really, that
God watched over all people, regardless of their religion.

With Anna and Kalesh close behind, Kerkin followed the
Imam into a small passageway along the side of the Mosque. It
was barely wide enough to walk through. Kerkin realized that
the place used to be part of a church. Along a side wall Kerkin
saw what looked like a hinged panel designed to cover something.
Not able to resist his curiosity, Kerkin reached to lift the panel.
The Imam immediately became agitated.

"You must not touch that."

Kerkin pulled his hand back.

"I'm sorry ... I did not mean to ..."

The Imam calmed down.

"Please ... allow me to explain. That panel covers a picture
of Christ."

"Christ?"

"Yes ... from Armenian days. This was a church ... an
Armenian church."

Kerkin glanced back at the panel, then at the kind eyes of
the Imam.

It's not his fault.

"Why did they not just paint over the picture?"

The Imam looked at Anna and Kalesh, then back to Kerkin.

"I know she is Armenian and her son is part Armenian."

Kerkin was slightly astonished that the Imam could talk with such certainty about Anna and Kalesh.

"How could you know?"

The Imam smiled.

"It's the way they react."

"React?"

"They know this was not originally a mosque. As Muslims ... or as Christians ... they know."

Kerkin could see that Anna and Kalesh were uncomfortable with the Imam's words.

"Muslim or Christian?"

"Exactly."

"I'm confused. Muslim or Christian ... there is no exactness."

"Many of the Muslims that pray here know that they are descended from Christians. That panel covers the truth of this."

The Imam looked at Anna and Kalesh with kindness.

"The panel of your heart has been lifted."

CHAPTER FIFTEEN

Kerkin and Agha Bey both knew all too well that to remain in their present position would only further weaken their chances of escape since more Turkish soldiers would surely arrive quickly. Before entering Kars they had prepared Anna and Kalesh for such an eventuality.

The situation called for Kerkin and Agha Bey to provoke a fight in the town. The hidden Peshmerga would then join in to help Kerkin and Agha Bey. During the ensuing chaos Jamal and Sadik would get Anna and Kalesh away from danger, then make their way to a rendezvous point outside of Kars that they had agreed upon.

Making sure that Anna and Kalesh were in a position to leave the Mosque without being detected, Kerkin and Agha Bey went back to the front of the Mosque. They then made their way to the center of the town. Kerkin wasted no time. They rushed a Turkish soldier who had seen them, knives in hand, the intended effect being to provoke the other Turkish soliders.

Before they realized it more soldiers started to appear. Agha Bey cried out.

"Allah be merciful."

Immediately Bedosh was seen to the side of one of the stalls. Knowing that Bedosh was responsible for the soldiers finding them, Agha Bey cried out to Kerkin.

"Bedosh is mine."

Agha Bey ran towards Bedosh. The Turkish soldiers could now be seen trying to surround Agha Bey and Kerkin. At that moment a group of Kurds surrounded Agha Bey.

"We are with you."

The Kurdish Peshmerga were here. It was all happening very quickly. Agha Bey yelled out to the Kurdish leader.

"We must try and kill this small group ... to prevent reinforcements from coming to their rescue."

From the back door of the Mosque fighting could be heard. People were running everywhere, some wielding knives and guns. Jamal indicated to Sadik that this was the opportune time to leave. They thanked the Imam then directed Anna and Kalesh to go with them, Jamal in front and Sadik in the rear. They were sure that the Kurdish Peshmerga were now engaging the Turks.

As careful as they may have been, Kerkin and Agha Bey knew that plans can and do go wrong, especially in conflict. Both men understood that while Bedosh was a detestable character of a man, he was nevertheless clever and willfully determined to get what he wanted and more.

This presented a choice. Do Kerkin and Agha Bey purposely ignore Bedosh until the decided moment, where all concerned, especially Bedosh, knew the outcome? Agha Bey did not even consider it because he knew from experience that conflict has a way of stumbling a well laid out plan. There was no predicting the outcome. For him it was pure chance that determined what would be.

Agha Bey thought it far better to leave Bedosh alive until the right moment.

Let him fear.

Kerkin glanced over at Bedosh who was now fully aware of the impending conflict.

"I will walk toward Bedosh even as I accuse him of stealing from me."

Before Agha Bey could say anything, Kerkin set off toward Bedosh, speaking in a loud voice.

"What have you done with my horse?"

Bedosh was startled to hear Kerkin's demands as the angry Armenian rushed toward him.

Kerkin again yelled out.

"You are a thief ... you have stolen from me."

The crowd looked at the tense scene developing. Agha Bey smiled as he realized that Kerkin had found a reason to fight. Bedosh was caught off guard and couldn't think of anything to say. He stumbled in speech.

"I ... I don't know what you are talking about. Who are you?"

Kerkin, now only about 10 feet from Bedosh yelled furiously.

"Now you lie ... that you don't know me. You dirty cheat."

The last statement caught Bedosh's pride, taking him from being caught off guard to anger. He drew his scimitar. The crowd was now anxious to see what would happen next.

Agha Bey now rushed to the aid of Kerkin. Drawing his scimitar as he approached Bedosh, Agha Bey addressed the crowd.

"This man has dishonored my good friend by not admitting the stealing of his horse."

Bedosh and Agha Bey stared each other down. Each man knew a confrontation was inevitable and that it was about to happen at any moment. Agha Bey motioned for Kerkin to step aside.

"Bedosh is mine."

Agha Bey had wanted this from the moment he first met Bedosh. The man represented for him all that was bad in the Kurdish culture. It was men like Bedosh that shamed the Kurdish people during the Armenian massacres.[1] Forever all Kurds must share in this shame for the terrible atrocities that some Kurds, like Bedosh, committed against Armenians. Now he had a chance to at least rid the Kurdish people of one of the worst of their kind.

For Bedosh there was no such feeling of ridding the world of anything. He only wanted to take advantage for his own good, not the Armenians, not the Turks, not even the Kurds. Bedosh was a man whose only concern was for himself. He would kill Agha Bey not because he represented something good about Kurds and Bedosh something bad, a way to rid himself of guilt because he was a bad Kurd. No, Bedosh would kill Agha Bey because to do so meant certain reward by the Turks for his service. Bedosh only cared about the certain rewards.

Agha Bey was coming for Bedosh, scimitar in hand. The fight was on. Kerkin could do nothing more but to watch the two Kurds fight.

Kurdish Peshmerga were now openly engaging the Turkish soldiers. Although the fighting was mostly being done with knives, gunshots could also be heard. At first glance the fight looked evenly matched. But the fighting skills of the Turkish soldiers, as good as they were, were no match for the experience of the Kurdish Peshmerga, many of who have been fighting since they were teenagers.

The Kurdish Peshmerga were particularly adept at fighting with knives in close quarter. They struck quickly with a knife slash to the throat then removed themselves only to again reappear to their next victim.

Bystanders were running about trying to get away from the fight that was quickly taking shape. Most of the fighters from the two sides had positioned behind structures to protect themselves from flying bullets. An exception was the fight between Agha Bey and Bedosh, which had become virtually a hand-to-hand combat.

In the midst of the violence, Jamal and Sadik were taking Anna and Kalesh away as planned, in the direction away from Kars. Frightened, Anna cried out to Jamal.

"How have I brought such violence?"

Seeing that Anna was about to go hysterical, Jamal quickly took her right arm and pulled her away from the view of the violence. This put her in place to see Kalesh's expression of both fear and interest of the unfolding events. Anna was about to break down in hysterics.

"Now I've put my only son in danger as well."

Kalesh put his arms around his mother, pulling her further away from the violence. Anna could not contain herself.

"I should go back to Bedosh and beg his forgiveness. Nothing is worth this."

Kalesh consoled his mother.

"You know him. It was only a matter of time before he ..."

Kalesh couldn't say the word. Anna looked up at Kalesh and finished the sentence.

"Killed me."

Kalesh nonverbally acknowledged the bitter truth of the statement. Anna turned back to look at the carnage. She watched Agha Bey and Bedosh fighting to the death.

Endnotes

1. After 1948 defined as the Armenian Genocide. See Powers, Samantha, "A Problem from Hell": America and the Age of Genocide Harper Perennial (2003) paperback, 656 pages ISBN 0-06-054164-4

CHAPTER SIXTEEN

Anna and Kalesh warmed themselves late at night by a small fire outside of Kars. Jamal and Sadik were on guard for either the unexpected or hopefully the expected that would mean Kerkin and Agha Bey's return. Did they make it out of the fight? It was the question all four people were thinking about that night.

Did they have a chance to still make it to Armenia? Anna again wondered if it was a mistake that she had left Pezme? There at least she had some kind of life. Granted it was with a terrible husband but at least she knew what to expect. Now she had no idea what the next day would bring. Even if Kerkin and Agha Bey returned and took her and Kalesh to Armenia, what then? Would the Armenians accept her and especially her son Kalesh who is half Kurdish? Unfortunately she couldn't know the answers to these questions. For now she could only wait for Kerkin and Agha Bey.

The camp was made near a small lake. Jamal made sure Anna was comfortable while he and Sadik took guard positions. Looking across the lake Anna saw the beauty of the area. It took her mind off the danger and regret she felt, and gave her pause to remember the past. She tried to remember her brother John and wondered how he had changed since she knew him as a little boy. Why she wondered, did she and John have to be separated as young children?

There was little Anna remembered really about her childhood or her life as an Armenian. Vaguely she remembered her father reading a book to her about Armenia with its tall mountains, especially Mt. Ararat.

Am I still Armenian?

The question haunted Anna. All she knew was how to be a Kurd and a Muslim. Could she become a Christian? Was that really possible for her? What can it be like to be an Armenian woman? Exhausted from these questions as well as the physical exhaustion of the day, Anna at last fell asleep.

It was early next morning when Anna was abruptly awakened. The sun had not yet risen when she saw through the dim morning light a familiar image of a man. She smiled in relief when she recognized the man. It was Kerkin. Looking around further as she became fully awake, Anna saw that Jamal and Sadik were hurriedly putting everything on the horses. Kerkin looked at her impatiently and spoke in a very hurried tone.

"Quickly Anna, we must go now."

Kerkin reached for Anna's arm then gently helped her up. She looked for Agha Bey but couldn't find him. Then she looked up at Kerkin.

"Where is Agha Bey?"

Kerkin hesitated to answer.

"He did not make it."

Anna put her hand up to her face as if about to cry.

"Did Bedosh kill him?"

Kerkin started to gather up Anna's bedding in a way to avoid answering the question. He then relinquished an answer.

"Agha Bey killed your husband but was killed by Turkish soldiers as he was getting away."

Anna could say nothing. Was she supposed to feel happy, sad, guilty, what? The situation was all too much for her to consider at this moment.

Although the Kurds prevailed against the Turks in Kars, Kerkin knew all too well that Turkish army reinforcements would soon be coming. Even as he contemplated this, a plane could be heard circling overhead. Kerkin determined that it was likely a

Turkish army reconnaissance plane looking specifically for them. He motioned to Jamal and Sadik while trying not to alarm Anna or Kalesh.

"They are most certainly looking for us. We must get out of the open now."

Jamal looked in the direction of a rock outcropping.

"I know a cave where we can hide."

Kerkin helped Anna up to her horse then mounted his own horse. He then motioned to the group in the direction of the rocks.

"We must ride fast while we are in the open. If not we will surely be found out. No cave will save us then."

Even as he said this Kerkin was concerned about Anna. She almost appeared in a state of shock now. Nevertheless he considered this the lesser of evils compared to not letting her know the danger, thus putting all of their lives in jeopardy. Kerkin pointed his horse in the direction of the rock face.

"We ride."

Kerkin knew that riding out in the open left them vulnerable to being spotted, especially given the reconnaissance plane that was seen earlier. If that plane came again then they must somehow hide. Fortunately there were some hills that offered ground cover.

Just as sure as Kerkin considered the possibility, the plane was again spotted in the distance. It was approaching their position. Not sure if they had yet been spotted he called out "Everyone ... quick ... get behind this hill."

Kerkin rode and the others followed him to a gathering of thick trees on a hill. They dismounted under the trees and waited for the plane to pass overhead. It was a close call. Probably too close as Kerkin feared their position had been spotted. It was only a matter of time before Turkish army reinforcements would be on the scene.

Despite what he felt, Kerkin forced himself not to believe they had been spotted. He knew that if he gave in then most certainly they would be captured. At least now they still had a chance. With the plane in the distance, Kerkin motioned the others to start riding again to the rocks. They were close now, just about a five minute ride to the cave Jamal knew about.

Jamal took the lead as a network of caves became visible. He glanced at Kerkin as he pointed to a particular cave.

"This is it."

Jamal had been here five years before with Agha Bey. They were looking for sheep and exploring the area. Jamal thought about the death of Agha Bey.

My Sheik ... my friend ... is gone.

It was a Kurd's natural way to look for places that might be useful in the future. This seemed to be one of those times. The cave Jamal pointed to had a very small opening but looked to be part of a large cavern, evidenced by the huge mass of rock overhead.

Kerkin was apprehensive about the small opening.

"Can we get our horses through there?"

Jamal nodded in agreement although somewhat hesitant about giving the answer.

"We should be able to get through."

Kerkin was a bit aggravated by the situation.

"Should?"

Jamal was concerned.

"I know that others have done it."

Kerkin reluctantly motioned the group forward towards the cave opening. The only way to get in was to dismount from the horses. It was going to be close. To make matters worse, the plane was again approaching from a distance.

They had to get into the cave quickly. What was apparent was a sizable boulder resting at the bottom of the cave entrance. If they could just move that boulder then the horses could get through without problems. If not then the horses would not be able to get through, the result being that their position would be given away to the Turks.

Working quickly, Kerkin and Jamal lifted an old log from a dead tree to try and pry the boulder loose. The boulder started to budge but then fell back to its old position. Meanwhile the plane was fast approaching. They now had only a brief moment to make this happen. Calling Sadik and Kalesh over, they put all their strength into prying the boulder. With as much force as could be mustered, they heaved the boulder. It budged then again started to fall back.

Kerkin refused to give up.

"Come on ... lets do this ... now!"

The four men gave it their all. It was just barely enough to budge the boulder so that it would not fall back. The cave opening was now clear.

Kerkin yelled out.

"Come on ... everyone get inside ... quickly."

Anna and Kalesh quickly followed Kerkin and Jamal with their horses into the cave. Sadik picked up the rear. Immediately upon entering they realized that the cave, besides being very dark, dropped off quickly. Jamal lighted a torch to provide some kind of visibility. They proceeded cautiously down into the cave. After only about 50 feet in, they could hear the roar of the plane's engines. Had they been spotted?

They proceeded further into the cave to a level spot where they could set up a makeshift camp of sorts. It was makeshift only in the sense that as soon as it was determined that the Turks could be evaded, then they would make their move from the cave, back into open terrain. It was now a waiting game to see what the Turks would do.

Just one day later, Kerkin cautiously went to the entrance of the cave. There were no Turkish troops within sight. Unless they were being duped, certainly a possibility or maybe the Turks didn't see them. Otherwise they would have checked the caves if they knew they existed.

"It's time to go."

They gathered up their meager belongings and lead the horses out of the cave entrance. It would be a day's ride to Mount Ararat, the ancient volcanic mountain where Noah's Ark was said to have landed after the Great Flood. Kerkin told Anna and Kalesh that they should expect to ride fast this day, as the Turkish Army would soon be approaching.

That Mount Ararat was part of their journey was significant not only for strategic reasons but also for a kind of spiritual reason. This mountain is to Armenians their heart and soul. Although Armenia is for the most part a barren highland, it is Mount Ararat that symbolizes the Armenian spirit, that which rises up towards the heavens despite the hard earth below it.

For Anna and Kalesh this land was a different place than Pezme. There were no wooded forests here. To the north was the Arax river. It ran along the border of Turkey and the Soviet Armenian Republic. This was the river that must be crossed near Mount Ararat to make it safely into Armenia. Kalesh had heard much about Mount Ararat, though always from a Kurdish point of view.

As they rode closer, Kalesh rethought what Mount Ararat meant to him. This was especially important now that he knew he was actually part Armenian. He did not know too much about the Armenians, only that they were an ancient people that were killed and deported in mass during the 1915 massacres.[1] Kalesh had heard that they were an industrious people, devout in their Christian religion. He wondered just why they were killed and deported. Was it their religion or because they were so industrious? Perhaps he would find out when they reached Armenia. There was much to learn.

Mount Ararat was fast approaching. The great snow capped mountain reached to the sky. It was here that Kerkin decided the group must try to enter Armenia. There were some significant problems though.

One such problem was the vast open plain in front of the Turkish side of Mount Ararat. Kerkin knew that the only way to surmount this problem was to stay close to the border and travel at night, all the while not being spotted by the pursuing Turkish troops.

The second problem, making it through the border, would also be difficult. Because Armenia was a republic of the Soviet Union the border guards were typically of Russian descent, giving them no national loyalty to Armenians trying to cross into Armenia. Kerkin knew that appeals of being Armenian would provide no special favors with these border guards.

About a mile from the border entry Kerkin decided the time had come to cross the plain in front of Mount Ararat. Towers along the Armenian border could be seen dimly in the distance. If they were lucky Kerkin could get Anna and Kalesh across without being noticed. If not, there would be sure trouble to pay.

So far there had been no sighting of the Turkish troops that had followed them all along. Kerkin wondered if perhaps they had given up after the fight at Kars. Most likely though he acknowledged that at least some remnant were probably hiding in wait for a moment just like what was about to occur, that is exposure under the shadow of Mount Ararat.

As this was no longer their journey, Kerkin bid farewell to Jamal and Sadik. The two Kurdish Peshmerga insisted that they must see Anna and Kalesh to safety. Kerkin explained, "Your courageous generosity is much appreciated but the fewer people to get across the border ... the better in this case."

Jamal and Sadik accepted Kerkin's advice to leave. They rode up to Anna and Kalesh. Jamal spoke for both of them.

"We must leave you now but know this ... that even though you go to the country of your people ... you will always be Kurdish. Remember ... the only friend of a Kurd is the mountains."

Jamal and Sadik respectfully acknowledged Anna as is proper in Muslim tradition then embraced Kalesh as a brother. Before riding off Sadik looked to Kalesh.

"A son's obligation is to watch over his mother."

Kerkin decided to wait until dark before leading Anna and Kalesh across the plain of Ararat to the Armenian border. Unfortunately the moon was full this night making the chances of not being spotted much harder. For her safety Anna would ride between Kerkin at the lead and Kalesh to rear. Kerkin looked back at Anna and Kalesh.

"We must ride fast. Remember, the Turkish troops could be in hiding, just waiting for us to come into the open."

Riding just inside the cover of some trees, Kerkin brought up his hand for Anna and Kalesh to halt before making a dash across the plain. The situation was tense. Taking a deep breath, Kerkin waited for the right moment. Then, with a deliberate act of determination, Kerkin lowered his hand to start the dash across the plain. They rode fast against the backdrop of a moonlit Mount Ararat.

The distance to the border gate was about one mile, certainly enough time to be spotted by Turkish troops. Kerkin couldn't escape this possibility as he led Anna and Kalesh towards Armenia. With every gallop of his horse he felt the stress of being watched.

Does John's quest for his sister die here?

If so, then no one, certainly not John, would ever know what happened. This would be the worst in Kerkin's mind, to simply disappear. There would never be reconciliation between him and his wife. He would never see his son grow up. No, he, along with Anna and Kalesh, would simply disappear. No one would ever know.

To Kerkin's surprise, no Turkish troops had emerged from hiding in pursuit. This didn't make sense at all to Kerkin. He was sure that Turkish troops were waiting for an opportune moment. Did they have another agenda? Surely they must know that once in Armenia, there was nothing more they could do. Perhaps after all it was some kind of divine providence. Whatever the reason, he was grateful as the Armenian border drew near.

Kerkin could now see the watchtowers on the border. A few seconds later a guard was visible in the closest watch tower. At last, they had made it to Armenia. Almost!

Kerkin motioned for Anna and Kalesh to slow down as they drew near to a border gate. Guards were posted at each side of the gate. Both guards drew their rifles. Pointing his rifle directly at Kerkin one of the guards spoke.

"Halt."

Kerkin put up his hand for Anna and Kalesh to halt. The guards were still pointing their rifles at Kerkin, whom they assumed was the leader. Against his better judgment, Kerkin had hoped that once the guards knew their reason for entering Armenia, all would be fine. With that in mind and noting that the guards were likely Russian, Kerkin spoke.

"This woman and her son as am I, are Armenian. We are seeking asylum in Armenia from pursuing Turkish troops."

The guards brought down their rifles. With a calmer disposition on his face, one of the guards approached Kerkin.

"You can not enter Armenia through this gate."

Now surprised, Kerkin looked over to the guard.

"Why not? We are Armenians."

The guard looked at Anna and Kalesh before responding.

"By order of the Soviet Union ... no one enters the Soviet Socialist Republic of Armenia without diplomatic orders."

Although neither Anna nor Kalesh spoke Russian, they could sense that something was wrong. Kerkin was now becoming highly agitated. He looked directly at the guard.

"What shall we do then? Should we wait for the Turkish troops to get here so they can kill us in front of this guard post?"

The guard was embarrassed by Kerkin's question. He could see that Anna and Kalesh were concerned. Anna in particular looked frightened. With sympathy he responded to Kerkin.

"Look ... I'm sorry but we have our orders. Even if I let you through this gate you will be stopped at the next gate. It's simply not possible. There is however another way ... through Iran then through Azerbaijan."

Kerkin still irritated but now curious inquired further.

"Why such an out of the way route and why Azerbaijan, it's also a Soviet republic?"

The guard motioned for Kerkin to dismount from his horse, then walked him a few feet to the side. He spoke quietly, almost in a whisper.

"You can easily get into Iran and then to Azerbaijan. Lets just say that with some money ... it's no problem. Once in Azerbaijan you can go to Karabakh. Do you know of Karabakh?"

"I've never been there but I know of this place ... that there are lots of Armenians there."

The guard acknowledged.

"Almost all Armenians. Once there it will be easy enough to get proper papers for entry into Armenia. It's the best chance you have."

Kerkin walked back to his horse then mounted up. He told Anna and Kalesh that they must now ride south to Iran. Surprised by this information, Kalesh looked at the guard that had been speaking to Kerkin.

"Why to Iran?"

Not being able to speak Kurdish, the guard could not answer Kalesh. Kerkin spoke for him.

"I will tell you later. For now just know it's the only way for us to get into Armenia."

These words were enough for Kalesh as he turned his horse in the direction Kerkin was heading, due south. Kerkin glanced back for a moment at the guard, gratefully acknowledging the information provided.

The situation gave Anna reason to again have doubts.

How could I have brought my son into this mess?

It was all too much for Anna. She began to cry.

Kerkin could see that Anna was distraught and so decided they must rest. Laying out camp, he and Kalesh took special care to offer sympathy to Anna. The world she knew had collapsed. Kerkin knew the feeling. When a marriage dissolves for whatever reason, it is tragic. Sure Anna's husband was a terrible man. Nevertheless, their marriage was a point of balance. Take that balance away and there is instability, and it's close cousin, vulnerability. Kerkin knew this all too well. His life was never the same after he separated from his wife. He lost his balance and had yet to regain it. Life managed on but that sense of well-being, was gone.

Enough about himself. Now was Anna's time of mourning. Kerkin gently sat down gently beside her. He brought out some locum, a favorite jelly candy from the region, that is covered in powdered sugar. Without saying a word Kerkin offered some locum to Anna. Smiling gently, she took a piece of the candy.

Endnotes
1. After 1948 defined as the Armenian Genocide. See Powers, Samantha, "A Problem from Hell": America and the Age of Genocide Harper Perennial (2003) paperback, 656 pages ISBN 0-06-054164-4

CHAPTER SEVENTEEN

As the journey continued south towards Iran, Kerkin still couldn't believe that Turkish troops had not yet exposed themselves in pursuit. Any time now, he could just feel it. If he could just get Anna and Kalesh to Iran then at least they would be safe from Turkish troops. There was still ample money for bribing border guards so getting through at least to Iran was doable.

Kerkin decided it was best to stay close to the Armenian border all the way to Iran. This way, when and if the Turkish troops showed themselves, there might still be a chance to get through into Armenia somehow, even though he knew that this was not very likely.

With three days still left to reach the Iran border, Kerkin saw a plane flying in the distance. Since the region was not a military theater, Kerkin suspected that this was evidence that pursuing Turkish troops were near. Indeed, the plane circled low upon approach. That the plane had not fired a gun was Kerkin's confirmation that the Turks wanted them alive.

What was it he wondered, that the Turks were after? Certainly Anna and Kalesh could not be considered a threat to the Turkish state. As for Kerkin, perhaps they considered him some kind of spy. But for whom? Kerkin had heard rumors that with the war's likely end in less than a year, the Soviet Union was planning an invasion of eastern Turkey on the pretense of liberating historical Western Armenia. In actuality their real aim was the same as in the days of the Czars, a seaport on the Mediterranean.

After circling a few times the plane headed off due north back towards Mount Ararat. Kerkin believed that within a day

Turkish troops could be within eyesight. With a kick to his horse he alerted Anna and Kalesh.

"There's no time to waste. Turkish troops will be here soon. We must cut our time to Iran. If we ride fast and sleep little we can make it in two days."

Kerkin looked especially at Anna.

"Are you up to it?"

Anna and Kalesh acknowledged Kerkin's request and picked up the pace. The next two days ride was arduous in terrain with mostly arid grassland. They only slept a few hours each night in order to make good time.

The sun was just setting when Kerkin spotted men on horses in the distance, about three miles away. Using his field glasses Kerkin confirmed what he believed inevitable, Turkish troops in pursuit. The Iran border was at least six hours away. Kerkin put away his field glasses and yelled out to Anna and Kalesh.

"There will be no sleep tonight ... not until we get to Iran."

It was going to be close, perhaps too close. Kerkin knew all too well that Turkish mounted troops ride fast. This is what they train for. In six hours they will surely close the distance. Kerkin hoped that in the dark of the night the distance would not be too close.

Five hours later the Turkish mounted troops were spotted again. The riding had been hard. There was real concern that at such a fast pace the horses would not be able to go much further. Kerkin demonstrated with a swift kick to his horse that they must not slow down too much.

Because of the darkness they couldn't tell how close the Turks actually were. What Kerkin did know is that they must be getting closer.

A shot was heard. Then in the sky overhead a flare illuminated the terrain below. Glancing back, Kerkin saw Turkish mounted troops in hot pursuit. It would not be long before they were in firing range.

The catch here was that Kerkin didn't know if the Turks would risk killing those they pursued. Kerkin thought likely not, an advantage as he saw it. He knew all too well though that this could change if the Turks thought they would lose their prey.

The Iranian border was very close now, just about a 20 minute ride as Kerkin estimated. Anna and Kalesh were however becoming exhausted with the fast pace and the stress of the Turks in pursuit. Kerkin needed to find a way to invigorate them.

"We are so close now ... just a little more and we will make it to Iran ... to safety."

Kerkin's words empowered Kalesh but Anna remained despondent. She was simply too exhausted both physically and emotionally. Kerkin had no other choice but to accept this. Nevertheless, the Turks were pressing ever so furiously and could catch up before the Iranian border was reached. Kerkin thought back to his last meeting with John back in the United States.

John will never know how Anna died?

Never mind that he also would die today. No, Kerkin determined that he must not give in to the pressing fear. Somehow they must, they would, make it to the Iranian border, and from there freedom.

Gunshots from the Turks were now being fired in volleys. The shots were still out of range but were converging ever closer. Kerkin decided an evasive action was necessary. Riding furiously between Anna and Kalesh, Kerkin yelled out.

"Spread out but keep your pace. We don't want to make an easy target for them."

As his words were spoken, Kerkin could vaguely see the Iranian border in the far distance. He yelled out to Anna and Kalesh.

"Look there ... the Iranian border. We can make it."

A volley of shots was fired. This time the bullets were able to reach their target distance. Kerkin knew that now it was a matter of accuracy or just plain luck. Whichever the case, they had to reach that border.

We have to make it.

Kerkin was obsessing about the border. Then, as if waking from a dream to find that it is really true, the border was upon them. They had arrived to safety.

Seeing the pursing Turkish army, the Iranian border guards abruptly halted Kerkin. Anna and Kalesh stopped right behind him.

Kerkin exclaimed "Come on ... the Turks are trying to kill us."

The border guard was very suspicious. Looking at Kerkin and then at Anna he asked "Your wife?"

Kerkin was becoming more agitated.

"She is not my wife ... now please ... let us through. You have no love of Turks."

The border guard was still puzzled.

"Why do they pursue you?"

Glancing at the approaching Turks, Kerkin knew it would only be another minute before capture or something worse, was upon them. If that happened, then just to save themselves trouble the border guard may give them up. Kerkin couldn't allow this to happen. He reached into his saddlebag. The guard was alarmed that Kerkin may be grabbing for a gun. Kerkin motioned to the guard.

"It's not a weapon. It's something much better."

Kerkin pulled out some money from the saddlebag.

"Now please sir. We are just Armenians, nothing more. Please take this money as a thankful gift from Armenians to the Iranian people."

The guard looked at the money appreciatively in a way that did not give away his intention as to whether he wanted money all along or not. It did not matter to Kerkin what the guard may have thought. All that mattered to him was to get into Iran.

The guard took the money then motioned for the gate to be opened. Kerkin followed by Anna then Kalesh rode past the gate and into Iran just as the Turks approached. Realizing that they had lost their mark, the Turks stopped just short of the border gate. Kerkin glanced back at the Turkish soldiers in relief.

We made it.

CHAPTER EIGHTEEN

Knowing that the journey through Iran to the southern tip of Armenia would be short, only a days journey, and that the Turks were no longer in pursuit, Kerkin could at last relax, at least until reaching Armenia. Crossing the Armenia - Iran border would present a new set of challenges. For now he decided it would be a good time to relax. Passing by a small lake of water, not much bigger than a very large pond, Kerkin motioned for Anna and Kalesh.

"Let's rest a bit by the lake."

Anna and Kalesh, exhausted from the previous day's harrowing run from the Turks, gladly dismounted. Kalesh walked over to the shoreline of the lake and ran some water through his hands onto his face, an entirely refreshing experience for him. Anna was more subdued in her approach to the lake. Kalesh joked.

"Come on mother ... enjoy the clean water. You deserve to drink of this water. We are nearly in Armenia now."

Kalesh noticed Kerkin's attentiveness to his statements and looked for a response. Kerkin took the cue from Kalesh.

"Almost in Armenia."

It was not the response Kalesh expected, much more cautionary, instead of optimistic. Kalesh couldn't conceal his concern.

"Do you expect problems getting into Armenia?"

Kerkin threw a rock into the lake as he looked to Kalesh.

"Not so much. But ... you can never know about border crossings. You have to see when you get there."

The remainder of the short journey through Iran was hot and arid in the landscape traversed. Despite this, the road was well traveled. Trucks could be seen on local roads heading between Armenia and Iran. Kalesh and Anna had never seen such motor traffic. Kerkin smiled as he looked at Kalesh's astonishment.

"It's a new world we live."

Kalesh watched a fast passing truck.

"But how can there be so many trucks? Where are they all going ... to Armenia?"

Kerkin looked in the direction of Armenia.

"They go to progress ... the Armenian Soviet Socialist Republic."

Kalesh was confused by the long name attached to Armenia.

"Soviet Socialist?"

Kerkin responded to Kalesh's confusion.

"It's still Armenia ... but also part of the Soviet Union. Think of it as the Russian empire. This empire stretches from the Pacific Ocean all the way to Europe. If this empire has its way, the lands of the Mediterranean will be its prerogative as well."

The confusion of Kalesh diminished slightly when he heard the familiar word Mediterranean.

"Turkey as well?"

Kerkin looked westward ... towards Turkey.

"The Soviet Union indeed has its sights on Turkey ... at least the Straights of Marmara so it can send its ships through the Black Sea and into the Mediterranean Sea. Another way is through the historical Armenian provinces."

Kalesh was drawn into the idea of a Russian advance into the historical Armenian provinces.

"How would Turkey allow such an attack?"

Kerkin looked at Kalesh then back in the direction of Armenia.

"They may not have a choice?"

By evening the Armenian border crossing was spotted. Tall gun posts were positioned on each side of the gate. It was an imposing site that gave Kalesh and Anna reason to be afraid. Kerkin motioned for them to halt their horses.

"Be careful now ... not to show your fear. These are Armenian guards and we should be okay to get through. They have no reason to deny us."

Anna did not understand how this could be, especially given the situation near Mount Ararat where they were denied entry into Armenia. Kerkin sensed Anna's perplexity.

"Here they welcome Armenians from other countries to immigrate. Armenians everywhere are coming back to their homeland."

Anna still had a question.

"But why was it not possible at Mount Ararat?"

Kerkin motioned for Anna and Kalesh to follow him towards the border.

"The situation back there was too political. It might have caused an incident ... or at least that's what the border guard thought. Here there are no such political problems."

As they came near the border gate a guard drew his rifle and ordered them to halt. Kerkin was calm. Anna and Kalesh were afraid. They did as Kerkin said, trying hard not to show their fear. Kerkin acknowledged the guard.

"We are Armenian and have come to Armenia to live."

The guard brought down his rifle with a slight smile.

"Are you here to immigrate?"

Kerkin acknowledged.

"To come back to the homeland."

The guard's smile grew bigger.

"Then I welcome you on behalf of the Soviet Socialist Republic of Armenia. Please enter your country."

Anna and Kalesh could hardly believe what was happening as they rode past the border gate into Armenia. They had made it to the homeland.

The terrain that lay before them was hardly different from what they left behind in Iran with the exception that groups of people, peasant farmers of sorts, could be seen tilling the ground. Kalesh spoke out.

"Why so many people working together?"

Kerkin looked over at the group of farmers.

"It's communal farming. They say this is the way of an egalitarian culture ... the culture of communism."

Kalesh became even more curious.

"Egalitarian ... communism?"

"Here there is no private ownership. It's only the state that owns anything. In return the people have food to eat and a place to live."

Kalesh was not so enthusiastic.

"Those people look like slaves. Are they free to work and eat and live where they want?"

Kerkin purposely did not answer the question but instead thought back to life in the United States, to the kind of freedom that Americans have, at least in theory. He wondered how the United States and the Soviet Union, despite now being allies, would treat each other after the war. These two great empires will likely fight it out. The question was how?

Kerkin was suddenly surprised when he saw what at first appeared to be a border crossing that they were approaching. As they drew near, a guard ordered them to halt.

"Papers?"

Kerkin pulled out identity papers drawn up for himself and handed them to the guard. The guard then motioned for Anna and Kalesh to produce identity papers as well. Kerkin looked at the guard.

"They are from Turkey. They have no papers."

The guard looked over Kerkin's papers.

"You are fine to go on."

The guard looked up at Anna and Kalesh.

"These two can not go through."

Kerkin was astonished.

"But why? They are Armenian."

The guard looked especially at Anna.

"I'm sorry but without papers their Armenian identity can not be established."

Kerkin tried to maintain his composure.

"But what are they to do? I can't just leave them here."

The guard looked east.

"Go first to Azerbaijan ... then to Karabakh. Proper identity can be established there."

Kerkin looked at the guard with apprehension.

"Money?"

The guard took note of Kerkin's concern.

"Not for me here ... but in Karabakh it can be arranged. Do not be concerned about crossing into Azerbaijan. We are all part of the Soviet Union. When you get to Karabakh go to the immigration office in the capital ... Stepanakert. Your situation can be worked out there."

Although relieved that there was a remedy, Kerkin was still in a kind of disbelief about the situation. He considered it a big mistake for not having papers for at least Anna. This was his mistake alone and now consequences would have to be paid.

The guard waved goodbye as Kerkin lead Anna and Kalesh east towards Karabakh. Kerkin estimated that it would take about one day to get to Stepanakert. Just like they had seen so far in southern Armenia, the terrain was dry and arid. As they continued to ride east however, the terrain appeared greener. This became even more pronounced as they continued east to the point where the beauty of the land was everywhere evident. They had entered Karabakh.

A small village could be seen in the distance. Coming upon a makeshift wooden marker inscribed with Armenian script, the name of the village read 'Artesh'. Kerkin motioned for Anna and Kalesh to follow him.

As they entered the village Kalesh was caught by the beauty of a young woman. Her smile was slight but intentional as Kalesh rode by. Until starting the journey to Armenia, the idea of being with an Armenian girl was something Kalesh never would have considered. So much had changed for Kalesh now that the look of a beautiful Armenian girl, especially after such a perilous journey, gave him a sense of renewal.

With amorous thoughts running through his mind, Kalesh glanced back at the young Armenian woman. He noticed that she acknowledged his interest as well. Without thinking, Kalesh turned his horse around and rode over to the young woman.

Kerkin smiled as he watched what was happening. Anna watched with some apprehension.

As he approached the young woman, Kalesh was concerned about his ability to speak Armenian. Over the last few months he had the opportunity to practice with Kerkin and even his mother, but neglected the opportunity.

Why didn't I learn when I had the chance?

Despite his trepidation of language, Kalesh was determined to speak with the young woman.

"Hello ... I ..."

Kalesh realized he did not have any words to speak.

The young woman saw that Kalesh was nervous and spoke to him in a consoling voice.

"My name is Tamira."

Tamira's introduction of herself gave Kalesh the confidence he needed.

"I am Kalesh."

Tamira was surprised by the name.

"Are you Armenian?"

Kalesh felt vulnerable with the question, a first test of his new identity.

Give her the truth.

"I'm half Armenian ... on my mother's side."

Tamira smiled warmly at Kalesh.

"The mother's side is the most important."

Kalesh smiled back but still was at a loss for words. He glanced back at Kerkin and his mother for an excuse to leave the situation in an unassuming way.

"I must be going now."

Tamira looked intently at Kalesh.

"Will you be staying here ... for a while?"

Tamira's words encouraged Kalesh.

"I am ... may I ... see you again?"

Tamira's eyes sparkled.

"I would like that."

Anna watched her son with mixed emotions. On the one hand she had a sense of optimism for Kalesh. He had met a beautiful Armenian girl that he was attracted to. On the other hand she had a fear that her son, being only half Armenian, would never fit in with their newfound home of Armenia.

That Armenia could even be considered home was still an idea that had not yet proven itself to Anna. She again wondered if leaving Pezme to come to Armenia was a good idea. Although Pezme for her was a place of shame, it was at least a place known. Here in Armenia she had no place from which to start, at least it felt that way to her at the moment. Kerkin had told Anna that family existed for her in Yerevan, that the anchor she could hold onto here was her Armenian blood.

Is blood the same as identity?

The question had been haunting Anna ever since she left Pezme. As it stood, she did not feel Armenian and even worse, the identity she knew in secret, that of a Kurdish woman had been stripped clean from her. Anna now found herself in a place where she felt no identity.

Kalesh's encounter with Tamira provided Kerkin a kind of contemplative calm. He smiled inwardly as he saw the glimmer of love, or at least infatuation, in the eyes of Kalesh and Tamira. Those were the best days, as he remembered them, for love. The first moments it seemed, so vaguely between himself and his wife.

How is it that love can be lost in despair?

Kerkin caught himself drifting into a chain of thoughts he so often had gone through, into a past with no recourse, no closure, only a dim reminder of what once was and what had been lost.

This was not the time. Kerkin forced himself from the chain of thoughts, back to the reality of the present moment. The task ahead of him was the commitment to John, to bring his sister Anna to safety.

The requirement now was to get the proper identity papers so that Anna and Kalesh could get to Armenia proper, likely Yerevan. Kerkin had determined that it was best for Anna and Kalesh to stay in Artesh while he went alone to Stepanakert. Considering Kalesh's newfound love interest, Kerkin mused that this would not be too difficult for the young man.

The local magistrate of Artesh had come by to introduce himself to the new visitors. In a strong Karabakh accent that Kerkin had a bit of difficulty understanding, the magistrate motioned to a small house about 100 yards in the distance.

"This house is here for visitors to our village. You are most welcome to stay there as long as you need."

Kerkin acknowledged gratefully.

"My thanks to you and your village for welcoming us. The woman and her son will need to remain here while I travel to Stepanakert."

The magistrate acknowledged the unspoken necessity that Kerkin needed to go to Stepanakert for identity papers. In an attempt to put Kerkin at ease he responded.

"They may stay here as long as needed. We are all Armenians here."

CHAPTER NINETEEN

The next morning Kerkin bid farewell to Anna and Kalesh. He told them that he was going to Stepanakert, which was just a few hours journey from Artesh by car. Driving away, he could not help but think that anything could happen while he was in Stepanakert. It was likely that the local people in Artesh could be trusted, but still he thought, you never know.

Beyond leaving Anna and Kalesh, his own situation could be precarious. Once in Stepanakert he would have to negotiate, through bribe, identity papers for Anna and Kalesh. These days, with the war still going on, there could be problems. He would have to see when he got there.

By late afternoon Kerkin arrived in Stepanakert. Although it was the capital of Karabakh, Stepanakert was little more than a provincial town. Karabakh itself, despite being declared an autonomous region of the Soviet Republic of Azerbaijan, was distinctly Armenian in culture and population.

Not wanting to waste any time, Kerkin told the driver to get to the immigration office so that he could start the paperwork, which he expected would amount to a negotiated bribe. Kerkin asked the driver "Is there enough time to get through the immigration office today?"

The driver hesitated a bit before answering.

"We can make it into the office but I can not tell you if the people you want to talk to will be available. Here in Karabakh people can be on their own schedules."

The driver laughed.

"This is after all a place for Armenians."

Pulling up to the immigration office, the driver pointed to a small hotel across the street.

"I will arrange for a room in the hotel for you."

Being in a hurry, Kerkin glanced over at the hotel.

"Thanks. I will see you over there."

Kerkin left the car and entered into the immigration office. Guards were posted at the entryway. Kerkin reached for his papers then handed them to one of the guards. The guard looked through Kerkin's papers then back up to Kerkin.

"You are Armenian but a foreign national?"

"I'm here on diplomatic matters concerning matters of interest to the British government."

The guard knew that Kerkin would not be forthcoming with any more information, as this was standard protocol. He motioned for Kerkin to enter the building.

Kerkin walked down the corridor to a room with a sign overhead in Russian 'Identity papers'.

Taking a deep breath before entering the room, he opened the door. A woman, approximately 30 years of age and exotic looking, stood behind the counter.

"Good day."

The woman responded in kind.

"Your request?"

Kerkin approached in the most confident manner he could, given the potentially difficult situation. He pulled out his papers and handed them to the clerk. As she looked through his papers he inquired "Would it be difficult to obtain duplicates of such papers?"

The clerk at first looked puzzled then realized the strangeness of the request actually suggested an alternative motive. She knew the drill. This man wanted identity papers for someone else.

She answered.

"Such papers can usually be obtained but they can be difficult depending on the circumstances."

"What kind of circumstances?"

The clerk smiled a bit so as not to say the obvious.

"Lets just say that if these papers were for someone else ... then the costs could be higher."

Kerkin now knew the game was on, negotiation through bribe.

"So how would these additional costs be paid?"

The clerk began writing on a piece of paper then spoke concealed.

"All will be explained at this place."

Kerkin looked at the paper. It had scribbled directions to an apartment on 22 Abramov Street. The woman waited until Kerkin finished reading.

"Tell them that Ursula sent you."

What if this was a setup? How would Anna and Kalesh survive?

I have no choice.

The directions to the apartment were straight forward enough. Take Tigranes Ave. about two kilometers, then make a right on Abramov Street. Kerkin thought about walking it but then decided having a car ready, in case of trouble, would be at least a measure of security.

The taxi drove up to the apartment building. It was typical Soviet style, a multi-story structure that demonstrated utility but was devoid of character. Kerkin became used to seeing these kinds of structures. They were everywhere. A blessing or a curse, depending on one's point of view.

Walking up the stairs to the third floor of the building, Kerkin saw nothing that made him suspicious. He knocked at the door. A gruff voice answered.

"Who is it?"

Kerkin could feel his anxiety.

"Ursula sent me."

The door opened immediately. Kerkin's heart immediately sank. There in front of him, in full uniform, was a KGB officer.

"Come in quickly."

Don't panic.

Kerkin tried to reassure himself even as the KGB officer spoke further.

"We will conduct our business and you will be on your way."

Just the way it's done over here.

That's what Kerkin told himself as he heard the words of the KGB officer.

"You need documentation for how many people?"

Kerkin composed himself the best he could.

"There are two people, a woman 34 years of age, and her son. They want to settle in Armenia. That's all."

The KGB officer could see that Kerkin was stressed.

"My name is Yuri. My mother was Armenian before we moved to Moscow. I welcome you to Armenia and will help you get your papers."

Kerkin wondered if the man's name was really Yuri. Probably not.

"$200 ... pay me now."

Kerkin was taken aback for the moment, especially that payment was to be in United States dollars. With the war going, it made sense, he supposed.

"Yes ... but can I trust you?"

Yuri laughed.

"You can't ... but it doesn't matter. I will get you the papers nevertheless."

Yuri waited for Kerkin to give him the money.

"Here are the details. Listen carefully."

Kerkin payed strict attention to Yuri's words even though he wondered if this was all a setup. It didn't matter though. The situation offered no luxury of choice.

"In two days ... return here at this time to pick up the papers. Are we clear?"

Kerkin looked at his watch. It read 10:15 AM.

"Clear."

Yuri's expression became very serious.

"If you do not come at that time ... do not come at all."

Two days later, exactly at 10:15 AM, Kerkin knocked on the apartment door. There was no answer. He knocked again. Still no answer. Kerkin checked his watch. It read 10:17 AM.

It was just two minutes.

Kerkin tried to reassure himself that all would be fine. Yuri was just a few minutes late. All would be fine.

A woman and a boy passed by Kerkin as they made their way down the stairs. The boy turned around to look at Kerkin. His mother quickly pulled the boy away to continue down the stairs. Kerkin could feel the obvious awkwardness of the situation. Every second waiting was becoming intolerable for him.

Kerkin checked his watch. It read 10:30 AM.

Get out of here ... now.

Kerkin hurried down the stairs. The woman and boy he saw were waiting just outside the building. Once again the boy looked at Kerkin. The mother again pulled him away. Another obvious awkward situation. There was nothing Kerkin could do about it. All he could do was to get away as fast as he could. He opened the door to the car waiting for him.

"Let's go ... now."

Kerkin had all his luggage with him. There was no need, he assumed, to go back to the hotel once he had the identity papers. But now, without the papers, he realized his decision to leave Stepanakert right away was hasty. Should he tell the driver to go back to the hotel? No. It was too late now. Something had gone wrong.

Heading out of Stepanakert Kerkin thought about what to do next. The only course of action he could see would be to get Anna and Kalesh away quickly. Somehow he would get them into Armenia. He had to. There was nothing else that could be done.

Kerkin's planning was suddenly interrupted by a roadblock just ahead. What now, he thought? That they were the only car on what seemed to Kerkin an isolated road, did not feel right. The driver pulled the car to the side and parked. Kerkin took note that the two cars blocking the road were government issue, KGB to be specific. That no one was standing outside the cars was even more alarming to Kerkin.

Something is not right here.

TAP- TAP – TAP. Kerkin was startled. Yuri's face peered into the window. He motioned for Kerkin.

"Get out of the car."

Kerkin tried not to show any emotion as he got out of the car. Whatever was going to happen will happen now.

Yuri stood with stern expression. Three other men were next to him. Without a word spoken, Yuri took out a gun, then pointed it at Kerkin. He motioned to the three men accompanying him to stand by Kerkin's car and driver.

Kerkin could feel the gun in his back as Yuri pushed him into the woods that ran along side the road. A sense of dread ran through Kerkin.

So this is how it ends.

Yuri had taken away the gun from Kerkin's back. He motioned for Kerkin to continue into the woods. As they walked, further and further from any kind of chance of safety, a sense of calm came over Kerkin. There was nothing he could do to change the situation really. He could of course make a run for it, or even try to fight. But realistically the outcome would be the same. He would be dead in few minutes. That's all there was!

Perhaps, Kerkin thought, it was for the best. His life had not turned out the way he had hoped anyway. Thoughts of his wife and son ran through his mind. How was it that his life, so promising at one time, so hopeful, had turned out the way it did? He had not deliberately set out to ruin it. Life just turned out that way, or had it?

The sound of shuffled dirt ran under his feet. At that very moment Kerkin could feel a splitting off of himself, as if the man walking was not him, but someone else. He could watch that man walking, that man filled with fear, with regret. It was all in that man, not the one watching, not Kerkin.

"Stop."

One word from Yuri caught Kerkin's attention. He turned around to a kind Armenian face.

"There were problems. I'm sorry for this."

Kerkin was confused.

"I don't understand. What are you ..."

Yuri interrupted.

"Someone was alerted to your presence."

"How?"

"I don't know. It should have gone without incident."

"What are you to do with me now?"

"I have to kill you."

Yuri put his gun away.

"That's the way it has to look."

Yuri pointed in the direction that he and Kerkin had been heading.

"Continue this way. About three kilometers out you will come to a clearing. A truck will be waiting."

Yuri handed Kerkin an envelope.

"Get on that truck."

Before Kerkin could say anything, Yuri walked away, out of sight, in what seemed a vanishing moment. Kerkin stood there alone, envelope in hand. There was no need to check. He knew what was inside. Walking away, in the direction Yuri had told him, Kerkin no longer sensed the split of himself. All he could think about now was that he was walking in the direction of what had to be done. But what was it exactly, that had to be done?

Kerkin knew that John had to be told that his sister was alive and safe, that she had a son, that all was well. A simple message through the telex out of Yerevan would suffice.

ALL IS WELL JOHN ... ANNA FOUND ... SHE AND HER SON ... ARE WELL.

But was all well, really? It did not feel that way. The sense of calm had gone. He was no longer the watcher. Was this good or bad? He did not know.

CHAPTER TWENTY

A safe harbor is a provision of a statute or a regulation that reduces or eliminates a party's liability under the law, on the condition that the party performed its actions in good faith. - Wikipedia

The funeral procession made its way to the Masis cemetery in Fresno California. Although the procession was not large, there was a sense that the person being buried was important. As the casket finally came to a halt where it was to be buried, there were many mourners with tears in their eyes.

An Armenian priest began his oratory.

"This is the funeral of John Avedisian ... well known in Fresno and throughout California's Central Valley as a very important financier of agricultural business. John lived a long and dignified life of some 101 years. We want to remember him today ... not only as a man rich in material possessions ... but also rich in those qualities that can't be measured in any sort of objective way."

The priest went on to talk about John's life, of losing his family when he was very young, and of his resilience and forcefulness, especially in finding his lost sister.

Qualities such as personal integrity and kindness were what John's grandson David remembered most. For him, Grandpa was someone to look up to and feel special about. Serving as one of the pallbearers of his grandfather's casket, David remembered the long walks with Grandpa through the furrows of grapevines on a hot evening at the family farm near Fresno.

The farm was small, only about 40 acres. It was John Avedisian's first real investment in the Central Valley and although profits from the farm were far outweighed by the agricultural financing business, the farm was never given up. For John Avedisian, this small farm was where it all started. David knew this intuitively as a little boy. He would walk with his Grandpa up and down those furrows checking for water breaks that separated the rows of vines, an unspoken peace remembered.

John's daughter Debra, David's mother, did not share the fond remembrance of her father that her son reminded himself of. For Debra, memories of her father couldn't escape her own shame of failure. Watching her son serve as one of the pallbearers only drove home the point that she never measured up to the expectations of being the daughter of this very special man, John Avedisian.

It was not that John looked with disapproval at Debra. On the contrary, she was, as John use to call her, his special flower. John never gave up on his daughter. Even up to his death and despite the fact that Debra had consistently made messes of tasks given to her, John never gave up hope that Debra would take a good turn. This was perhaps what made thoughts of her father so painful to Debra. She could only blame herself for her misfortunes.

Not present at the funeral, in what was very conspicuous to David but convenient for Debra, was John's beloved sister Anna or her son Kalesh. David had expected his mother to contact them about his grandfather's death. Debra had purposely not called them, using the excuse that they lived too far away to be present. David knew better though, that his mother wanted that side of the family to be completely estranged from their side of the family.

What David did not realize was that not inviting Anna and Kalesh was of much more practical significance. It was not about familial jealousy. No, it was about Debra not wanting Anna or Kalesh to share in any kind of material wealth from her father's estate.

As David lay down to the earth the casket upon which his dear Grandpa would rest, he began to fight back thoughts that perhaps there were other, more sinister, reasons for Anna and Kalesh not being present. He would not however allow himself to give into such thoughts because to do so would bring him to the very cause of his mother, whom despite her faults, David loved very much. No, he pushed into his subconscious. His mother would never do such a thing.

Walking to a small lectern where he was to give a final eulogy, David fought hard to not allow such thoughts of his mother's selfishness to take hold of him. But it was no use. The thoughts were there. He glanced at his mother hoping to see in her eyes an honorable sadness reflecting the death of her father. Instead what he saw was the coldness of self opportunity. It was horrible for David to contemplate.

Whatever Debra's feeling towards her father or David's feelings toward his mother, David knew this was not the time for him to consider any of the consequences of such feelings. His job now was to deliver the eulogy to memorialize his dear grandfather. This he would do to the very best of his ability.

Setting his notes down on the lectern he prepared his initial words.

"John Avedisian was a very special man."

David fought back tears as he heard himself saying these words. They were so prim and proper, what everybody expected for the great man, John Avedisian. But David knew that they did not capture in the least, what his grandfather was really about. No, David knew there was so much more to John Avedisian. This was his beloved Grandpa.

Because his father had died before David could remember him, Grandpa was much more to David than a grandfather, he was also a kind of father, the one who showed David how to be a man. There were in fact even some remarkable physical similarities between John and David. Friends of David use to remark unknowingly that photos of what they thought were of

David were actually those of a young John. David gratefully took heart at such mistakes.

Preparing to continue the eulogy David wondered if he would be able to live up to the legacy of his grandfather. The man was certainly larger than life. David's words followed.

"John Avedisian had a very successful life in America. He had made a fortune through the Avedisian bank. That bank, which he had founded so many years ago, stood up under the Great Depression of the 1930's. He started this bank ... not to make money ... but instead to help those in need of economic recovery from what had been real devastation."

David paused for a moment to glance around at some very old faces, those of nearly the same age as his grandfather. He knew that these were people his grandfather had helped in those times. These people had suffered during the bad economy. Yet through the help of John Avedisian, went on to prosper financially.

David looked back at his notes then continued.

"When soldiers came back from World War II it was the Avedisian Bank that was there to help them buy houses."

David again paused to glance at some older faces that reflected the era of young soldiers going off to war. These were faces of men that had known what it was to provide for their family. David continued.

"It was men like these, the ones my grandfather had helped, that have built Fresno, and indeed the entire Central Valley, into the agricultural giant that it is today."

Listening to David's words from the audience was a man that desired to be inconspicuous in a way that repeated that of his own father. This was the son of John's closest friend. The man's name was Mark. He was the son of Kerkin.

Even though he had the same name as his father, Mark never went by Kerkin Jr. Perhaps it was because Mark, although he loved Kerkin, never could quite think of him as a father. He thought about John Avedisian, how his father's search for John's sister forged a friendship. That friendship would last throughout their lifetimes and span continents. Mark could not think of his father without also thinking about John Avedisian.

Mark knew well how John made every effort to help in the reconciliation of his mother and father. A moment of sadness was fought back at the thought, that despite John's best efforts and the love between his mother and father, their reconciliation was never to be. Kerkin in fact was never able to fully come back to a life in Fresno.

A reluctant adventurer at heart, Mark remembered the exciting stories told to him by his father of those days past. How Russia almost attacked Turkey in an effort that could have created a Greater Armenia. Although it never became reality, the idea of a Greater Armenia gave reason for Mark to admire men like his father and John Avedisian, men who were committed to 'Hye Tad', 'the Armenian Cause'.

Mark also knew of the practical realities set up between his father and John Avedisian. These involved a trust set up for John's sister Anna with the hope that she would one day come to live in the United States. Because of her own family commitments she never did come to the United States. Instead Anna happily settled in Yerevan. Her son Kalesh eventually returned to Karabakh where he married his first love Tamira, and had two children. All of this, Mark considered as he heard David's words, came out of friendship between his father and John Avedisian.

David spotted Mark as he continued to speak out the eulogy. Despite their generational and age differences, the two men shared a kind of bond that both believed would one day come to fruition in a way reminiscent of John and Kerkin.

Considering such a reality, David's reminded himself of the many achievements of his grandfather. He talked about these achievements out loud.

"My grandfather's achievements came directly from his desire to help Armenia. He left there as a young boy ... running for his very life. John Avedisian would spend the remainder of his life giving back to that very Armenia from which he barely escaped.

Despite the loss of the independent republic of Armenia in the 1920's ... John Avedisian found ways to help the country ... even under Soviet occupation. When Armenia once again became independent in the early 90's ... it was John Avedisian that helped immensely with the finances. This included support for the Karabakh war and it's aftermath ... especially the construction of village communities throughout Karabakh.

David paused then looked around at the entire audience.

"My grandfather dreamed of ... and worked diligently for ... an eventual lasting peace for Karabakh ... a place of safety that all Armenians could call home."

CHAPTER TWENTY-ONE

It was already starting out to be a hot summer day as David walked up the steps of the Fresno County courthouse. As he entered the building David felt a pit in his stomach, a dreadful feeling really, that came from what was about to take place. It was the reading of his grandfather John's Will. Although much of the family would be there, hoping to get something, this was not what was bothering David. No, the trouble would be coming from the one woman he was closest to so far in this life, his mother Debra.

David approached the security counter at the courthouse. Looking at David in a bored but somewhat suspicious way, a security guard handed David a tray for his belongings that needed to go through the X-ray machine. David checked his wallet as he motioned to the security guard.

"Do I need to put my wallet in?"

The security guard made effort to look professional. As he looked at David he could not hide his annoyance at a question he heard all the time, every day. His response was gruff.

"Everything metal."

David hesitated for a moment, wondering if there was some kind of metal in his wallet. The thought flashed through his head about how annoying this all was. Then he took another look at the security guard and realized that he was just doing his job.

With a grin David asked, "Is this about the millionth time someone has asked you about wallets?"

The security guard laughed.

"At least a million times."

David picked up his belongings as he made his way through the X-ray machine. The security guard noticed a man watching David at a distance from the security counter. Surmising the situation he motioned to David that the man was watching him. David looked over then back to the security guard.

"The press will never let this alone."

The security guard then realized the situation.

"Now I know where I've seen you before. You are John Avedisian's grandson ... right?"

David responded back a bit reluctant.

"That's me alright."

The guard sensed reluctant sadness in David.

"Sorry to hear about your grandfather. He was a good man to this valley. His bank gave my grandfather the money for their farm."

David was grateful to the security guard for sharing a personal note about his grandfather. It cheered him up hearing how his grandfather's legacy lived on.

The security guard continued.

"I still live on that farm ... couldn't have done that without your grandfathers help."

Trying to hold back a tear as he put the wallet in his pocket, David looked over to the security guard.

"He was a good man."

David walked down the wide corridor in the direction of the man watching him. He assumed the man was yet another reporter keen on picking us some news about John Avedisian's estate. The man held up the day's edition of the Wall Street Journal as David approached. Plastered on the front page was the headline,

20 billion dollar estate likely to be contested.

The man revealed himself to David as a reporter.

"Mike Stanton Fresno Bee – Is it going to be contested?"

David held back his irritation at having to answer this question so many times in the last few weeks. But then he thought to look back at the security guard who had a big grin on his face.

The security guard yelled from a distance at David.

"Now you know how I feel about the wallet question."

David laughed and put up his fist as an act of defiance at the question.

"We haven't even read the Will yet."

The security guard raised his fist with David, the two men acknowledging this bit of life's futility. David glanced back at the Wall Street Journal and said nothing. The reporter, realizing he was at a loss here, tried one more time.

"Oh come on ... give a guy a break. How often does a Fresno Bee reporter get a chance at a story like this?"

David felt a kind of sympathy for the reporter so he decided to say something.

"My grandfather was a rich man ... not only because of his money ... but more important because of his family."

Encouraged by the answer, the reporter pressed on.

"But did John Avedisian mean something to his family ... besides his money?"

The question struck to the heart of David's anxiety about what was coming with the reading of the Will. David glanced back at the reporter as he walked away.

"What do you think?"

The door read, 'Room 105 – Probate Law'. Entering, David took a deep breath. As he expected, all eyes were fixed on him, all except his mother, that is. Looking at his mother, David couldn't help but be angry. The very fact that they were at the courthouse today instead of a lawyer's office was because of his mother.

Having suspected that the Will would be in favor of her son instead of her, Debra was insistent that it be read in the court. This added inconvenience said a lot about her. She didn't care what others thought or how much inconvenience her actions might cost others.

David knew all too well how his mother thought about such matters. If she couldn't control the situation then she would create all kinds of surrounding havoc. The result of causing the inconveniences was a much longer than needed drawn out reading of the Will. David was reluctant to recognize this tendency in his mother but couldn't escape the blatant history having to do with her approach to life. He thought back to his childhood, how she was always with a new boyfriend that just never seemed to work out.

David had liked most of her boyfriends. They had generally treated him well. His mother made sure of that, but just as he was feeling comfortable with one of them, his mother would promptly change to another boyfriend. It was never ending and continued even into the courthouse today. Yet another boyfriend was sitting there with her. His name was Mike and just like most of the others, David got along with him.

Mike acknowledged David.

"Here we go."

David and Mike both looked at Debra to see if she would respond to Mike's friendly gesture. Not a chance. Withstanding his mother's attitude, David took it upon himself to answer Mike.

"Seems the verdict ... or whatever they call it ... will be read by the judge any time now."

The judge entered the courtroom with documents in hand. As he walked towards his desk, an officer of the court spoke out loudly.

"The honorable judge Lawrence Conners presiding."

As the judge sat down he laid the papers to the side then struck the gavel.

"The court is now open."

The judge picked up the documents then read.

"Concerning the estate of Mr. John Avedisian, the deceased has laid out a clear direction. His grandson David is to be made executor of the Will. Further, with the exception of specified distributions to various parties present, and perhaps not present at this meeting, Mr. David Jandian has been given full control of how the remaining estate will be handled."

Debra was aghast at what she heard. Her boyfriend tried to console her but it was of no use. She glared at the judge then lashed out.

"He was my father ... I have a right. I can ..."

The judge cut Debra off with the striking of the gavel.

"Such outbursts in my courtroom will not be tolerated under penalty of contempt of court."

Debra was furious and started to speak again when both her boyfriend and lawyer each grabbed one of her arms. It took about 15 seconds for her to settle down, enough for her lawyer to whisper.

"Be patient ... our strategy is sound."

Debra bit her lip so as not to speak. Instead she just glared at her son. For David, to see such a hateful expression directed at him by the mother he loved was almost too much to bear.

Continuing with the reading of the Will, the judge spoke out clearly.

"To Ms. Debra Avedisian, the amount of $10,000,000 is to be assigned immediately."

Reading the words, the judge was incensed at how ungrateful Debra Avedisian could be. She was a rich spoiled brat he thought.

The judge read off other details concerning minor distributions to various parties. John Avedisian had also included Armenian and American charities. Notably, Kerkin's son Mark was pleased to find out that a sum of $1,000,000 had been given to him as heir of John Avedisian's lifelong friend. Special mention was made of an endowment to the St. Agnes hospital in Fresno and to the Fresno State University, California.

Concerning these last distributions, the judge spoke.

"I had the privilege of personally knowing John Avedisian. The man was always about giving, and although I know how much he cared about things Armenian, I can say here today on the record that he cherished his adopted country, the United States of America."

The judge hesitated for a moment, becoming just a bit choked up.

"He used to tell me how the United States was the best place in the world. His contributions to the Central Valley during his lifetime, and now after his passing, gives testimony to this statement."

The judge glanced over at David to acknowledge a sense of rightful duty now being given to the young man to do the will of his grandfather. David for his part acknowledged back this responsibility. With that, the judge struck his gavel.

"This court is adjourned."

Immediately with the striking of the gavel, Debra almost leaped out of her chair towards David. She was furious as she spoke.

"So now you have it all. Well, are you proud of yourself today ... now that you have hurt your mother?"

David started to respond but was cut off by his mother.

"You think you are like him but you're not. You are my son too and what burns in me burns in you. Do you think you will just give away all the money to Armenia like Daddy tells you even now? Let me tell you something ... that money should be with our family. It's not for Armenia. We need that money."

David was embarrassed by his mother's blatant selfishness, especially since she had been given $10,000,000 dollars. He would give her more if she needed it. Kerkin's son Mark came over to support David. Seeing this, Debra again lashed out.

"Oh yes ... here he comes for his money too, a $1,000,000 to the son of a vagabond."

Mark lashed back.

"My father was no vagabond."

David motioned for Mark not to respond to his mother. Debra continued.

"Oh I see ... he found Daddy's lost sister in the Old Country. How do we really know that was his sister? She was probably just another Armenian looking for a handout."

David now jumped in.

"How can you say such things about your own aunt?"

Debra fumed at the accusation.

"My aunt huh ... someone you and I have never met. Are we supposed to care about such a person?"

David started to speak, then waited until Debra's boyfriend and lawyer approached them. Fired up by the heated exchange with his mother, David looked directly at the lawyer to get across a message.

"I'm going to Armenia ... to meet my great aunt and to see for myself what can be done for Armenia and ... Karabakh. My grandfather asked me to do that."

Hearing David's words put Debra into a near frenzy. She again lashed out at her son.

"You do what you want. I will do what I want. This Will is not finished yet. I will..."

Debra's lawyer quickly pulled her away from the conversation. He spoke in a near whisper to her. "Remember our strategy."

CHAPTER TWENTY-TWO

David knew he must call Armenia to talk to his great aunt's son, the man Kalesh. Although he had never met Kalesh, David had heard much about him. For David, men such as Kalesh were a kind of legend. They were much like Armenia itself, almost mythological in what they represented.

The fabled Mount Ararat, even though within the borders of Turkey, was a majestic site from the streets of the Armenian capital, Yerevan. David remembered wondering as a boy if Mount Ararat was a real mountain or maybe just a dream of Armenians. During his youth the question could hardly be answered since Armenia itself was part of the Soviet Union.

People did go to Armenia in those days but it was not an easily arranged journey. Because so few actually went to Armenia the mythology, in David's eyes, was further perpetuated. Now with his planned first trip to Armenia, David would discover for himself the reality of Armenia.

The same would be for Kalesh. David wondered if the man would live up to the legend. Was it right he wondered, to even consider such a question? Likely not, but nevertheless, the question remained. One way or another the day was soon coming with the answer.

It was with some reluctance that David considered just how to break the news of his grandfather John's death to the family in Armenia. Of course, they likely had already heard through the news media about the death of the important Mr. John Avedisian. But that was not the kind of news that was spoken between families. This kind of news spoke from the heart, at least that's what David hoped for.

It was not until the day after the funeral that David decided to make the call to Armenia. He had purposely waited until after the Will was read, a week after his grandfather had died. This, he justified so as not to hurt his great aunt Anna whom he knew was not in good health. In actual fact David was too distraught and hated the idea of telling her.

David knew that his grandfather and Anna had come to grips with the past but that they were estranged from each other in ways that could not be spoken. Although his grandfather talked often about the history of what had happened, he would become silent when the subject touched him personally, especially with Anna.

There was only one time when his grandfather spoke about what happened to the family in the Old Country. A young cousin from out of town had wanted to learn about the history of the family. She had asked John unassumingly how it came to be that he and his sister were separated?

John began to recount the events that lead to the separation, that is, what actually happened to his parents. It was too much for John to bear. David still remembered as a boy of twelve years of age how shocked he was to see his strong Grandpa John sob uncontrollably. It was the only time he saw his grandfather cry.

Such were David's thoughts as he picked up the phone to call Kalesh. As he dialed Armenia's international call prefix of 011 374 David realized that he was now embarking on the journey to Armenia. Although it was just a phone call, this would surely be the start of his involvement with the part of the family so dear to John but so distant to David.

The phone rang. David felt tense about how to start the conversation. Should he introduce himself formerly with full description of his position now within the family, that he was the executor of his grandfather's Will? Or should he speak to Kalesh with familial warmth expected of close cousins? David thought this to be the right way but then considered just how much he actually knew of Kalesh. The legend came to mind.

The phone rang three times, then an answer.

"Barev."

It was the familiar Armenian greeting of 'Hello' that David recognized. More importantly than the words themselves was the voice saying it, a voice that suggested age and experience with life. David instinctively knew that this was the voice of Kalesh. Taking a breath he replied.

"Barev Kalesh."

"This is John Avedisian's grandson, David."

Immediately the conversation lighted up as Kalesh jumped in.

"David ... I have been expecting your call. We heard the news of John's death. I'm very sorry."

David slightly choked up by hearing the words spoken of his grandfather's death.

"Thank you Kalesh for the kind words about my grandfather."

Kalesh sensed the sadness in David.

"How are you doing with this?"

David fought back the sadness to the point of tears.

"The best I can. My grandfather was really like a father to me and now I must also continue running his businesses and estate."

Kalesh asked gently "Running the business ... in what way?"

"My grandfather made me executor of the Will."

Kalesh straightened himself up with the news.

"Well then, you have much responsibility with such a position. Are you prepared for it?"

Taken aback a bit by the directness of Kalesh's question, David remembered his grandfather's words concerning Kalesh, that he became through the years a forceful man, getting right to the point. It's one of the reasons that his grandfather allowed him much responsibility in Armenia to disburse funds for the various charities John was concerned with.

Before David could respond, Kalesh spoke again.

"It's a good time for you to come to Armenia."

A dead silence came over the phone.

Kalesh spoke again.

"It's a good time for you to come to Armenia."

David did not know how to respond. There was so much to do here, in the United States. The New York office was clamoring about the direction of the banking interests of the former John Avedisian. Farmers in California that were depending on loans to see this years crops through to harvest needed to know if these loans would still be made available. Then there was the matter of charitable interests to Armenia and throughout the world. All of this taken together was just about more than David could handle. After all he asked himself, "Am I the man my grandfather believed me to be?"

David took a breath before responding to Kalesh.

"Why now?"

Kalesh became firmer in his response.

"Because you need to get your grandfather's vision. Do you know what kept your grandfather going all these years?"

David paused, remembering that he had asked the question many times but never came up with a definite answer. Kalesh did not wait for an answer.

"I will tell you David. It came from his heart that was lost as a boy running for his life ... having to leave his sister alone and defenseless. That suffering he held all his life. It was that very suffering which kept him to his mission in life ... to first help his close family ... then his extended family. For John ... they were the Armenian people."

David took to heart what Kalesh had said, the words ringing true about his grandfather. The question he asked of himself was if he had that same mission? His life really was so much easier than his grandfather's. Never had he been in danger and never

had he been in any kind of real want.   David's life was one of
privilege.

Can I really do what my grandfather wanted?

"If I come to Armenia then what? What do I do there?"
Kalesh's response was quick.
"You will know when you are here."

CHAPTER TWENTY-THREE

John Avedisian Dead

Memet Taletglu, an attaché with the Turkish embassy in Washington considered the situation as he continued reading the New York Times article describing the death of the billionaire. Was this the chance to propel his career from what was currently bureaucratic routine, likely to end with nothing more than a pension after 30 years?

It had been this way for 20 years now, ever since Memet joined the modern counterpart of the Turkish National Security Service, the Milli İstihbarat Teskilatı or MIT, straight out of the army. He had such high hopes then, that he could have a real impact in Turkish foreign affairs in the spirit of a modern, forward-looking Turkey. Although he would not admit it openly these days, Memet knew what his colleagues in the embassy considered a taboo subject. That is, what happened to the Armenians.

Massacre or genocide?

Memet knew all too well that to ask the question openly would be career suicide. He simply kept quiet about the issue. Still, Memet had hoped that he could be a player within a new cadre of Turks that would come to grips with the history of what happened to the Armenians. In so doing this could create cooperation between Turks and Armenians rather than the now close to 100 years of simmering conflict between the two peoples.

It was this kind of career aspiration that motivated Memet to keep track of such influential Armenians as John Avedisian.

Memet took particular notice that a daughter survived John Avedisian, but that she was given only a small portion of the billionaire's fortune. Most of the money was instead given to her son. The article spoke clearly to Memet that there could be resentment on the part of the daughter. There lay the opportunity.

As Memet continued to read on, a colleague Adem, tapped him on the shoulder.

"Interesting piece ... don't you think?"

Memet looked up.

"Indeed ... especially the bit about Debra Avedisian not getting much money."

Adem spoke quietly, almost in a whisper.

"Lets not talk about it here. Come on then ... in my office."

Memet knew the drill. Do not act interested. He inconspicuously put the paper in his brief case, taking note that he and Adem were being watched. It was no surprise. This was the business of espionage. It was completely expected that others at the embassy would see opportunity in John Avedisian's death as well. Then again, perhaps not as much as Memet and Adem could see. They really were the agents most interested in anything related to the Armenian problems. Still, quick action would be required if they were to be assigned what Memet hoped, would be the associated case.

Adem unlocked the door to his office while speaking in a noticeably loud voice. His intention was to divert attention.

"Did you catch the match? Manchester United ... amazing club."

Memet glanced to his side to see some approaching agents trying not to look noticed.

"Great match against that club from Mexico. What was the name of the guy that got the ... second goal?"

Memet acknowledged the approaching agents as he entered Adem's office. They walked by with no apparent interest. Hopefully the ploy was working, at least for enough time to come up with a plan to present to their boss.

Adem shut the door then motioned for Memet to sit at the desk.

"Can you believe he's dead?"

Memet acknowledged.

"We've watched him for so long now. It is a bit difficult to get a hold of. Not sure why actually. I mean ... he was an old man. It's just ..."

Adem completed Memet's sentence.

"Just that he was so larger than life."

Adem took notice that Memet was studying an overhead fluorescent light.

"I just had the office checked. We are clear of any bugs."

Memet relaxed.

"Ok then ... well yes ... John Avedisian... what will our world be like without him?"

Adem unlocked his desk and pulled out a folder. Memet tried to hide his surprise when he noted the folder was earmarked - 'Debra Avedisian'. Adem grinned.

"Oh come on now ... we've worked on this far too long. Did you think I was not on her?"

Memet smiled.

"Always the better researcher."

Adem laid the folder on the desk.

"Indeed ... and that is why you are the field agent and I am the guy stuck behind this desk."

Adem sat down across from Memet.

"Now ... lets get down to business."

"So do you think you have a chance with her?" Adem's loaded question caught Memet slightly off guard. Hardly any woman could resist Memet. It was not so much Memet's good looks, although none would argue his handsomeness. Rather, Memet possessed that certain quality so valuable in a field agent, charm.

Adem had only seen Memet work his charm once, during a training mission about five years back. The site – the end of a movie theater ticket line. The mission – to engage an attractive woman in conversation as a prelude to going home with her.

The selected woman had no information that was of interest to them. She was merely a training assignment to demonstrate to new recruits such as Adem, how a field agent got the job done. Although a young man at the time, Adem knew well enough that to manage such an assignment was not so particularly difficult if you were as handsome and experienced as Memet. No, the challenge was that the woman was with a man. Adem worked hard to contain his grin as he wondered how in this world Memet was going to pull it off?

Then it happened. Memet nonchalantly stepped in front of the man accompanying the woman. The offended man of course could not contain his irritation.

"Hey ... do you mind?"

Memet paid no attention as if he had done nothing wrong. The man's irritation was simmering now. It was clear to Adem that the offended man's pride had been pricked.

The irritated man again tapped Memet on the shoulder.

"Hey ... did you hear me?"

Memet's magic began. Just before addressing the offended man Memet momentarily looked at the woman with his deep blue eyes. Then he looked apologetic at the man.

"I'm sorry ... did I do something to offend you?"

The offended man was so caught off guard by Memet's naïve politeness that he failed to realize something of much more critical importance that was happening. His date could not take her eyes off Memet.

In only a moment the tables had turned from Memet being the offender to the offended. Adem had been amazed to witness how the woman's date was now actually compelled to apologize for his rude remark.

"Uh ... well fine then."

The original offended man looked at his date embarrassed. Memet smiled politely. She nudged her date who acknowledged his offense.

"Look ... I did not mean to ..."

Memet politely interjected.

"I'm so sorry to have stepped in front ... please..."

Memet stepped back to the end of the line. The offended man, now feeling completely embarrassed and also a bit rude, turned to Memet in apology.

"I'm Tim and this is Linda."

Memet graciously accepted the presumed apology using an alias and friendly handshake to Tim.

"I'm John."

Linda couldn't take her eyes off Memet's deep blue eyes. Memet for his part played on Linda's attention, pretending not to notice but then also throwing her a provocative glance with polite conversation.

"Have you heard much about this film?"

Tim was quick to take the opportunity to befriend Memet.

"Yes actually. It's supposed to be a kind of Hitchcock thriller. No name actors that I know of though."

Memet replied in a sophisticated manner to impress Linda but not to as yet aggravate the Tim.

"Hitchcock ... well then ... I will certainly be interested in the film."

Tim still had not noticed that Memet was captivating Linda. He inquired of Memet.

"Are you a Hitchcock fan?"

Memet's answer was well crafted to send a subtle message to Tim and Linda that he was the superior man here.

"Oh Hitchcock is indeed a favorite of mind. I try to capture his style in my films when appropriate."

Linda eagerly entered the conversation.

"A filmmaker ... wow ... that's exciting."

Memet once again caught Tim off guard. This time though Tim was forced to be polite without realizing it. What he didn't notice however, without consciously realizing an actual threat, was that Linda was all too impressed with this handsome man that had inadvertently come into their lives.

At this point Tim's annoyance was outweighed by relief that the earlier altercation did not go further and that they were enjoying of as yet, a polite conversation of no consequence. Adem of course knew better. He watched Memet work the couple like a game of chess.

Inside the theater Adem watched with increasing amazement how Memet played the situation between himself and Tim to look ever better the man in the eyes of Linda. Although the physical distance of the unfolding drama prevented Adem from listening to the conversation, he could tell by the admiration and fawning of Linda towards Memet, along with the apprehension in Tim's face, that the situation was likely to erupt in some kind of crisis by the end of the movie.

Sure enough, as the credits rolled, the look of apprehension on Tim's face turned to irritation.

"Ok then ... Mr. What is it ... filmmaker ... I think we are duly impressed by your qualifications about film."

Linda was obviously annoyed.

"Really Tim ... could you be any more rude?"

She looked at Memet apologetically.

"I'm so sorry."

Her words sent Tim through the roof.

"Rude ... this guy steps in front of us and then comes along on our date for the ride."

Memet said nothing in reply. Instead, his silence craftily broadened the rift between Linda and Tim. Linda lashed out.

"I've so had it with you."

Linda looked sympathetically at Memet.

"He's done nothing except be a nice guy who's enjoying a film."

Adem could hardly believe the words he heard from Tim as he sat inconspicuously while the drama unfolded.

"Nice guy huh. Why don't you just continue this date with the nice guy then?"

Linda glanced at Memet's deep blue eyes.

It's a look that Tim at last noticed and all that he was willing to take.

"I'm out of here."

Tim stormed off as Linda and Memet engaged in conversation. Adem considered what had just taken place.

The work of a pro.

Coming back to the present situation at hand, namely how to influence the life of Debra Avedisian, Adem opened the folder.

"So ... what do you think?"

Memet quickly glanced at a recent photo of Debra looking rather distraught and sitting alone.

"What is the name of the bar ... in Fresno did you say?"

Adem thumbed through some notes.

"Ah yes ... in Fresno. It's called the Blue Angel."

Memet took a closer look at the photo. Somehow the name fitted the lonely woman's face.

"Yes ... I think we have a chance here."

Adem was encouraged by Memet's confidence. At least it was enough to tell him of his plan. Memet knew his colleague too well.

"Get on with it then ... your plan please."

Adem joshed Memet.

"You are so very sure that I have a plan?"

Memet joshed back.

"Well of course you do. We've been working for too long on this. Come on with it now."

Adem brought out another folder earmarked 'Confidential'.

"This is of course strictly off the record."

Memet thumbed through the folder.

"Understood."

The folder contained dossiers on both Debra Avedisian and her son David. Memet noticed in particular the repeated mention of Karabakh.

"How much of a concern is the son David?"

Adem was circumspect in his answer.

"He is a very American young man which would lead one to believe that he will not be involved with Armenian issues the way his grandfather was. Then again ... he is the grandson of John Avedisian. Which brings up the plan. It seems likely that David will indeed follow in his grandfather's footsteps ... at least in some minimal fashion. But with the kind of money that John Avedisian's estate represents ... even a minimal effort could be highly effective against Turkish State interests. I should mention that as we speak ... even now David is traveling to Armenia and probably Karabakh."

Adem pulled out a one page planning sheet from the folder.

"The plan then ... as I have devised it ... is to focus not on David ... but on his mother Debra. She is by far the weaker link ... the one that can be exploited."

Memet caught on quickly to what Adem was suggesting.

"Let me guess ... I will become acquainted with Debra at ... let us say ... the Blue Angel bar."

Adem grinned.

"There is certainly no lack of confidence that you will have Debra in quick fashion. Seriously though ... the approach will be to develop a relationship with Debra in order to influence her ... specifically to get her to challenge the existing Will."

Memet took a last look at the planning sheet.

"We better get this plan to the boss ASAP."

Adem agreed.

"Not a moment too soon. We both know that others ... although not as well versed as we are about the issues of concern ... nevertheless will want to take an opportunity here."

Memet joined in.

"Worse yet ... they could end up doing more damage than good."

Adem took note.

"Indeed ... in regards to Turkish State interests."

Adem and Memet walked hurriedly into the office of Dr. Ali Ugur, their boss. Memet saw through the open blinds of Ali's office a not too welcome sight.

"There we go ... as you predicted ... opportunists."

Adem took notice of the two men talking with Ali.

"Of course we should have guessed it would be Teshkur and Salem. They know virtually nothing of Armenian interests but thought they could make a big catch."

Even as he and Memet walked into Ali's office, Adem couldn't resist a word of contempt.

"I can imagine a brute force strong arm approach from these two. Utterly useless!"

Ali was briefly distracted from discussion with Teshkur and Salem. He glanced at Adem and Memet entering his office.

"So you think by taking David out ... the situation could be remedied?"

Adem bristled at Ali's words knowing that was exactly the approach that would likely do more harm than good to Turkish State interests. He was curious though, about the specifics of their plan.

Adem listened carefully to Teshkur's response.

"David is the one with the money. Get rid of him and you get rid of his aid to Karabakh."

Salem took notice of Adem and Memet entering the office. He looked at Ali, irritated that they had been invited to the meeting. Ali knew the score here between the two pairs of agents. Adem and Memet generally preferred a strategy requiring a more sophisticated well thought out plan. Teshkur and Salem preferred not to depend so much on details. They just wanted to get the job done, often with violence.

Ali did not judge either approach. Rather he saw the utility of both when used in the appropriate situation. This was in fact very much a part of his overall management style. For the most part it worked well. Of course this could and often did lead to problems between agents but Ali couldn't care less as long as the job was done. The agents themselves realized this, if only in a vague, subconscious way.

Adem couldn't resist jumping into the discussion between Teshkur and Ali.

"Just how likely is it to actually kill David ... and if you miss ... then what?"

Teshkur was furious about the interruption that directly aimed at his plan. He knew however that to demonstrate his anger in front of the boss was, well, not what a good agent does if he wants to keep his career in the right direction. Instead he took a more passive aggressive approach to Adem's remark.

"Well certainly Adem has a point ... that we must be careful if ..."

Adem interrupted again.

"No ... that's not exactly what I said ... that is ... how likely ..."

This time Teshkur interrupted Adem.

"Certainly we can debate all day about how likely such and such an event may be. The main point is..."

Teshkur looked at Salem before continuing.

"That the job is done professionally."

In some ways the two pairs of agents were opposite counterparts of each other, Adem versus Teshkur as strategists and Memet versus Salem as field agents. It was again a consequence of Ali's deliberate management style, to bring together pairs of agents that contrasted with other pairs of agents.

For the problem at hand, the prevention of John Avedisian's money from helping Armenia and Karabakh, these two pairs of agents were the ones to solve the problem. Already with Adem's interruption of Teshkur's plan, the internal conflict between pairs of agents had begun. It's just what Ali wanted.

Adem and Memet took their seats directly facing Teshkur and Salem. Ali called the meeting to order.

"I have invited you all to this meeting because of the necessity to solve a long standing problem ... that is ... John Avedisian's money. When he was alive, there was hardly anything that could be done to prevent him using his money for Armenian causes ... usually in direct conflict with Turkish national security. However, now that he is gone we have a chance to stop this money flow. I have had private discussions with both Adem and Teshkur on approaches to solving this problem. You will find these plans described in detail..."

Ali paused for a moment to hand out dossiers to the four agents. He then continued.

"You will note certain differences in style of approach between the two plans. This is necessary ... I believe ... if we are to give ourselves the best chance here. You four were in fact personally chosen by me because of your ... differences in style of approach. It is essential that the two approaches will coordinate with each other."

Ali paused to look at the four agents sternly then continued.

"I again emphasize ... it is essential that we work together here. The stakes are far too high. Let us now continue with Teshkur's briefing of his plan."

Teshkur steadied himself internally as he prepared to continue discussion of his plan. He knew that despite the words of Ali about the importance of working together for the common good, the reality was that he had been placed in direct competition with Adem. It was almost humorous for him to consider this, as he and Adem had once been friends of sorts at the University in Istanbul. Even then they always seemed to be in some kind of competition, especially in the case of women.

There was one woman in particular. Her name was Nadja Tancheli. She was entirely captivating in those days, with a flowering beauty that would send any guy into dreams of a perfect life.

Teshkur still remembered the party where he first saw Nadja. The best and brightest of Istanbul's elite were all invited to celebrate election results of the Turkish parliament. The party, set up officially by professors of the university, was really brought together unofficially by top political bosses of Turkey. It was a way really, depending on one's point of view, to groom, or conform, the best and brightest to the government's point of view.

Teshkur knew this all too well. But that did not concern him at that moment. No, what concerned him was this gorgeous girl that Adem just happened to be talking to. What could he do but to play the game of being the best of friends with Adem in order to meet her? That he did, and he suspected Adem had never forgiven him for what happened afterwards. A year later, Nadja and Teshkur were married.

Teshkur opened up a slide presentation on his computer. A photo of Kalesh came up.

"This man worked many years with John Avedisian. His name is Kalesh. He is in fact, the nephew of John Avedisian."

Before continuing, Teshkur looked directly at Salem with the intent of letting all know in the room that Salem was the man to take out David.

"We are currently implementing specific methods to prevent the vehicle from arriving at its intended location."

Adem saw a point of weakness here.

"You say specific methods but lets be clear ... these methods ... if they fail ... will make it obvious that external parties, namely us, are intent on killing David."

There, I said it - killing.

Teshkur was quick to respond to Adem's critique.

"Of course there is the possibility of a particular implementation failing, but no matter, because we have many such particular implementations that will, one way or another, achieve the objective."

There was a palatable competitive fire in the room now. Teshkur rapped up the description of his plan with the response to Adem's question. Sensing this and wanting the meeting to keep moving efficiently, Ali motioned for Adem to start the description of his plan.

As he started up his computer Adem couldn't get the phrase, 'One way or another', so typical of Teshkur, out of his mind. Nevertheless Adem brought up a first photo. It was the same photo shown to Memet earlier, the one of Debra Avedisian sitting at the Blue Angel bar in Fresno.

Adem looked up at the photo.

"Debra Avedisian ... a woman with so much potential." Adem brought up another photo of Debra graduating from college.

"She was top in her class at Harvard Business School. Considered by many to be the heir apparent of her father's vast business empire."

Adem brought up another photo of Debra on her wedding day. She stood beside her husband, a handsome young man in his early 20's.

"She met her husband at Harvard. Few would argue that they were an ideal couple."

Another photo was brought up of Debra at her husband's funeral, her father comforting her as she cried in his arms.

"A hope cut short."

The photo of Debra at the Blue Angel bar was again brought up.

"Potential gentlemen ... that is all it seemed ... or at least what many think, Debra ever possessed. It is this failed potential that we intend to exploit. We have the advantage here that this lost potential is very much connected with lost love."

Adem now looked directly at Memet. His intent was to remind everyone in the room how successful Memet could be with women.

Teshkur considered this his best moment to critique Adem's plan. A tit for tat for Adem's critique of his own plan. Interrupting Adem's description Teshkur raised a question.

"So if I understand it properly ... the plan is entirely dependent on striking up some kind of relationship with Debra Avedisian? Seems a bit on the touchy feel side to me ... quite an assumption to be made given the importance of the problem to be solved."

Adem understood that Teshkur had raised a valid point. He nonchalantly glanced at Ali to see any expression of what his boss might think of Teshkur's critique. As usual, no meaningful expression of Ali could be ascertained. It was a kind of reassurance as he addressed Teshkur.

"Granted we are relying here on intangibles of the human experience ... but it is this very quality of intangibility that protects us from direct exposure of a threat to David or anyone else associated with John Avedisian's fortune."

Adem breathed easy as the words came out of his mouth. He knew that Teshkur dared not continue the discussion further for fear of rehashing the critique of his own plan.

Ali was quick to make sure no further argument broke out between Adem and Teshkur.

"Very well then. We have heard the summaries of the two plans. Read carefully these plans in their entirety."

Ali paused for a moment before continuing.

"Let us implement these plans successfully. This is what we get paid for."

All in the meeting rose up from the table and walked towards the door. Adem was walking along side Teshkur. It was a bit of an awkward moment given the exchange of critiques of each other's plan. Attempting to break the awkwardness or maybe just continue the jab of critique, Teshkur asked Adem casually, "So how's the single life treating you these days?"

Hearing these words, all Adem could think about was Nadja. How on earth he wondered, could she have fallen for a guy like Teshkur?

A *tragic waste.*

CHAPTER TWENTY-FOUR

Mount Ararat stood majestic through the clouds as David looked through the airplane window at this great mountain. He wondered if Noah's Ark was down there somewhere. His grandfather would often kid him of how, since Mount Ararat was where Noah's Ark had landed, then it must be that Noah was an Armenian.

David smiled at the thought of his grandfather telling him the story. It was the kind of story that made a young boy endeared to his grandfather. For David this was certainly the case.

The plane made it's heading downward towards Yerevan International Airport. David took one last glance at Mount Ararat and remembered his Grandpa.

The pilot had warned passengers of a rough landing due to a runway in need of repairs. As the plane slowed down to a taxing rate of speed an applause went out throughout the aircraft cabin. David joined with the applause and in so doing felt the spirit of Hayastan, the name Armenians gave to their country that originated from the legend of Haik, the founder of the first Armenian kingdom.

The plane taxied to a gentle stop, then was towed to the gate. Even before the plane had stopped moving everyone was bustling about gathering his or her belongings. David, exhausted from the trip and not wanting to join in the chaos, just sat in his seat, waiting for everyone else to exit. When the aisle was clear he got up and grabbed just the one carry-on bag that he had brought with him. It contained only gifts that he knew were important to have on hand for the people he would be meeting.

Bringing gifts when arriving for a visit to Armenia was a tradition that David knew well. Even though he was an American through and through, his ethnic culture, learned as a second generation Armenian American, was ingrained in his psyche. This had of late been a point of amazement to David. How was it he wondered that this Armenian culture, so far removed from everyday life in the United States, had such a remarkable resilience with him? There was no logical reason for it but somehow, some way, his Armenian culture seemed to permeate much of what he believed. More and more the actions he took reflected this. It was after all, the very reason he now was getting ready to step off the plane onto Armenian soil.

Making his way down the aisle David exited the plane through the gate. There he saw to his surprise, Russian security guards. A moment's thought provided the reasoning he needed to understand why the guards were Russian instead of Armenian. It was the strong connection that had existed for so long between Russia and Armenia. David remembered his grandfather saying that Russia was Armenia's big brother.

As he exited the airport terminal, David surmised the man he saw before him, a man that looked to be in his early 60's but still physically strong. More noticeable was the strength of character that showed on the man's face. It was a look of determination and gentleness all in one blend of face. This was the man Kalesh whom David had heard so much about.

At first Kalesh looked at David in a stern serious way. He then broke out in a smile as he forcefully shook David's hand.

"It's a good day when I meet the grandson of John Avedisian."

David could say nothing. He was lost for words. Somehow meeting the actual man from whom the legend came was surreal for David. He didn't know how to feel about it.

Kalesh intuitively sensed David's apprehension. He looked David directly in the eyes and laughed loudly.

"Am I what you expected?"

David smiled then began to laugh out loud as well.

"I suppose there is no choice."

Kalesh continued to laugh.

"Well then ... it's settled. Now I will show you the beautiful city of Yerevan."

A driver was waiting by a car just outside the airport. It was a black Mercedes-Benz CL600, which apparently was typical for the very wealthy of Armenians these days. The black color especially seemed to be trade mark Hyastansi, signifying the status of wealth.

To see an example of upper class wealth in Armenia demonstrated to David what had been simply an intellectual understanding. It was not just the car waiting for him that reinforced the notion for David. All around him were expensive cars, Mercedes, BMW's, Lexus's, and even a Ferrari.

If it had been New York, Los Angeles, or London, to see expensive cars would have been of no surprise for David. But this was Armenia, a country which just some ten years previous was in dire poverty due in large part to the country just emerging from a fallen Soviet Union.

The breakdown of the vast Soviet empire, with its centrally planned economy, was a deathblow for the individual republics. Essentially these individual republics lost their economic connection with each other, each republic originally being dependent on each other for resources.

This loss of connection was especially problematic for the newly formed republic of Armenia. In Soviet days Armenia had abounded with highly educated people that could develop and manufacture resources from other republics. The resulting products could be transferred back to other Soviet republics as income revenue.

Armenia had found itself with no resources to work with and no outlets for their manufactured products. The result was a complete breakdown of the Armenian economy with massive unemployment.

David of course had read all about this. It's why he was so shocked to see expensive cars in Yerevan. The experience was so unexpected that he remarked to Kalesh, "How is it that there are such expensive cars everywhere?"

Kalesh's disposition became serious.

"You are only seeing a small part of Armenia. Wait to see more before making a judgment."

Kalesh's response gave David reason to consider that indeed there were other parts of the Armenian population, likely lots more, that were not sharing the newfound wealth of the upper class.

The car departed from the airport roundabout. David took notice of the countryside. It was mostly shrubs interspersed with some trees. At first sight there was a kind of drabness to what he saw. It was not an unexpected feeling, rather it was exactly what David expected of Armenia. He knew full well the harsh history of this country since the fall of the Soviet Union, the loss of economy and even more after the war with Azerbaijan over the fate of Karabakh.

Indeed Karabakh was one of the main reasons David had come to Armenia. Literally an Armenian enclave within the borders of Azerbaijan, Karabakh had been a continual source of strife between Armenia and Azerbaijan since it was declared an autonomous region by Stalin's regime in the 1920's.

Although the population of Karabakh had been predominantly Armenian for centuries, political calculations of the early years of the Soviet Union overrode what made sense demographically. That miscalculation created a simmering tension. At long last during the late 80's, as the Soviet empire was beginning to show signs of cracking, Armenians decided to take back what was wrongfully taken.

Open protests within Yerevan for Karabakh to be reunited with Armenia proper boldly challenged the status quo. David remembered as a teenager hearing about these protests. At the time it all seemed far removed from his reality. After all, in those days Armenia was not an independent nation but instead was a small republic within the larger Soviet Union. Could anyone have imagined in those days that Armenia, let alone Karabakh, would be independent?

Thoughts of independence of Armenia and Karabakh ran through David's mind as he and Kalesh rode through Yerevan towards the city center where David's hotel was located. Situated on the perimeter of the city center, Hotel Yerevan was an elegant place. Attendants promptly greeted David as he got out of the car. Without a word they took his two bags into the hotel lobby.

There was certain seriousness about these attendants that impressed David. It was the way they handled themselves which let everyone know that they took their job very seriously. David had wondered if he would see this in Armenia. He had heard some in the United States claim that Armenia, like other Soviet republics, still suffered from a lack of individual initiative. So far though, at least from the behavior of these hotel attendants, the Armenian people were demonstrating clear initiative in their work.

Kalesh and David followed the attendants into the hotel for check-in. Because of David's association with Kalesh, the check-in clerk required no paperwork for him to fill out. Clearly he was a VIP. The clerk gave David his keys then instructed the attendants to escort David to his room.

Leaving the lobby, Kalesh said, "Please get some rest now. I will be back later this evening to take you to see mother."

David took a deep breath as he heard Kalesh talk of his mother, his great aunt Anna whom his grandfather had said so much about.

Once in the hotel room David was able to relax a bit. It had been a long journey from Fresno to Yerevan. All total almost 24 hours had passed since he left Fresno by car to Los Angeles International Airport and then by plane to Yerevan. Feeling that he would almost certainly drift off to deep sleep, David first called the hotel lobby.

"Please wake me at 5:00 PM."

This gave him at least three hours sleep. David figured he would need at least this in anticipation of meeting Anna. Drifting off to sleep David felt a sense of deep peace. At last he was in Armenia.

The phone rang. David was so tired from jet lag that he barely managed to pick up the phone. A friendly voice with a strong Armenian accent was heard.

"Hello sir. This is your wake up call scheduled for 5:00 PM."

David steadied himself then responded.

"Thank you."

Forcing himself to get up from the bed, David walked to the shower, turned on the water, then stepped in. The hot water ran over David's head, refreshing his entire body.

Toweling off, David then sorted through his bags to find a blue pin-stripe suit. He specifically brought this suit for his meeting with Anna. The reason; his grandfather John always wore a blue pin-stripe suit. It was his trademark so to speak. David hoped that wearing such a suit would in some way comfort Anna.

Straightening his tie, then combing his hair once through, David left the room and went to the hotel lobby. Coming out of the elevator he saw Kalesh sitting in a lounge chair. David checked his watch. It was 6:30 PM. He was on time.

Kalesh saw David coming out of the elevator and waved him over. Seeing David in the blue pin stripe suit gave Kalesh a reason to smile.

"In that suit ... I see your grandfather."

Kalesh started to choke up a bit but then contained himself.

"The car is waiting just outside."

David followed Kalesh outside to the car. Kalesh told the driver.

"Take us to the Cascade."

As they drove towards what is known in Yerevan as the Cascade, Kalesh asked, "Have you heard of the Cascade?"

David responded.

"Well yes ... a bit. The statue of Mother Armenia is at the top I think."

Kalesh smiled.

"It's good that Mother Armenia is known in the United States. My mother's house is nearby the statue."

The car drove in the direction of what appeared in the distance as a massive set of stairs. At the top was a statue that David couldn't quite make out. He figured that this must be the Cascade. Kalesh motioned to the driver to stop at the base of the stairs. He looked over to David.

"A good night for a walk ... don't you think?"

David looked up at the stairs. They looked to go on and on. David had not figured he would be doing such a walk in his blue pin-stripe suit. Kalesh smiled as he looked at David's reaction to the steps.

"Here in Armenia we walk whenever the weather is good. Tonight the weather is perfect. So we walk."

David grinned a bit.

"Ok then ... a perfect night for a walk it is."

Kalesh motioned to the driver.

"We will walk to my mother's house from here. Pick us up there later in the evening."

Kalesh and David started to walk up the stairs. David considered the September night, how it truly was perfect for a walk and how very much this felt like something that should be done in Armenia. Kalesh started off the walk briskly. David was surprised to see how this older man could walk up the stairs with such vigor. Kalesh smiled back at David.

"Do I surprise you with my pace?"

David was a bit embarrassed to answer.

"Strength seems to run in our family."

Kalesh grinned.

"Indeed young man ... it does."

The stairs ran in sets of about 50 steps each. All total it looked to David that there were at least 20 sets of stairs. He couldn't help but laugh to himself that he was climbing such steps in a blue pin-stripe suit. Somehow he imagined that his grandfather had arranged this.

Walking up the steps David noticed lots of people either going up or down. It seemed to be an activity well liked here in Yerevan.

Kalesh took a deep breath.

"The Cascade is well appreciated here in Armenia. Did your grandfather talk to you about my mother and I, how we walked for miles and miles in the old days? It was a way of life in Soviet Armenia, especially during the war years. People were very poor. There were very few cars available so we walked. To tell the truth, I miss those days. I think my mother does too.

When you walk there is time for finding presence. Do you know what I mean?"

David was puzzled.

"I'm not sure what you mean by presence. Is it thinking ... what?"

Kalesh looked up at the remaining stairs. They were about half way up the Cascade by now. Looking directly at David Kalesh pointed to the statue of Mother Armenia.

"How do you feel when you look at that statue?"

David looked up at the statue.

"I feel a sense of belonging, a kind of identity I guess."

Kalesh smiled.

"Then you do have some understanding of presence. But it's not in the thinking. More or less it comes from the heart. Do you understand?"

David did not know how to answer Kalesh's question. Instead the question of presence remained in David's mind as he and Kalesh continued up the Cascade. A few minutes later with no words spoken between them, David and Kalesh at last made it to the top of the Cascade. David turned around to look down at most of Yerevan. The city was brightly lit up.

Kalesh and David were standing directly under the statue of Mother Armenia. It was a magnificent statue depicting a woman with a sword. She was the protector of Armenia as the legend went. Kalesh looked up at the statue.

"I think of my mother in a way ... like this statue. She has protected me since as long as I can remember."

David studied Kalesh as he spoke, considering how Kalesh specifically did not mention his father as a protector. Vaguely David knew the story of Kalesh's father, how he was Kurdish but more importantly, that he was abusive. David was tempted to ask Kalesh about his father but decided it better to leave this alone. For now it was enough for David to learn more about Anna because she was so important to his grandfather.

Kalesh looked down the road at a beautiful house.

"We are going there."

Approaching the house, David could see it was very stylish. There was a distinctive Armenian look and feel to the house. This largely was due to it being made of Tufa, the beautiful pinkish-gray stone that it seemed most of Armenia was built of. Originating from volcanoes, Tufa is slightly porous. The rock is a mixture of colors giving it a kind of violent character. David reflected how this very nature of Tufa, that it was from a volcano, itself described Armenia's past and present. That Armenia was from a volcano, Mount Ararat itself. From there violence originated.

Chapter twenty-five

The reality of Anna's house was in stark contrast to what David had imagined. This came not from photos or actual descriptions of the place but instead from his grandfather's emotional description. It was a place for John and his sister to relive, if ever so briefly, all the years they were denied.

For John especially, this house was a place of healing for the guilt that never quite left him throughout the years for leaving his little sister alone to face the Turks. This was what David remembered most about his grandfather's thoughts of this place.

Seeing the house himself gave David pause to contemplate how it was that his grandfather's emotions about Anna came through so clearly even though such thoughts of healing were never expressed in words.

As David well knew, his grandfather was known, even to family, as the legend, John Avedisian. It wasn't that his grandfather was not a warm man. This was certainly not the case. But as it often seemed, great men have a certain persona which acts as a kind of wall where no one can enter. A last wall of defense, so to speak, that prevents opportunists from taking advantage.

John Avedisian, having managed to survive and even flourish during so many upturns and downturns of the world economy, was especially keen to such opportunists. He knew all too well that with wealth came people who would attach themselves not for good, but for a chance to take what they could. Perhaps, David reasoned, this was why his grandfather's emotions about Anna's house came through.

Somehow, someway, this emotion of healing got through to David. Was this a connection between himself and his grandfather that was revealing itself to David? At this point it was only an intuitive reaction to what appeared before him. All David knew was that ever since coming to Armenia, this connection between himself and his grandfather was showing itself in ways that David had never before considered.

Kalesh turned to David just before opening the door to his mother's house.

"Are you ready to meet your great aunt?"

David took a deep breath.

"I've heard so much about her. Now at last it's really here ... the woman my grandfather told me so much about."

David started to choke up a bit, then got a hold of himself.

"My grandfather really cherished her ... but you know Kalesh ... I don't know how to feel about her."

Kalesh could see that for David this was an entirely important moment. So much so that David had certainly the right to feel anxious. Even though he had only known David for such a short time, Kalesh had already felt connected beyond just a common relative, something akin to a good friend.

What Kalesh was beginning to realize was that this young man was not just a grandson of his uncle John by name only. No, he was indeed the grandson by essence of character, that real quality, which went beyond simple imitation, something innate that is defined not so much by spoken words, but through natural presence.

For Kalesh the realization about David was especially comforting at this very moment of introduction to his mother. He had seen all too well that in the short time of just a few weeks since his uncle's death, the effect on his mother had been serious.

Of course, Kalesh realized that his mother's emotions were entirely to be expected. Still, not since the days when he and his mother first came from Sasun to Soviet Armenia had he seen his mother so distressed. Except for those days and now, his mother had always been such a strong woman emotionally. For a son to see his mother the way she was now; it was difficult to bear.

Even as David and Kalesh were continuing to anticipate the meeting, the door suddenly opened. In an unexpected cheerful attitude Anna smiled warmly at David.

"My ... my ... I see John in you. Oh yes ... this is my brother's grandson."

David was startled that Anna could make such an affirmation in only a moment's time. Could she really see his grandfather in him or was this just a sentimental moment for an elderly lady? David knew that there was no way to really get the answer to this question. For now he could just enjoy the smile on the face of the woman that meant so much to his grandfather. If he was the cause of such a smile, then so be it.

For Kalesh to see his mother smile again was not something he needed to ask questions about. That she was smiling was answer enough.

With expected Armenian hospitality Anna took hold of David's hand with a fragile grasp. That she was very old in the physical sense was more than obvious to David. Still, what came through to David about Anna was not old age but youthful vigor of spirit. That Anna possessed without question.

"Come now and have something to eat."

David couldn't help but smile back at the words of his great aunt. It so reminded him of what he always knew to be true, at least in a kind of fantasy of Armenian women, that it is an honor to demonstrate hospitality.

The possibility for fantasy existed only for David because of the lack of such hospitality in his own mother. This had been a primary cause of contention between his mother and his grandfather. It was obvious to David that his mother's refusal to practice sincere hospitality the way Anna now showed with such ease, was in effect, some kind of open rebellion against his grandfather.

As a young boy David could only be sad about how cruel his mother could be to her own father, especially because John Avedisian was such a good man and good father. There was no way for David to really understand this as a young boy. He merely accepted it as part of the depressed personality of his mother. Was it depression or something else, anger perhaps at a life gone wrong? Whatever the answer, it was his mother that showed what to David, amounted to hatred for his beloved grandfather.

Anna could sense some apprehension, on the part of David, to her hospitality. She knew from her many years that it was not possible to know the reason why right now. Instead she instinctively acted to make the young man that so reminded her of John, welcome. Anna looked David directly in the eye with her warm smile.

"Now I see that look in you David ... I don't know why ... but come and eat. There is ... I think you Armenian Americans call it mezze ... to start."

David couldn't help but again be pleasantly distracted by the determined hospitality of Anna. That he loved the favorite Armenian appetizers known as mezze, made the experience all the more pleasant. The mezze Anna had prepared included basturma – a thin pastrami like meat, sojuk – a spicy sausage, humus, baba ganosh – a mashed eggplant dish, Armenian string cheese, bitter olives, and Armenian pickles known as tushi.

Most of these dishes David knew well from back home. This was a bit curious for him because he had heard that mezze common to Armenian Americans was typically different from what they eat in Armenia. In large part this was due to Armenian Americans being greatly influenced by non-Armenian tastes from the Middle East, humus being a typical example.

David remembered that even here in Armenia the word gets out about what kind of food Armenians from all over the world enjoy. Of course there was the possibility that his aunt remembered those dishes from the Sasun region in the Old

Country. For David such concerns were only on his mind for an instant as he was hungry now to enjoy this wonderful mezze.

David joked with Anna.

"Well my dear auntie ... the mezze is what we Armenian Americans expect."

Kalesh laughed.

"Already he is behaving like a real Avedisian."

David looked at Kalesh in a kind of a half joking half serious manner.

"You know about us Armenian Americans ... no pretense here. Just bring on the food."

Anna, now seeing she was getting through to David, lead him by the arm to the table. Despite her very slow gait, David was amazed that this sweet frail woman that was his great aunt, could still command a presence of vitality.

The beautiful spread of food included David's favorite, grape leaves stuffed with a meat and rice mixture. He couldn't resist expressing his delight.

"My favorite ... sarma."

Anna looked at Kalesh.

"Now see this boy says the real name ... sarma."

Kalesh put his arm around his mother then looked to David.

"She always insist I call them by the Old Country name. But you know here in Armenia we call them dolma."

David was confused.

"Now here just a minute ... auntie is right. Dolma are stuffed vegetables like peppers and cabbage ... not the grape leaves."

Anna laughed back at the purposely-contrived grimace on Kalesh's face.

"You see Kalesh, David knows. They are called sarma."

Kalesh looked back at David who was trying to resist laughing.

"Okay mama ... tonight in honor of our Armenian American guest we call them sarma."

Pleased with Kalesh's answer Anna answered back as she put baba ganoosh onto David's plate.

"Good boy my son ... you are learning."

The meal was well past the mezze with lamb kebab, rice pilaf, and green beans in a tomato sauce. These were all favorites of David. What he was not so familiar with was a pork kebab known in Armenia as khoravatz. A particular favorite of Hyestansi Armenians, khoravatz was largely unfamiliar to Armenian Americans due again to influences from the Middle East where pork was generally considered prohibited.

Kalesh noticed David's apprehension about the khoravatz.

"Now you must try real kebab from Armenia. Do you know khoravatz?"

David shook his head.

"I've heard about it but never tried it."

Anna looked on silently, smiling inwardly at the site of Kalesh and David becoming more familiar with each other. Without hesitation Kalesh forked a piece of khoravatz onto David's plate. David laughed.

"I guess it's time to try."

Anna and Kalesh both watched in anticipation as David took a bite of khoravatz. Both were pleased when David's face expressed great taste.

"Hey ... I like this."

Kalesh laughed back.

"You see what you are missing in America."

David joked back as he forked another piece of khoravatz onto his plate.

"Yes indeed cousin ... I think we are missing this great khoravatz in America."

The dinner finished up with Anna serving Armenian coffee and balklava. As his great aunt sat down David sensed that the conversation was about to become serious. This was expected partly because Anna had announced that she would read David's fortune from the coffee grounds in his cup. Often such fortune telling using coffee grounds was purely for fun. There was however always some notion that such fortune telling could be taken seriously, that there were reasons to take it seriously.

It was understood by all in the room that this was one such occasion where serious talk should take place. David had come to Armenia after all, not just for a nice pleasant visit, but also to decide if he was to continue the work of his grandfather for Armenia. It was a very serious decision for David, one he was not sure of, to say the least.

Anna knew David's imperative intuitively. While she did not want to force David into any action that he was not committed to of his own accord, she was nevertheless determined to present all that was necessary to convince him of the worthiness and continuation of her brother's work.

Anna studied the coffee grounds in David's cup. She smiled.

"Ah ... I see love in your future ... a love like you have never had before. She is a beautiful Armenian girl. You will not be able to resist her and she will not be able to resist you."

Kalesh punched David on the arm.

"You see cousin ... your destiny is here in Armenia."

David laughed.

"I like that word beautiful ... tell me more auntie."

Anna smiled as she continued to study David's cup.

"This girl will give you more than love. She will inspire you."

The mood suddenly took on what David had known was coming, a serious discussion about his role in Armenia. David looked intently at Anna.

"I'm listening."

Anna put the coffee cup down.

"What I tell you now is beyond what your cup tells you. This comes from me, the sister of your dear grandfather. Do you know how much I missed him during those years? If I'm honest then I will tell you that from the day we were separated as children until Kerkin told me that John was alive ... I ... did not want to be Armenian. As far as I knew ... my whole family was gone ... killed. Without family there was no Armenia for me. Then when Kerkin said those words ... that John was alive ... that's when I became Armenian again."

A tear fell down Anna's face.

"Now my brother is again ... gone from me."

David could hardly bear the intense grief, which Anna portrayed as she continued.

"But here you are ... the grandson of my dear John. I believe there are no coincidences in this world. Everything happens ... everything ... because God directs it. But we must choose if we are to follow where God would direct us. You are here David to make a choice. I cannot choose for you. Kalesh cannot choose for you. It is you that must make the choice of what you will do ... or not do ... for Armenia."

Anna hesitated for a moment then went on.

"You have heard about what is happening in Karabakh?"

David acknowledged.

"I know something ... but not enough."

It's the answer Anna was intending. She looke at Kalesh then back at David.

"Then I ask Kalesh to take you to Karabakh ... for you to find out what is happening there. Are you willing to go with him ... to find out?"

David went silent for a few moments as he looked away from Anna. He then looked directly back at her.

"I will go."

CHAPTER TWENTY-SIX

"There is a place I want to show you."

David heard the words of Kalesh as they headed south out of Yerevan in a Hummer H3. He looked outside to his right to see Mount Ararat.

"I suppose there are many places for me to see."

Kalesh shifted to 3rd gear increasing the speed along an open road that was now fully outside Yerevan. "Between here and Karabakh ... indeed there are. But this place ... you must see. We are almost there now."

They drove for another half hour until having reached their destination, the ancient church of Khor Virap.

David was awestruck at the site of Khor Virap, not only of the church itself, but also because of where the church sat. Khor Virap lay in the backdrop of Mount Ararat. The great mountain with its snow covered peak dominated against the ancient church.

Kalesh could see that Khor Virap overwhelmed David.

"Do you know of this place."

David was still overwhelmed.

"I've seen pictures of Khor Virap but could not imagine it really like I see it now."

Kalesh took a good look at Mount Ararat.

"This is why you needed to see this place. To really be here David ... that is the only way for you to make your decision. Do you understand why?"

David looked at Mount Ararat.

"It's all real ... everything I read about ... this great mountain ... this Armenia ... the place my grandfather loved so much. Now I begin to see why. Yes Kalesh ... I understand why I needed to come to Armenia."

"The origins of Khor Virap date back to the 4th century AD, that is to the very time of the Armenian nation's conversion to Christianity. History records it was here that the evangelist missionary St. Gregory the Illuminator was put in a prison dungeon for many years. The reason; his efforts to convert the Armenian people from their traditional pantheistic religion to Christianity in the late 3rd century AD.

King Tiridate, who saw Christianity as a threat, had St. Gregory put in a pit deep in the recesses of Khor Virap. Legend says that St. Gregory was kept alive during the many years of his imprisonment through the devotion of a woman who would bring the missionary food daily."

Events however were to dramatically develop in favor of St. Gregory. King Tiridate was struck by a sickness that rendered him utterly hopeless. St. Gregory was called up, out of the pit at Khor Virap, to heal the king. His prayers brought healing to the sick king.

Grateful for what St. Gregory had done, the king issued a decree that all of Armenia was to become Christian. St. Gregory then went about throughout Armenia evangelizing the population. This mass conversion to the relatively new religion of Christianity along with the date of the decree by King Tiridate in 301 AD made Armenia the first nation in the world to officially accept Christianity as it's national religion."

Kalesh pulled the Hummer onto the site of Khor Virap. It was a rugged setting of high altitude barren terrain characteristic of much of Armenia. David noticed a magnificent bird perched on a tree stump that lay on the edge of a cliff that was the limit of the Khor Virap site.

"Is that an eagle?"

Kalesh gazed at the bird.

"An Armenian Eagle ... magnificent, is it not?"

David couldn't help but relate what he saw to the American icon.

"We have such an eagle in the United States ... the Bald Eagle."

Watching the eagle launch itself into the open sky, Kalesh considered David's statement.

"I think Armenia and America have much in common."

David looked at Kalesh apprehensively.

"Both may have eagles but believe me ... there are many differences."

"Well of course there are differences ... but I'm not talking here of things such as America being large and Armenia being small. One could say it another way that America is so powerful and rich and mighty ... but Armenia is so weak and poor and lowly."

David was embarrassed that he may have over spoke.

"Please ... I did not mean to say that Armenia is somehow weak."

Kalesh reassured David.

"No David ... I did not take it that way at all. You are simply noticing what appears on the surface ... an allowed point of view. What I'm talking about is what is on the inside ... the character of what makes a people ... a nation. You see ... both America and Armenia have that spirit of independence ... to strive for what can be ... that certain element that makes a people really free. America is such a young country. Their independence has only been tested briefly. Armenia is an ancient country. Their independence has been severely tested over the long time of history."

David watched the eagle swoop down then back up along the cliff line.

"The history of Armenia ... it's certainly one of tragedy."

Kalesh reacted.

"Be careful David ... Armenia was once large and powerful and now it is reduced to a small remnant. It has indeed been through much and yet just watch that eagle. It still flies. That is the spirit of Armenia and I believe ... time will tell ... the spirit of America."

David followed Kalesh into the church. There was a sense about the place that David felt immediately. It was the history of the place, that it was here in ancient times that Armenia was forged. This went far beyond the kind of history read in books. Rather, it was that intangible essence of a place, of times long gone but which somehow offered traces of what once was. What was it like, David wondered, in the time of King Tiridates and St. Gregory? Were they but ordinary men thrust into extraordinary circumstances? What was it that made them into legend?

David considered his grandfather. What was it that made him into legend?

A guide interrupted David's thoughts.

"Would you like to see the pit St. Gregory was held prisoner in?"

Kalesh pointed in the direction of a crowd of people. They surrounded an opening in the floor that was just slightly larger than the width of an average sized man. It was the pit of Khor Virap. David displayed an obvious anticipation.

"I must see this."

The guide escorted David to the pit. Kalesh followed. A woman was just climbing out of the pit, breathing hard as she pulled herself up to level ground. The crowd applauded and cheered her on. Smiling, the woman yelled out.

"Whew ... I made it."

David could see that the crowd of people made up a tour group of Armenian Americans. One young man of the group, just about 20 years old yelled out.

"Right on Kate. What's it like down there?"

David listened attentively.

"It's another world."

Kalesh joshed David as he followed him down the pit.

"Are you ready to see what St. Gregory saw?"

The passageway to the pit was extremely narrow, barely wide enough to climb through. It was straight up and down vertical. David climbed down carefully to the room below. He walked away from the passageway to allow Kalesh to enter. Surmising the area, David looked to Kalesh.

"How is it that St. Gregory could have survived down here? I would go crazy."

Kalesh looked up through the passageway.

"A man of God ... with a purpose."

David walked around the room.

"Purpose or not ... it's so small down here. I just can't imagine not knowing if I would ever get out."

Kalesh touched the earthen ground.

"But that's just it. With purpose ... time is not considered."

David was intrigued.

"What do you mean?"

Kalesh brushed up some dust from the ground into his hand, then stood up to face David. He sparingly released the dust into the air to fall to the ground.

"The purpose of this dust is to fall to the ground. When it happens is not so important as that it will happen."

David watched the dust fall to the ground.

"For the dust it's an easy task ... to know it's purpose. It has no choice."

Kalesh sensed uneasiness in David's words.

"Choice does offer the appearance of difficulty."

The last bit of dust left Kalesh's hand as he continued.

"It is only appearance. If one allows himself to fall freely ... accepting what is ... then the choice is easy."

Kalesh put the Hummer into first gear and slowly drove away from Khor Virap.

David had enjoyed the visit. He looked back at the ancient church.

"My purpose ... here in Armenia ... it's not so clear to me."

Kalesh allowed silence for a moment then spoke.

"Your purpose here will reveal itself in proper order. Do not be concerned when it will reveal itself. You will know."

Kalesh shifted into second then third gear, picking up speed.

"For now we go to Karabakh. There you will see much purpose."

David looked straight ahead.

"This I have heard, especially since the war. Has it changed much ... since the war?"

Kalesh rounded a curve.

"Much has changed. I remember Karabakh even before the war, in the days that mother and I first entered into Armenia. Of course the Azeris would say Azerbaijan. There is a saying you know ... that Karabakh Armenians remain in the land one way or another ... either above ... or below ... ground. The first moment I entered Karabakh I knew ... without having ever heard the saying ... this to be true."

David put his arm out the window, feeling the cool air blowing against his hand.

"I've heard much of the bravery of Armenian soldiers during the war ... how they would not give up even when it seemed that the war was all but lost."

Kalesh glanced over to David then shifted to fourth gear.

"They found their purpose. It was then an easy choice. They knew it was not just about Karabakh. No ... it was about the fate of Armenia itself. For a thousand years Armenia has been loosing ground to Turks ... be they Azeris or any other kind. The war in Karabakh was a turning point. No longer would we watch as our precious land was taken from us. It was in Karabakh that a line was drawn. There would be no more Armenia lost."

David was greatly moved my Kalesh's words. Taken in with the sight of Armenia before him he felt compelled.

"What can I do?"

Kalesh smiled.

"You see my young cousin ... you are discovering your purpose ... how it's not ... when the purpose is found ... only that it is found."

David watched his hand in the wind.

"Yes ... the choice is easy."

Kalesh glanced to the right side of the road. A steep drop of at least one hundred feet lay below. It was a beautiful but dangerous site.

David again repeated his question.

"What then ... can I do?"

Kalesh hesitated for a moment then spoke.

"There is much to do. Of immediate concern are the mines. They must be cleared to give people confidence that it's safe to live in Karabakh. This is vitally important because we must settle people onto the land. It's then that they will call it their home. Everything about Karabakh invites them in. The soil is very fertile. Just about anything can be grown. What does it take ... what can you do? It's what your grandfather was doing before..."

Kalesh started to choke up a bit thinking about the death of John Avedisian. David noticed this and did not push Kalesh to continue. Regaining his composure, Kalesh continued.

"Your grandfather believed in community ... especially the idea ... something like what the Israelis have in their Kibbutz. He understood that for Armenians to survive and even flourish in Karabakh ... they would need to work together. That was his mission ... to get Armenians working together in Karabakh."

Suddenly the car lurched to the right. Kalesh tried to apply the breaks but the more he pressed the more the brakes pushed to the metal. They were now increasing speed down the dirt road. Kalesh was losing control of the car. It swerved wildly, heading first toward the mountainside to the left of the road then to the right. The Hummer was veering perilously close to the edge of the road and the steep drop that would follow. Kalesh barely managed to avoid disaster. He started down shifting the gears, to third, then to second, then to first.

Ahead Kalesh could see a section of grass that he decided was a chance to get off the gradient of the road. It was a slight incline upward. Shifting into first gear, the car now slowed. Kalesh was able to stop the car by steering into a bush. The car then stalled. Kalesh shouted.

"Get out of the car ... quickly."

The danger was now over with the Hummer locked into 1st gear. Kalesh switched the engine off.

That was too close.

Kalesh was visibly shaken. David was nearly in shock.

Kalesh got out then looked underneath the car.

"Look at this ... a missing bolt ... just under the front axle."

David came over to the right front tire along side where Kalesh was tugging at a loose rod just under the front axle.

"What part of the axle ... can I see it from here?"

Kalesh tugged again at the loose rod.

CHAPTER TWENTY-SEVEN

Memet had not expected so much traffic at seven o'clock at night. Then again, this was Los Angeles. Wanting to portray the impression of wealth he rented a Jaguar from the Avis office at the Los Angeles International Airport. The image of wealth even went to the extent of Memet buying a new Armani suit at a one of his favorite mens shop on Wilshire Blvd. He was then off to Fresno, about a three hours drive from Los Angeles.

Memet looked forward to the drive, especially the stretch between Bakersfield and Fresno, Highway 99, with it's great expanse of grapevines as far as could be seen. He was not sure exactly why, but seeing those grapevines, row upon row, had a calming effect on him.

For a brief moment Memet daydreamed of being a farmer. Memories drifted from his childhood days in Turkey. He grew up on a farm not too far from where John Avedisian himself was born. Even though a lot of work, those early days on the farm were the best years of Memet's life. Had his father not sold the farm it was at least possible that Memet would be what he daydreamed. Instead he found himself in route to Fresno to seduce a woman for reasons deemed by others, important.

The Blue Angel club was right off the Highway near downtown Fresno. Having pulled his car into the parking lot, Memet knew from another agent already in place that Debra would be at the bar that evening.

Coming to the entrance a six foot six inch fighter type was acting as the bouncer and trying to look aggressive. Seeing him at the doorway, Memet decided to let the big guy feel confident about himself. Memet joked,

"Do you want to see my ID?"

The bouncer was glad to see Memet's friendly disposition.

"I'm sure that's not necessary sir."

Walking into the club, Memet surveyed the scene. It was fairly typical as far as clubs go with a bar off to a corner and open floor space for dancing. It wasn't hard for Memet to identify Debra. She was sitting at the bar and had three men standing around her.

"Another round."

Debra asked to anybody listening, just as Memet walked up to the counter behind her.

"May I join in?" Memet asked, looking directly at Debra's back. She turned around to face Memet. He immediately saw some interest from Debra. What surprised Memet though was that he also found her taking his interest. An unexpected turn of events Memet thought. Perhaps this assignment could turn out to be more interesting than he had originally thought.

Debra was obviously on her way to getting flat on her face drunk but was not yet too far gone to accept Memet's self invite.

"Be my guest."

She toasted with the three men drinking with her. Memet then joined in with the three men and Debra.

"I just closed a deal . Allow me to buy you drinks."

Although initially a bit threatened by the good looking self invited guest, the three men became a lot friendlier when they were served free drinks.

Memet leaned in towards Debra.

"Young lady ... what can I get you?"

Debra was flattered.

"It's a long time since someone called me young lady."

Memet and Debra continued talking, each becoming more interested in the other. Realizing that they likely couldn't compete with this handsome newcomer, the three men gradually moved over to some other women also at the bar.

Now that he had Debra to himself, Memet decided to work the conversation in the direction of family, specifically her father. He did this with intention of bringing out her emotions that he knew from experience, offered him a way into Debra's inner turmoil. Once there, Memet knew he had a good chance of winning her over.

Debra spoke out in an emotional voice.

"I loved my father but he never wanted me to help him. Still ... I always had helped with the business."

What she omitted to tell was that she had nearly run the business into the ground. Memet of course knew this already from reports back in the DC office. Debra continued to reveal herself.

"I love my son but he was always taking my father's side."

She went on.

"Daddy didn't trust me. I think it was my son that gave him the bad ideas about me."

She hiccuped.

"Oops ... sorry."

Debra and Memet continued to talk, oblivious to the crowd that was now forming in the bar. Memet then said, "Excuse my rudeness. My name is Richard Davidian."

Debra smiled.

"You are Armenian?"

Memet smiled back.

"Ah ... you can tell by the name. I'm part Armenian ... on my father's side. I guess here in Fresno it's more common than not."

Debra was intrigued.

"You are not from around here then?"

"No. Actually I'm from Washington D.C. I'm here for a meeting today."

Memet had a hunch that Debra's interest was caught so he continued.

"I'm with farm equipment."

"So how was your meeting?" Debra asked.

Richard played the part of a humble yet successful man.

"Well today ... can you believe ... I made my company two million dollars."

Debra reached out to shake Memet's hand.

"Well let's shake to your good fortune."

Richard took Debra's hand.

"Indeed ... thank you ... and your name?"

Debra hesitated knowing that when she gave her name the handsome man she was getting to know may recognize her from the newspaper headlines. Still she was almost drunk so who cared anyway. She gave her name.

"Debra Avedisian."

Memet smiled.

"Your name gives you away."

Debra frowned a bit.

"Yes ... the newspaper headlines."

Memet pretended to not understand.

"Newspaper ... I just meant that you are Armenian."

"Oh ... wait a minute ... you are."

Debra was embarrassed.

"Yes ... I'm afraid so ... that Debra Avedisian."

It was a perfect opportunity for Memet to show some understanding for Debra's plight. He did not miss a beat.

"I can imagine ... you must be sick and tired of the media coverage."

Debra sighed.

"It really is getting to be too much."

Memet took Debra's right hand gently.

"Say ... I enjoy talking to you. Would you care to join me for dinner?"

Debra straightened herself.

"Are you flirting with me Richard? By the way ... you do look like a Richard."

Sitting with Memet over dinner Debra could not help but fall for him. He was charming but without pretense. She found him so easy to talk with and noticed that he actually listened to what she had to say, something Debra was not used to with many other men, especially she thought, her current boyfriend Mike.

The conversation took on many different directions that Debra found fascinating. Surprisingly for himself, Memet also found the conversation very stimulating. At one point he had to remind himself that this was not a real date that he was very much enjoying. He reassured himself that the enjoying part was okay, a perk of the job.

Following the main course, Memet ordered some Port wine. They sipped the wine as Memet readied himself to get to the main subject.

"You seem to be quite bitter about your father."

Memet paused before continuing.

"Please excuse me for asking ... do you think your son poisoned his mind against you."

Debra was caught by the question.

"Yes ... I'm bitter. I get ten million dollars and the billions go to my son. Do you know what he will probably do with the money? Give most of it to Armenia and their causes."

Debra began to get tears in her eyes.

"Probably Karabakh."

She went on.

"Do you know that Daddy once wanted me to go to live and work in Karabakh ... on one of the communal village type places. We had a big argument. I told him that I didn't even speak Armenian. How could I survive there?"

Memet tried to be consoling.

"I remember my father telling me to do things I didn't want to do. Life gets very unfair sometimes."

Memet now saw the opportunity to start influencing Debra according to plan objectives.

"From what I hear ... it would be a waste to put time and money into Karabakh since that territory will eventually be back in the hands of the Azeris. Azerbaijan will never sign a peace treaty with Armenia because they believe Karabakh is their land. Probably there will be another war soon."

Checking to see that he had caught Debra's attention, Memet continued with a smile.

"Ok ... now I'm on my soap box but you ..."

Debra smiled back.

"No ... please continue."

Memet took his cue.

"It's a bit like the Falklands to Great Britain. The people want a choice to whom they identify with. In that case ... Britain or Argentina. Ultimately for Karabakh ... the people will have no choice due to larger politics at work. It will be part of Azerbaijan."

Debra studied Memet's face as the conversation continued.

He's smart and handsome.

Debra's boyfriend Mike had not been around for quite a few days. She was pretty sure that he was only after her money anyway. Given that she only received a small portion of her father's estate, the likelihood that Mike would stay in her life was remote at best. So, she considered it time to make a move.

Debra joked.

"A decent man would escort a young lady home."

Memet took his cue.

"Most certainly ... it would be an honor to make sure you get home safely."

Debra accompanied Memet to his car. Taking note that Memet drove a Jaguar ranked up another good point in Debra's mind.

He has money too.

Memet drove Debra home. She lived in a high-class area of Fresno overlooking Millerton Lake. As they drove through the gates to her house Memet was suitably impressed.

"Beautiful place you have here."

Debra smiled.

"Thank you. I do love this place."

There was a brief somewhat awkward pause more common than not at such moments when two people are attracted to each other.

I can't let him go so quickly.

"Would you like to come in for some coffee?"

Memet smiled graciously.

"That would be really nice ... thank you."

Getting out of the car Memet quickly came around to Debra's side. In true gentleman fashion he took her left arm with his right arm. Feeling his masculine touch sent Debra into a kind of infatuated trance. Memet noticed the moonlight shining on the lake.

"What a magnificent view. Do you mind if we walk to the lake shore?"

Debra was enthralled at the opportunity.

"By all means ... lets do. There's a path we can walk on."

Debra motioned to cobblestone walkways that lead to the lake shore.

"It's just over there."

Walking to the shore Memet himself was noticing that he was truly enjoying himself. He wondered if somehow he should be more serious about what was taking place. But then hey, he thought to himself, why not just enjoy the moment. Then, before he could understand what was happening, the moment came, when attraction between a man and a woman occurs in a romantic setting. The first kiss.

Pulling away gently from the kiss, Memet saw the moonlight reflecting from the lake onto Debra's eyes. For an instance he forgot all about his mission and just felt the beauty of her. There was no anticipating this attraction. It was not that Debra was the most beautiful of women that he had been with. No, it was much more than that.

Debra possessed a kind of kindred spirit that Memet had not experienced in a long time, not since his days in Turkey. A legend came to Memet's mind, that the eyes of an Anatolian woman can reach into a man's soul. Could it be that Debra was reaching into Memet's soul? Memet wondered as he looked at Debra's eyes.

Debra smiled.

"That was nice."

Memet smiled back.

"Indeed."

Debra grabbed hold of Memet's arm in a more confident fashion.

"Come on then ... I will serve you some Turkish coffee. It's a specialty of mine."

Memet was caught off guard by the mention of 'Turkish' with the coffee. Then he remembered that Fresno Armenians do call their coffee 'Turkish', a remnant of their Anatolian roots.

Debra unlocked the back door of her house. It was a very nice place. The home itself was on three floors with a patio outside. A ground floor held the kitchen, which was tastefully laid out. The second floor provided a kind of living room loft that could be seen from the kitchen. A desk was noticeable on one side of the loft with the remaining area being occupied by a flat screen TV and couch adjacent to a fireplace.

Debra took Memet's hand and lead him up the stairs to the couch. Memet now noticed it was positioned with a view of the lake. Glancing at the lake, Debra let go of Memet's hand.

"I will get us that coffee."

Memet smiled.

"Thank you."

Sitting down on the couch and admiring the view, Memet felt at peace. It was a wonderful feeling that he had not experienced in quite a while. A few minutes later Debra brought the coffee. She laughed.

"Now I must warn you. I have been known to tell a man's fortune from the coffee."

For a split second Debra caught herself with those words, not spoken since the days with her deceased husband.

How is this man effecting me?

As they finished the coffee both Memet and Debra automatically put their cups upside down on their saucers. This allowed the grinds to be prepared for a fortune telling reading. Whether Turkish or Armenian, it was the Anatolian way. Memet lead off.

"So what do I pay for such a fortune telling?"

Debra laughed seductively.

"I will let you know ... later tonight."

Memet glanced at Debra in a passionate look that he couldn't help but give.

"Very well then."

Debra took Memet's cup and saucer then lifted the cup up to read the grinds. With inquisitive voice Debra studied the cup.

"I see a future for you that you do not expect ... a dramatic change of life that will bring you back to your roots."

Watching Debra read his cup took Memet back to his childhood days in Turkey. His grandmother would read the cups. Although never taken completely seriously, it was Anatolian tradition to at least take note of what the fortune could portend. As such, Memet could not take what Debra said with no regard.

"Will I like the change?"

Debra's face became very serious, holding the expression to a point of tension. Then suddenly she laughed.

"I had you there now didn't I?"

Memet laughed back.

"Whew ... you sure did."

Debra continued.

"Okay then ... you will like the end result ... but I must be true to the cup ... getting there will be a challenge for you. Can you accept that?"

Memet hesitated before answering in a half laugh.

"What can I do then? I can only accept my fate."

Debra's face turned serious as she put down Memet's cup and saucer.

"I suppose that's all any of us can do."

The next morning Memet awoke to see that Debra was not on the other side of the bed. He got up and went in search of her. Predictably, she was sitting at the bar having a drink. Even though it was already eleven o'clock in the morning, she was still in her nightgown. Memet had been around women long enough to notice when they were bothered by something.

Memet prepared himself before speaking.

"Good morning."

Debra took a drink before responding in a somewhat subdued way.

"Oh ... good morning."

Memet choose his next words carefully.

"You seem upset. Is everything okay?"

Debra stared down at her drink.

"I'm sorry ... it's nothing really."

Memet carefully continued.

"If you feel like telling me ... I'm here to listen."

Debra was so moved by Memet's concern.

"Are you sure ... I don't want to bother you with..."

Debra went silent. Memet took the initiative.

"Please ... I will be glad to listen."

Debra took confidence to continue.

"It's just that I can't get the idea of my son getting away with all of Daddy's money. I was his daughter after all. He doesn't deserve that money."

Debra's last phrase, that her son doesn't deserve the money, woke Memet up from what could only be described as a love affair, back to his mission. It was the break he needed. Memet took a seat next to Debra.

"There's something I must confess to you."

Debra paid close attention.

"Confession?"

Memet realized he might have come on a bit too strongly.

"What I mean is that I have heard of you ... from the papers."

Debra sighed.

"It seems the whole world knows of my humiliation."

Memet took hold of Debra's hand.

"Please ... there is no need for you to feel humiliated. When I first read the story and now especially ... after knowing you ... what comes to my mind is injustice."

Debra inquired back.

"Injustice ... do you really think so?"

Memet was resolute in response.

"Absolutely! How is it that a grandson should get nearly all the money while a daughter is denied what is rightfully hers? My thought is that your father was unduly influenced in the writing of that Will. Such a Will in my opinion should be declared invalid."

Debra was startled by Memet's statement.

"Invalid ... if only that were the case."

Memet went silent until Debra spoke.

"What?"

With calculated hesitation Memet continued.

"Perhaps it can be the case."

Again silence until Debra spoke.

"But how?"

Memet took hold of Debra's other hand, both of her hands now in his.

"I have a friend that may be able to help. Are you interested?"

Debra paused before speaking, knowing that continuing this line of discussion would almost certainly lead to actions that may be laced with regret. The temptation was however too great for her to resist.

"I could be."

Memet's eyes took on a serious expression.

"Very well then. My friend is a lawyer specializing in probate law. He can ... shall I say ... be creative in establishing alternative Wills."

Debra felt a pit in her stomach.

"But isn't that forgery?"

Memet kept a serious focus.

"Couldn't it also be said that the current Will is a forgery. Who can determine that really?"

Debra couldn't quite believe that she was having such a discussion, but listening to the words from such a handsome gentleman, could what he said really be all that wrong. Memet continued.

"Would you be interested in at least talking with my friend ... just to see what could be done?"

Debra hesitated.

Just stop right now before it's too late.

The temptation was too great for Debra to resist at this point.

"Okay ... why not."

Chapter twenty-eight

Memet opened the restaurant door for Debra. It was a classy place in Beverly Hills called the Crescent. Debra had just flown into Los Angeles from Fresno on a commuter flight specifically for the purpose of meeting the friend Memet had mentioned. The friend would help Debra with a new Will. That friend was actually Adem. His purpose was to close the deal with Debra, to get her to agree to the creation of a new Will.

A very expensive restaurant, the Crescent under normal circumstances would have caused Memet's boss to question the outlay. However, it was vitally important to give Debra a good feeling so Memet had chosen a place that would impress and where they could also talk quietly.

Based on Memet's report of his arrangement with Debra so far, Adem knew that he could take nothing for granted. Despite his colleague's way with women, it still could prove to be a hard sell. Even one mistake could wreck the deal. He told himself this as he waved Memet and Debra to his table. Adem stood up from his chair to greet Debra. He shook Debra's hand in American fashion.

"My name is Hovanes. It's a pleasure to meet you."

Debra acknowledged back.

"My pleasure too."

Sitting down at the chair that Memet had pulled out for her, Debra hesitated momentarily before speaking again to Adem.

"I'm trying to place your accent."

Adem tried to maintain his cool.

"I'm from Istanbul originally. There are still many Armenians there today."

Memet gave Adem a look to take it easy with the explanations. Adem took note that this is why he never made it as a field agent. Despite his concerns, Debra acknowledged Adem's explanation.

"Well ... that's us Armenians ... from all over the world."

Adem was inwardly relieved and appreciative of Debra's graciousness.

"Thank you."

A waiter came by asking if they would like to order drinks and appetizers. Memet by now knew the drink of choice for Debra and so ordered it for her.

"She will have an apple Martini."

Realizing that he may have taken too much prerogative with Debra, Memet paused.

"Sorry ... I did not mean..."

Debra smiled.

"Thank you dear. I like it when a man knows what I want."

Adem noted a smile of relief on Memet's face at the hearing of Debra's words. He thought it curious that an agent so experienced with women would appear to care about what Debra thought. Adem admitted to himself that despite what he read in reports about Debra, she did have a charming quality about her. It was clear to Adem that Memet saw this as well.

Memet continued with the waiter.

"I will have a Scotch on the rocks."

The waiter looked at Adem.

"Gin and Tonic for me."

Adem laughed inwardly that if the mothers of Memet and himself could only see their good Muslim boys drinking liquor, they would be furious. But then that was the life of an agent in the Turkish MIT.

The waiter then asked.

"Have you decided on any appetizers?"

Adem was beginning to feel more comfortable and so took the initiative in ordering. He looked at Debra. "They have marvelous stuffed mushrooms with crab here."

Debra took a glance at the menu, then at Memet.

"Do you like crab?"

"Stuffed mushrooms with crab does sound good."

Debra looked back politely at Adem in the affirmative. Adem then looked up at the waiter.

"Stuffed mushrooms with crab it is then."

The waiter acknowledged.

"I will get that right up to you along with the drinks."

Adem surmised that if Memet had already made such progress in getting Debra's affection then his job of convincing her about the new Will may be much easier than anticipated. Then he checked himself.

"Hold on there. This is just drinks and stuffed mushrooms ... a long ways away from a forged Will."

The word 'forged' stuck in Adem's mind.

The dinner was going well with excellent food and conversation. Adem couldn't help but keep noticing that the chemistry between Memet and Debra was really quite remarkable. If he did not know better he would be convinced that Memet himself could very well be falling for this remarkable woman.

Contemplating his own perspective, Adem reflected on how such a woman with the qualities of Debra could have fallen from grace so to speak. It spoke to him of the human condition, so prone to tragedy. There was a momentary feeling of guilt. How he and Memet were using Debra's tragedy to achieve their aims. Then he checked himself. They were not here to enjoy a lovely meal with a lovely woman. No, he and his fellow agent were here to work, to serve the Turkish state.

With the mission in mind Adem initiated the topic of concern with Debra.

"So, Richard tells me that you have some concerns about the Will."

There was an awkward silence at Adem's words. Memet stepped in for Debra who looked distressed by being put on the spot.

"Hovanes, my good friend ... you do have a direct way of starting such conversations."

The gracefulness of Memet's words brought out a laugh from Debra that Adem himself couldn't help but join in with. Adem then continued.

"Indeed ... I must confess that being indirect is not one of my strong points."

Debra smiled as she gently tapped Adem on the arm.

"That's quite all right. It's a sensitive subject and I do appreciate that you are here to explain the opportunity."

Debra checked herself to not be so coy with something that from her perspective was at best questionable and at worst, illegal.

Memet could sense that Debra was uncomfortable with how the conversation would likely be going so he decided, given that they have just finished dinner, to order a coffee. He looked to Debra and Adem.

"What do you say to a Cappuccino?"

Debra knew that Memet was looking after her interests.

He's a real gentleman.

Adem could see the practical usefulness of Memet's suggestion.

"A Cappuccino sounds perfect ... and you Debra?"

Debra acknowledged.

"Why yes ... I would love one."

Memet then motioned to the waiter.

"May we order three Cappuccinos?"

The waiter acknowledged.

"My pleasure ... I will get those to you right away."

After thanking the waiter Memet looked at Adem to continue his explanation. Adem took the cue.

"As an Armenian I can certainly appreciate your concern for how your father's vast estate will be spent. Let me be frank, this kind of money, if not used properly, could cause great harm to Armenia and indeed, to the entire Armenian people."

Memet couldn't help but admire the eloquence of Adem's initial argument, couched in terms of concern for Armenian interests when in reality it was designed to thwart those very interests. He listened as Adem continued.

"It is of course widely known that if your son significantly funds projects in Karabakh, specifically the settlement of Armenians in that territory ... well then ... it will only antagonize Azerbaijan and by extension, Turkey."

Debra interjected with concern.

"I may not be a politician but why should Armenians be concerned about antagonizing Azerbaijan and Turkey?"

Adem purposely paused circumspectly then continued.

"You raise an important question. Certainly we can all acknowledge that traditionally these two countries are sworn enemies of Armenia. However, long term they are neighbors of Armenia and as such they must be approached to become friendly. Let's face reality. Karabakh has proven to be a thorn in the side of Armenians."

Adem purposely bit his tongue just long enough to allow his words to settle with Debra. He then continued.

"So many of us died in the war to claim that territory and today Armenia suffers economically because of the blockades of its exports. It is forced to ship its goods primarily through Georgia and Iran. Can this continue indefinitely? I think not. Anything then that overtly antagonizes either Turkey or Azerbaijan is detrimental to the Armenian Cause. Your son's intended funding for increased settlement of Karabakh is indeed antagonistic."

Cappuccinos were being served just as Debra raised another question.

"I can see what you're saying but he is my son and honestly ... I can't say that he is committed to helping Karabakh, at least not yet. He's only just visiting Armenia and Karabakh for the first time."

Memet appreciated Debra's defense of her son. It reminded him of his own mother, how she would always come to his aid no matter what she believed herself.

Adem could also sense a mother's concern for her son. He responded carefully to Debra.

"Of course we can't presume your son's disposition on the matter. However it is well known ... please excuse me here for being direct ... that he greatly admired your father. Indeed ... he followed in your father's very footsteps."

Debra interjected.

"No offense taken. Please continue."

Adem acknowledged Debra politely.

"As an Armenian I dare say ... to allow your son ... however well intentioned ... to fund the increased settlement of Karabakh is extremely detrimental to the Armenian Cause. Something must be done to prevent this."

Adem paused in anticipation of a question from Debra. She did as expected.

"I suppose then ... that this is the reason we are here tonight?"

Adem was circumspect.

"Indeed ... it is."

Debra looked around to make sure no one was overhearing the conversation.

"What I know is that what you are about to suggest makes me very uneasy. I mean a new Will ... if it's found out ... then I could end up with nothing. I know this because there is a clause in the present Will which states that all rights will be lost to anybody contesting."

Debra looked down at her cup of Cappuccino in embarrassment.

"You see ... my money is running out. Even the amount given to me in the current Will ... it is at least enough to keep me going."

Memet could plainly see that what Debra said was difficult for her to express. He took her hand. Adem continued.

"I can understand ... really I do."

Adem purposely hesitated just for a moment to show this concern, which in some unexpected way was partly genuine. He then continued.

"What you mention about loss of rights due to contesting is considered standard in most Wills. Fortunately there is a law that allows for what is called 'Safe Harbor'. It's a feature of the law that allows a Will to be contested if there is reasonable doubt about that Will. This protects the contesting party. Of course a judge would make the decision."

Debra interjected.

"But really ... there is no fraud here or other causes that I can think of. My lawyer has already looked into it."

Adem was prepared for Debra's concern.

"But there are other reasons. I strongly believe a case can be made to show that the present Will was ill intentioned at a time when your father was emotionally impacted by the plight of Armenia during the Karabakh war. A later Will would be far more reflective of your father's wishes later in life."

Debra was a bit shocked by Adem's argument.

"Are you actually saying that a new Will..."

She looked around to make sure no one was overhearing what she was about to ask.

"My father would agree to it?"

Debra knew even as she asked the question that her father would never have agreed to such expression in a new Will. Nevertheless she would gladly accept any kind of acknowledgment that it could actually be. Adem gladly gave the acknowledgment.

"I believe so."

Debra had now tasted the fruit of denial. It intoxicated her. Memet could feel this literally, as she let loose of his hand and turned directly toward Adem. The moment brought with it certain sadness even for Adem in that even though he had won over Debra through well executed argument and persuasion, what would be the cost for this woman?

A piece of her soul.

What did it say about Adem's own soul? Had he lost that part of humanity that cared about the ultimate fate of people? Adem could hardly bare to inwardly admit the question.

Chapter twenty-nine

"Do you think he will agree to it?"

Adem asked his boss Ali over the phone from his hotel room in Los Angeles.

Ali responded.

"I don't expect problems. He owes us ... so to speak. You are expected at his office tomorrow at 9:00 AM."

Adem hesitated briefly before asking the next question.

"How much does he know at this point?"

Ali was reticent in his answer.

"I leave that to you."

Adem thought to himself.

"Never a straight answer ... it's why he is the boss."

There was only one response that made sense for Adem to say.

"Very well sir. I will be at his office as scheduled. Thanks again."

There was no thank you on the other end of the line, just a click that told him the discussion was over. So it went with the upper echelon of the MIT, always protecting themselves in the event that a case went bad. Adem wondered why his boss was careful not to divulge details about such an important person? Did it portend a lack of confidence in the ultimate success of this mission?

The important person here was an Armenian lawyer originally from Turkey, Aram Tertanian. His reputation was untarnished in Los Angeles. That was until about a year ago when his son Kevork was apprehended by the Turkish MIT in Istanbul on charges of smuggling historical artifacts out of Turkey. It was an honest mistake on the part of Kevork who did not know that the books he bought at a local Istanbul Bazaar were registered as historically property.

Under normal conditions a small fine would have sufficed to get Kevork off and back safely to the United States. But once the MIT became aware of the young man's predicament, they moved to step up the charges. The reason; use the son's incarceration to force his Los Angeles based lawyer father into doing the bidding of the MIT.

As Adem prepared to enter the office of Aram Tertanian he had this gnawing feeling that this mission was causing him ever-increasing anxiety. He knew why but refused to admit it to himself because to do so was to admit that maybe, just maybe, he was really not cut out for espionage work.

Until this mission, Adem's assignments were so detached from his personal reality that they were of no consequence to his self defined identity. However, with the manipulation of Debra, and now what amounted to blackmail of the man he was about to meet, well, this was beginning to cause the kind of distress that gets a man to wonder if what he is doing is right. Adem knew when he signed on for the job that working as an MIT agent would of course entail some compromise of personal values. At the time he deemed the compromise worthy to protect his nation, the Turkish Republic. Now he was not so sure.

Adem opened the door and immediately was greeted by an attractive receptionist that looked to be straight from Hollywood, a blond haired blue eyed beauty, about 25 years of age. Apparently the Turkish imposition on Aram Tertanian had not been so bad, at least as office aesthetics went. Still, Adem thought to himself, a pretty receptionist does not say much about the man's personal anguish over his son. Again Adem was reminded how much he dreaded meeting this lawyer even though he knew this was the guy for the job.

Adem snapped out of his minds wanderings upon hearing the receptionist.

"Good morning sir. Can I help you?"

As a single man, not too far in age from the attractive young lady, Adem smiled in response.

"Yes ... I am Hovanes Karazian. Mr. Tertanian is expecting me ... at 9:00 AM I believe."

The receptionist became quickly attentive upon hearing Adem's alias, necessary to maintain his cover. She was told by her boss to expect him.

"I will let Mr. Tertanian know you are here."

No sooner had the receptionist put down the phone did she tell Adem what he had expected.

"Mr. Tertanian will see you now."

She stood up from her chair and directed Adem through an open door then through a hallway.

Aram Tertanian sat at his desk, in his office, as Adem stepped through the open door.

"Good morning."

This is terribly awkward.

It was the only immediate thought that Adem could have. Here he was, a Turk, asking, no forcing, an Armenian man to do his bidding. Worse yet, the bidding was at the expense of this man's integrity. Adem wondered how he would feel if the roles were reversed?

Aram brought out a document from his desk drawer.

"Here it is."

No words of explanation needed to be said about the document. Adem knew exactly what it was, a forged Will.

"Are you confident of its authenticity?"

Adem felt a sense of disgust asking the question. Aram replied in a matter of fact way.

"It's all there ... prepared by one of the best ... whom I am not at liberty to say."

"The forg ..."

Adem caught himself before saying the word 'forgery'. Better to keep up the charade.

Nothing gained by telling the truth.

Had it really come to this, Adem wondered? To deny the truth, well of course that's part of the espionage game. Adem knew that all too well. But to have it slammed in his face, he was beginning to feel disgusted with the entire affair.

CHAPTER THIRTY

Just a few miles from their destination, a small village in Karabakh, Kalesh was rethinking the cause of the Hummer lurching sharply to the right.

"What do you think now David ... about the missing bolt?"

David was not surprised by Kalesh's question. What did surprise him was that this time at least, his internal questions were valid, or were they? Almost certainly Kalesh was going to ask the question about the bolt. That was a given. David would remain left with his own questions that, except for his own intuition, could not be validated. Nevertheless, David took some relief in answering Kalesh's question.

"It does seem that the missing bolt could be more than just a factory caused problem."

Kalesh glanced over to David, then back at the road.

"I tell you David ... there are those at work here that would see us dead. I never before saw this when I accompanied your grandfather. Why then are they after you?"

David looked straight ahead as he answered.

"Perhaps they consider me an easy target."

David laughed as he continued.

"But then so far they have been wrong."

David looked over to Kalesh.

"At least that's what is happening because you are accompanying me. My thanks to you."

Kalesh acknowledged David's thanks.

"My pleasure David ... especially because we are family."

David saw what looked like a small village in the distance about a half a mile out.

"Is that it?"

Kalesh took his hands off the steering wheel for a second "Yes ... that's it."

As they approached the entry point to the village, Kalesh continued.

"Is this what you expected?"

David did not answer right off. Someone he saw distracted him.

Kalesh laughed.

"Indeed ... it's not what you expected."

He was referring to a beautiful young woman that had caught David's infatuation.

David kept his attention on the young lady.

"Do you know who she is?"

Kalesh smiled.

"And why do you ask?"

David now laughed a bit.

"Come on now man ... you know why I ask."

Kalesh couldn't hold back his laughter any longer.

"Indeed ... I do know why and yes ... I know who she is."

David was waiting for more information but Kalesh went purposely silent. Finally Kalesh spoke.

"Her name is Ani Der Vardanian."

David wanted more information about Ani.

"So ... what do you know about her?"

Kalesh played David's question off.

"Her ... who do you mean?"

Both men started to laugh until Kalesh spoke again.

"Oh ... you mean Ani. Well let me tell you David ... her beauty is a lot more than just what you see on the outside. I've known her family for years and Ani ... since she was a very little girl. You see David ... I am Ani's Godfather."

David lighted up.

"Godfather ... now that's what I wanted to hear."

Kalesh suddenly became very serious.

"Hear me clear David. Ani is an Armenian girl through and through. She is to be treated as a special jewel. If you do this ... the jewel will shine for you as you could not imagine."

David went silent. Kalesh then continued.

"And yes ... I will introduce you."

David smiled.

Kalesh drove up to what looked to David to be a small schoolhouse. This was confirmed when David saw kids playing along the side of the building on a makeshift playground. Although the village itself would be considered relatively poor, the kids were impressively dressed. David noticed this throughout Armenia. It was an example of how kids in Armenia were treated with special care. There was a certain brightness in their eyes that David wished could remain throughout their lives.

What is it David wondered, which takes that special brightness from children as they grow up?

Searching back into his own memory David could just barely remember that brightness in his own eyes. Perhaps here in Karabakh David would get some of that brightness back. Just as he considered this, a reason for that possible brightness appeared. It was Ani. She was so excited to see Kalesh who greeted her with a traditional Armenian kiss on both cheeks. Ani spoke excitedly.

"We did not expect you here for another month."

Ani glanced at David then continued to speak to Kalesh.

"Why are you here?"

Kalesh looked at David who had come around from the other side of the car.

"I've brought this young man to meet you."

Ani displayed a shy smile at David then laughed at Kalesh.

"You embarrass me."

David reached to shake Ani's hand.

"I'm David."

Ani looked back at Kalesh.

"Is this him?"

Kalesh looked at Ani with a calm peaceful presence.

"This is the grandson of John Avedisian."

Ani took a good look at David.

"Well then ... I'm very pleased to meet you David."

Ani headed into the schoolhouse.

"I have to teach now but please..."

Ani gave David a smile that made him feel special.

"I must show you our village here."

David smiled back.

"I look forward to it."

As Ani disappeared into the schoolhouse David couldn't contain his excitement.

"Man Kalesh ... I see what you mean about her beauty being a lot more than what is on the outside. There's just something about her."

Kalesh motioned for David to get back in the car.

"Come on now ... there is someone else I want you to meet."

David was still thinking about Ani as they drove off. Her beauty caused him to notice the raw beauty of the surrounding landscape.

"This place is like heaven."

Kalesh looked at a big green hill that David was admiring.

"Indeed ... heaven ... it's why we fought for this place and why we continue to struggle for it."

David looked straight ahead at an old woman walking by the side of the road.

"I believe I'm starting to understand that struggle ... why it's worth it ... and what I must do in this struggle."

Two seemingly juxtaposed thoughts ran through David's mind, the close call where the car nearly went off the cliff, and now Ani. David could never have imagined it all, how it had caused him to reflect on his own brief life so far. He had a sense that here, in Karabakh, there was life and there was death. All of it was real. There was not much fantasy here. No, it's tough and beautiful at the same moment, a place where a man will, must, find out who he really was. David was not sure if he wanted to find out who he was, but whatever the outcome, he would at least know.

The wind blew briskly as David got out of the car near a humble looking house. Kalesh came around to his side. He and David made their way up some steps onto a porch. To his surprise David noticed an old wooden sign that was labeled 'Sun-Maid Raisins Fresno, California'.

David wondered how it was that the sign turned up here unless, and then David guessed whom they were meeting, that person was from Fresno.

The door opened. A very old man stood at the door. David knew immediately who he was. The old man standing before him was his grandfather's dear friend. It was Kerkin. Although David only met Kerkin once before, when he was just a boy, there was no mistaking that grin of his. It had a kind of mischievous quality that suggested a man who enjoyed playing life out no matter what the circumstances.

Kerkin was definitely the kind of man that thrived on challenges and who made fear his friend. Certainly just by his exploits, anyone would say that Kerkin's life was one of uniqueness and great adventure. What was also evident though, was a deep hurt that this man carried, the kind of hurt that never went away.

David vaguely knew about Kerkin's hurt through family stories. Mostly they had something to do with Kerkin losing his wife through divorce and never getting her back. These stories David had to work hard as a boy to hear, as they were something talked about in hushed voice, a kind of sad legend.

Kerkin looked at David once over then came back with the grin.

"How many years young man ... has it been?"

David smiled at Kerkin then without hesitation warmly grabbed his right hand with both of his.

"Far too long. It was in Fresno ... at an Armenian picnic in the summer."

Kerkin's eyes lit up.

"Ah yes ... you were just about 10 years old and eating shish kebab when your grandfather brought me around."

Kerkin stopped to motion David and Kalesh into his home. He then continued recounting his meeting with David.

"Do you still like to eat shish kebab ... as they make it at the Fresno picnics?"

David walked into Kerkin's home.

"I still do ... especially the way they make it at those picnics."

Kerkin motioned for an attendant to bring some food to a small coffee table where the three men sat down. As they ate Kerkin again looked David over.

"The first time I met your grandfather was in New York. I did not know much about him except that he had a lot of money from farming and banking in the Central Valley. What I realized early on though was a quality he had for not giving up. No matter what the circumstances..."

Kerkin shifted his attention to Kalesh.

"He never gave up."

David could see that Kalesh was choking up a bit. He then made the connection of how Kalesh and his mother, David's great aunt Anna, were found and brought to safety by Kerkin. David respectfully acknowledged Kerkin's statement.

"That was my grandfather."

Kerkin offered some dried apricots to David.

"I believe ... seeing you here in Karabakh ... it is a quality you possess as well."

As they finished the meal Kalesh glanced over to David, then to Kerkin.

"I have not yet told him."

David looked at Kalesh.

"Told me what?"

Kerkin finished eating a dried fig.

"Since you have left the United States there has been a development, one that could significantly effect efforts here in Karabakh."

Kerkin went silent then continued.

"Your mother has filed a motion in court ... to contest your grandfather's Will."

David became extremely agitated with the news.

"But how can she? The Will clearly states the wishes of my grandfather."

Kerkin responded in serious attention.

"She claims there is another Will ... newer ... that makes obsolete the previous read Will."

David's agitation increased further.

"I suppose this will give her control of my grandfather's estate?"

Kerkin responded.

"Yes ... so completely that any judge will likely hold your mother libel for such a dramatic move. She must have some kind of legal protection in mind to even be doing this. We will see soon enough what this legal protection is."

David sighed knowing what the answer to his next question would be.

"What must I do?"

Kerkin paused for a moment then looked at David directly in the eye.

"You must go back to the United States ... to Fresno ... where the court action is to take place. There you will likely have to confront your mother. Are you prepared for that?"

David thought about the question.

"I'm sorry to say ... my mother and I do not get along very well. We never confront each other on anything."

David paused for a moment to regain composure.

"That's just the point. We don't confront each other. We avoid each other ..."

Kerkin interjected.

"This time you will need to confront her. The stakes are simply too high."

David acknowledged.

"I know."

CHAPTER THIRTY-ONE

David's flight was just taxing into the Fresno airport. Listening to the conversation in the plane reminded him just how different life was in Karabakh compared to the hustle and bustle of life in the United States. He was quick to remind himself that neither place is necessarily better, just different.

This lack of judging ones place or person over another based solely on differences was something that David's grandfather taught him, not so much in words, but in action. David remembered his grandfather always being fair with those around him, despite their position or circumstances. It was the quality he admired most in his grandfather. Probably this was the reason, David thought that allowed him to keep an open mind about life around him.

Despite this, David now had to be aware of, or at least he suspected, that there were those who would wish him harm and would do whatever was in their power to stop him. If the car veering off the road on the way to Karabakh was any indication, he could even be killed.

David still didn't know why this was happening but almost certainly suspected it was associated with the fact that he had, at least for the moment, control over his grandfather's financial empire. The big question on David's mind as he stepped off the plane was, would whoever is trying to stop him be active here in the United States as well?

As David took his baggage from the overhead compartment he glanced back and noticed what looked to be a man watching him. This seemed odd to David since people were usually so concerned about taking their carry on luggage then getting off the plane. Why would anyone care about what David was doing?

Am I being paranoid?

Perhaps the guy was just noticing David for some personal reason, for any reason. Or, maybe he was just bored. David shook himself internally to get a grip. Then he noticed something else about the man. He looked like he was Armenian or Turkish or Kurdish or, some kind of Eurasian or Middle East type. This did seem suspicious given what happened in Karabakh. Perhaps this was reason enough, David told himself, to be just a bit careful here. Maybe there was a reason to be paranoid.

Keep it cool man.

David made an effort to take his luggage off the plane without overtly letting anyone know that he suspected being watched. He laughed inwardly at the absurdity of his thoughts. That is, if indeed they were just thoughts.

David made his way to the baggage claim. He would not have to go through customs here in Fresno since that had already been done at a previous stop in Los Angeles. It was the usual routine at the baggage carousel, everyone waiting for their luggage to come out the chute with most people wondering if it was lost somewhere in route to the destination airport.

While he waited for his luggage, David took the opportunity to check if he was still being watched. Surprisingly he did not see the man that seemed to be watching him as he was getting off the plane. Maybe the guy did not have any checked-in baggage. Just coming in from Los Angeles perhaps. David reassured himself. That had to be what it was. There was nothing to be concerned about.

Just go home now and relax.

That's what David told himself as he took his baggage from the carousel and made his way towards the terminal exit.

David could feel the sweltering heat across his face as he hailed an airport taxi. Having grown up in Fresno, David knew the hot summer weather all too well. It was a reminder to him of the days with his grandfather walking through the vineyards. What David especially appreciated about those walks was that even though his grandfather was rich beyond compare, he still took the time to walk the vineyards with David. He remembered his grandfather telling him that it was about feeling the earth. A good farmer had to know the land where his crops would grow.

More important to David was not so much what his grandfather told him but that he did tell him. That's what David remembered.

"Van Ness."

The taxi driver acknowledged David's request, heading off to the part of Fresno that, although not the newer part of the city, was considered tastefully elegant. David particularly liked Van Ness because it represented to him a classic Fresno culture with large custom houses and vast landscapes. As a child he spent many a hot summer evening at family parties in the house he was now going to. Those were great memories of good food, Armenian folk music, dancing, and laughing. He wished those times could have lasted forever.

With the death of his grandfather and now the contention with his mother, David wondered if those parties would ever be close to what they once were. The thought came particularly to David's attention when he glanced at a newspaper laying next to him in the back seat of the taxi. The headline read,

John Avedisian's Estate contested.

The taxi driver could see that David was reading the article.

"Can you believe that? The mother is fighting her own son. If that's what money does they can have it."

The driver's words put a pit in David's stomach over the thought of confronting his mother. It was a terrible thought.

The big house looked lonely as David paid the taxi driver, then headed up towards the front door. It was only for a few days anyway. Hopefully he would be back to Armenia soon. David was surprised at himself that he wanted to get back to Armenia so soon given that he had been there only once. Maybe it was that beautiful girl he met in Karabakh or maybe just the bad feelings he had about the pending trial. Whatever the case, the feelings were real.

David opened the door to the empty house. Entering the living room, something felt amiss. Was it just that the house was empty? In fact that was just the point. The house did not feel empty. Certainly it had been a while since he was in the house, but something seemed different, like someone else had been here. He put his luggage down and walked upstairs.

Then David heard something. It was a ruffling through one of the rooms. Alarmed, David's guard raised up. Could there be a burglar in the house? Fear rushed though his mind. What about the security system, the neighborhood security guards?

David hesitated to go further towards the room. He wondered now if the as yet not confirmed intruder had noticed him.

Then suddenly, a man came rushing out of the room. He had a knife in hand. Everything was happening so fast that David could barely notice what the physical features of the intruder were. What David did notice however was that the intruder had Middle Eastern facial features. That's all he could make out before the knife came down on him. Instinctively David broke the jab with his forearm. It was something he'd learned from years of martial arts training.

The intruder was surprised by David's defense. He jabbed again but this time David was able to kick the intruder's right leg out from under him. The intruder fell down the steps. David quickly grabbed the knife.

Realizing he had lost his chance at David, the intruder picked himself up and rushed toward the door. Just before opening the door, the intruder glanced up at David. There was a silent moment of exchange between the two men, each knowing that death was missed today.

~~~~~~~~~

Still alive.

Teshkur read the report concerning the attempted plot on David's life. He grabbed the report then rushed off to Salem's office. Teshkur especially wanted to mitigate the situation before his boss Ali got word of it or even worse, Adem found out. In the latter case, Teshkur knew that Adem would surely use the fact that David was still alive to quash his plan. This, Teshkur concluded, could prove extremely detrimental for his career.

Salem was reading the report just as Teshkur entered his office without knocking. He looked up at Teshkur embarrassed.

"What can I say?"

Teshkur did not play the game of guilt. From his experience it only worked for a while and then lead to later resentment. It's not that Teshkur necessarily believed in some kind of moral code of honor that directed him to not lay blame on Salem. Rather he just wanted to get the job done in the most efficient way possible.

Besides that, Teshkur's position was in no way superior to that of Salem. Both were agents at the same job scale level. While it was true that Teshkur was more educated than Salem, it was also true that Salem had by far more field experience than Teshkur. That potentially made Salem more valuable to the MIT simply because there were a lot of smart people around. There were not so many people like Salem that had proven themselves in the field.

Teshkur sat down across from Salem.

"Don't say anything. We are both in this together."

Teshkur paged through the report.

"I had thought David would be an easier target. Trying to take him out in Fresno seemed the logical choice. But as you can see from the report, David is more formidable than we assumed."

Teshkur shook his head.

"Why did we not know that he had some martial arts training? That was a serious mistake for us. I believe now that we must wait for David to go back to Armenia. It will be easier to deal with him there. But then, this Kalesh is a problem for us. Essentially we have two targets to take out and I would venture to say, Kalesh must be taken out first or at least at the same time as David. Would you agree?"

Salem stood up from his chair.

"Agreed ... but I think the job will not get done from here. This will require on site action."

Teshkur knew what Salem's answer would be before he even asked.

"What do you suggest?"

Salem paced a few feet.

"I need to go to Armenia."

Teshkur stood up from his chair.

"I could not agree more ... as soon as possible."

Teshkur took a deep breath as he and Salem entered Ali's office. He could see that Ali had the report detailing the failure to take David out.

Not good at all.

Teshkur wondered if Adem knew yet? Never mind he told himself. Now is not the time to give up. Salem was more than capable to deal with the situation.

Motioning toward Salem, Teshkur spoke first to Ali.

"Salem has had much tougher assignments in the past ..."

Before Teshkur could finish his sentence Ali interrupted.

"Then why is this David still alive?"

Salem motioned to Teshkur that he would answer the question.

"I need to be on site ... in Karabakh."

Ali sighed.

"Do you realize what you are asking?"

Teshkur dreaded Ali's words. He knew all too well how difficult it could be to get an MIT agent into Armenia, let alone Karabakh. There was still officially a war going on between Armenia and Azerbaijan, with only a cease fire in place. It would be impossible to try and make it into Karabakh through the border.

The only way would be to enter Armenia through standard channels, like a visitor to the country on a tourist or business VISA. They would be taking a significant risk that Salem would be apprehended upon entry to Armenia. If that happened then there would be much bigger problems than the taking out of David. The capture of an MIT agent by Armenian authorities was something that Teshkur did not even want to contemplate.

Salem knew all too well the risk involved and did not hesitate to address the concern right there in Ali's office.

"I have not kept this job all these years without full awareness of the risks involved."

Ali interjected.

"But are you aware that there is more at stake here than your success or failure to enter Armenia? If Armenian authorities apprehend you then we have a much bigger problem. To be frank ... I don't believe the risk is acceptable. Better to take our chances with the agents we already have in place in Armenia. They will either succeed or fail in your plan to take out David."

Teshkur took note of Ali's specific mention of 'your plan'. Ali looked right at Teshkur when he said it. It was Ali's way to let Teshkur know that his career would likely suffer if his plan continued to fail.

Salem on the other hand did not care about the nuances of Ali's words. He simply wanted to make his point in the strongest way possible. Point blank Salem addressed Ali's concern.

"I will assume the consequences of the risk."

Ali looked at the report then directly back at Salem.

"Meaning?"

Salem did not flinch as he responded to Ali.

"They will not take me alive."

CHAPTER THIRTY-TWO

Walking into the superior court David caught a headline of the Fresno Bee newspaper,

Billionaire John Avedisian's Will Contested Today.

How can my mother be doing this?

David's mother had often been a source of contention for his grandfather, but to take steps to contest his Will, David thought she must have been influenced by someone or something outside of her. To even come up with an alternate Will, this would require significant legal resources dedicated to some purpose beyond simply his mother.

David knew it to be a 100 percent fact that his grandfather would never have created a second Will without telling him. It just was not at all like his grandfather. This new Will had to be a forgery.

But how was it that his mother had allowed herself to be taken in by people that would stoop to such practices? How was it that she could be persuaded to lie outright to the point of clearly going against her own father's wishes? What was especially difficult for David to contemplate was that she directly made David her adversary, her very own son. She must have known this was wrong. What kind of a mother was she?

There was all kinds of activity outside the courthouse. Reporters were everywhere. David was surprised as he walked up the courthouse steps to be crowded by so many of these reporters.

Why should they care? Then again, there was a lot of money at stake here and that money had much to do with Fresno. A reporter shouted out to David.

"Have you been in talks with your mother? How can she do this to her own son?"

The question hurt David to think about, let alone try and answer. He found himself reacting to such provocation, wanting to lash back. But then he remembered what his lawyer instructed him to do with such questions. Don't answer them. Just keep walking.

Taking such advice was easier to adhere to when it came from Mark, his lawyer, but more importantly also his grandfather's lawyer. More important than that was that Mark's last name was Kerkin. He was in fact the son of John's old friend, Kerkin. Perhaps because of this, Mark had always served his grandfather extremely well and with much professionalism.

David remembered his first meeting with Mark as a boy. That was how long Mark had worked with his grandfather. Owing to these long years of service, Mark knew the financial as well as the legal aspects of John Avedisian's financial empire better than most. David felt very confident that with Mark on his side his mother did not have a chance.

Security personnel immediately met David as he entered the courthouse lobby. They escorted him to the X-ray machine. One of the guards, an older man near retirement, was extra polite as David took off his watch.

"Thank you sir."

David responded.

"By all means. I'm sorry for all this fuss."

The guard gave a professional smile.

"Quite all right sir. This is more excitement than we've had for ... well ... can't tell you how long it's been."

David smiled politely back as he went through the metal detector.

"Glad you can see the bright side to all of this."

The guard glanced forward to David.

"My pleasure sure ..."

The guard hesitated as if not to go beyond his professional duty. Then, seeing the stress on David's face, he continued.

"Just remember young man. You will get though this okay."

Seeing the humble face of the old guard as he spoke those words, took David, just for a brief moment, to the face of his grandfather. It's as if his grandfather was speaking those words.

"You will get through it okay."

David acknowledged the guard.

"Thank you."

Security personnel escorted David towards the elevator. He had inadvertently caught a glance to his right side of a man that looked at David in more than a way of just an interested bystander or reporter. It was the same look he had seen before but just couldn't place where. Then, just as he entered the elevator, David remembered. Was this the same man, the Armenian looking man, that he saw on the plane?

A few weeks ago David would have thought nothing of this, but now, with the attack that happened at his home, David considered it more than just a coincidence. This was the same man. He was sure of it. But what was the significance? As the elevator doors closed David watched the man to see anything that could have provided a clue.

The man did nothing. He did not even look at the elevator. This confirmed it for David. That man was purposely not looking. It was completely obvious to David, or was it? David could never be sure these days if his thoughts were reasonable or paranoid. Ever since going to Armenia it had been this way.

David was beginning to feel his life unraveling. People were trying to kill him and his mother was contesting the Will. A faint connection between the two thoughts glimmered in David's mind as he entered the courtroom.

There she was. David saw his mother sitting there in the front row of the courtroom, on the right side of the isle. Two men that David did not recognize sat on each side of her. Owing to information supplied by Mark, he knew that Tom Lawrence was his mother's lawyer. David figured that he was one of the men sitting next to his mother. The other guy David couldn't say. Perhaps, he thought, this was another lawyer assisting Tom Lawrence.

The other man was actually Memet. Also sitting in the front row but on the left side of the isle was David's lawyer, Mark Kerkin. David walked through the center isle, eyes fixed on Mark. He purposely refused to acknowledge his mother. Mark acknowledged David as he prepared to take his seat to the left side of Mark.

Then, as if the very bond of mother and child demanded it, David couldn't refuse, at least a glance, at his mother. She saw her son and held back a tear. Inwardly she told herself that this was for his good too. Debra knew, deep down in the remotest place of heart, that it was a lie. She was betraying her son and her father.

The court clerk announced.

"Please rise for the honorable Judge Jackson Conners."

Watching Judge Conners enter the courtroom, David now fully came to grips that the fight was on.

Mark whispered to David as they sat back down.

"The plaintiff's side will make first arguments."

David whispered back.

"I thought she had only one lawyer."

Mark responded again in whisper.

"He's not a lawyer ..."

Mark hesitated before continuing.

"His name is Richard Davidian. He is your ... mother's friend."

So this is what it's now become.

David was incensed that his mother brought her new boyfriend with her? Very well then, so it was.

Judge Conners announced in firm voice.

"I want to remind everybody that I have granted a 'Safe Harbor' request for the contesting of John Avedisian's Will. This protects the right of the plaintiff to contest the afore mentioned Will. I have done this because of information submitted to me concerning the possible existence of a later Will than the one probated. We are here then to determine the validity of the new Will."

Tom Lawrence approached the judge.

"Your Honor."

The judge acknowledged.

"Counsel."

Tom Lawrence called his first witness to testify. It was Aram Tertanian, the lawyer that claimed to have written the new Will. Following the swearing in, Tom Lawrence began his questioning.

"You are Mr. Aram Tertanian, an attorney of law by profession?"

"Yes I am."

Tom Lawrence now held up a document then continued questioning the witness.

"I hold here the Will agreed to by Mr. John Avedisian one month before his passing. This Will supersedes the previous Will. I submit ..."

Mark Kerkin interrupted.

"Objection – no evidence has yet been provided that this document be considered a Will belonging to John Avedisian."

Judge Conners acknowledged the objection.

"The court duly notes the exhibit but reminds counsel that until sufficient evidence is brought forth ... it shall not be considered a Will. It is deemed only a document at this point."

Tom Lawrence was careful to respond.

"Duly noted your Honor. I submit the document as exhibit B."

Tom Lawrence handed the document to the witness, then continued questioning.

"Did you prepare this document which governs the administration of John Avedisian's estate on February 10, 2007?"

The witness responded.

"Yes I did."

Tom Lawrence glanced at David then back to the witness.

"Did Mr. John Avedisian explicitly state that this document was to supersede any previous Will that governed the administration of his estate?"

The witness responded.

"Yes he did."

Tom Lawrence took the document from the witness before addressing him.

"Thank you."

He then handed the document to the court clerk before addressing Judge Connors.

"I have no further questions your Honor."

Judge Connors looked at Mark Kerkin.

"Is counsel to cross examine the witness?"

Mark Kerkin addressed Judge Connors.

"Yes your Honor."

Mark approached the witness. David glanced at his mother to check her reaction. He wondered what his mother was thinking, given that Mark was going against her. Of course she must have known that Mark would never represent her in a case so fraudulent, especially one that so explicitly went against her father's wishes.

Mark started his questioning of the witness.

"Have you known the counsel representing Ms. Debra Avedisian, Tom Lawrence, at least one year before today?"

Tom Lawrence called out.

"Objection - the question is irrelevant to the testimony of the witness."

Judge Connors responded.

"Overruled. Counsel may continue questioning but is advised to show relevance in quick order."

Mark Kerkin acknowledged.

"Thank you your Honor."

Mark continued questioning the witness.

"I repeat my question. Have you known Mr. Tom Lawrence for at least one year before today?"

The witness answered.

"Well yes ... but I ..."

Mark Kerkin cut the witness off.

"A simple yes will suffice."

Mark then looked directly at Debra to make a point that his next question would connect her to what he intended to show as fraud.

"Did Mr. John Avedisian ever mention that his daughter ... Ms. Debra Avedisian was aware of the said document that supersedes the governance of his estate?"

The witness hesitated to answer. Mark Kerkin waited for an answer.

"Answer the question please."

The witness answered.

"No ... but ..."

Mark Kerkin did not let the witness continue his answer. Instead he posed another question.

"Given the serious implications to Ms. Debra Avedisian ... is it not at least customary that she would be informed?"

The witness responded.

"I can't say."

Mark Kerkin pressed hard.

"But you are a lawyer by profession. Surely you know what is customary in such matters?"

Frustrated by Mark Kerkin pinning him down the witness responded irritated.

"He did not say."

Mark Kerkin had the response he wanted.

"Thank you."

Mark Kerkin could see that Judge Connors was looking at his watch. Knowing that it was about lunchtime he expected an adjournment until the afternoon. Wanting to save his punch until that time, Mark held his next question, instead addressing Judge Connors.

"May I approach the bench."

Judge Connors acknowledged.

"Both counsels please approach."

Mark posed his request to Judge Connors.

"With the court's permission I would like to continue questioning this witness after lunch."

Judge Connor looked at his watch, 11:30 AM, and then replied.

"We still have about ½ hour until lunch. You need to have a good reason."

Judge Connors had been a judge for too many years not to know the reason Mark was about to give. He knew when there was a clear set-up between lawyers, Aram Tertanian and Tom Lawrence, in this case. Mark Kerkin partly revealed, or at least in Judge Connors mind demonstrated, a plausible connection during his cross-examination of Aram Tertanian. Nevertheless, this by itself was not enough to legally declare the new Will to be invalid.

More evidence was needed. Perhaps after the lunch break and further witness testimony, Judge Connors surmised. With that in mind and against Tom Lawrence's mild objection, Judge Connors sent Mark and Tom back to their seats. He then pounded his gavel.

"Court is adjourned for lunch. I expect to see everyone back by 1:00 PM."

Chapter thirty-three

"Do you think she will crack?"

David asked Mark concerning his mother's presumed testimony coming up in the afternoon. Mark was circumspect.

"Your mother can be a tough lady when she needs to be."

David was surprised that he was laughing a bit at Mark's remark.

"That I do remember from growing up around her ... that is ... when she was around."

Mark could sense the anguish David was feeling from the trial, that it was bringing up a past he would rather just forget. Unfortunately for David, forgetting was not an option, especially not today. He would be called to the stand to testify about his grandfather's intention of how his estate should be run.

Mark had debated within himself the advantage against the risk of putting David on the stand. The cross-examination could prove to be brutal for David. However, given that Debra would be testifying about her father's wishes, Mark could ill afford to just have one side of the story told, albeit a false side on the part of Debra. Mark of course would still cross-examine Debra. That should prove to be interesting and yes, if Mark had his way, brutal.

Mark braced himself as he and David entered the courtroom. He took aim at his immediate target Aram Tertanian, a continuation of cross-examination from before lunch. This time though Mark would be directly attacking Aram's credibility on the surface. Between the lines he would be looking for fraud.

Aram should prove difficult, owing to the fact that he was a lawyer himself. Mark would have to attack him on the facts, to find a hole in what he was saying and then blow it wide open. Of course, Mark knew this was an idealization of a certain legal reality that would pitch itself against him. The opposing side and the judge himself would see to it that finding the hole in Aram's testimony would not be easy, and blowing that hole wide open, not without a hard fight and a bit of luck. All in a days work Mark told himself.

Taking the stand, Aram took a good look at Mark. The two of them had known each other for quite some time, since their days at Fresno Pacific Law School. Both lawyers had been top in their class. This lent itself for them to become friends, at least until recently. That was when it became known, but not yet proven, that Aram's integrity had been put in question by at least some of the Fresno legal community.

Aram had tried to cover his tracks, but being a key witness in the contesting of John Avedisian's Will was hard to keep a secret. Especially in the Armenian community, most knew of John Avedisian's consistent support of Armenian interests and it only made sense that any Will contrary to those interests was likely fraudulent. This would all come out in the light of day under Mark's cross-examination.

Aram almost hated himself for what he was about to do. That was to lie outright against what he knew was true. But what else could he do? He had always tried to do what was right but now his son was in real trouble back in Turkey. Why Aram anguished, did this have to happen? Now he had to hurt others because of it.

That the people hurt were Armenians made it even worse for Aram. He told himself it was only about money. People can recover from money problems. Really though, this was a lot more than just about money. It was about personal integrity. In this case, his own.

"Is it not true that this new Will ... and I emphasize the word new ... is a forgery?"

The entire courtroom was shocked by Mark's first question to Aram. Tom Lawrence could hardly wait a second to respond.

"Objection – counsel's question presumes without basis in fact."

Judge Connors was clearly irritated by Mark's question.

"Sustained ... and I strongly suggest to counsel that this is a court of law ... not an inquisition."

David cheered Mark on silently. This was the lawyer his grandfather had always counted on, not just for his absolutely keen knowledge of the law, but more importantly that he wielded the law in an almost artistic way, shaping words for maximum impact.

Certainly Mark's qualities had been hugely beneficial to John Avedisian's financial empire. More often than not lawsuits of all kinds were brought against John Avedisian's interests, both personal and business. Mark was always there to bring these lawsuits crashing down.

Besides the use of his amazingly effective legal mind, Mark was able to bring down fraudulent lawsuits for two reasons. The first reason was that he had the advantage of working on the right side of the law. John never tried to cheat anyone. If someone was genuinely wronged inadvertently by any interest of John's, then there was never a question of taking care of that person in the most ethical and legally sound approach possible. The second reason was that if someone deliberately attempted to cheat John, then Mark was given carte blanch to go after that person, no holds barred. There would be no side deals. It was winner takes all and John, through Mark's efforts, was always the winner.

Despite his objection, Tom Lawrence knew that Mark's use of the word 'forgery' was now stuck in everyone's mind, even someone as legally impartial as Judge Connors. He was going to have to get back a point, but how? Likely he thought, Mark would not gamble again with such a shocking force of words.

All Mark had to do now was work that word 'forgery' into a cohesive case. Mark's next question exemplified this.

"Allow me to rephrase the question. Is it not true that this ... new ... Will ... was dated April 10, barely just five weeks from today and only one week before the passing of John Avedisian?"

Aram straightened himself in his chair before answering. "Yes."

Mark continued.

"Would you not agree that this is highly irregular ... especially given the vast financial holdings of the estate?"

Aram decided right then and there that he was not going to make Mark's job so easy. After all, despite the fact that what he was doing was wrong at some level, he still was a good lawyer and was for many years respected by his questioner. He was determined not to lose all his respect.

"Irregular is a rather vague word ... don't you think. May I ask counsel to rephrase what you are attempting to say?"

Mark couldn't hold back a momentary gesture of respect to acknowledge Aram's still sound legal mind as well as his characteristic politeness. It was the politeness in particular that always impressed Mark. He had watched his old colleague in many a court case that had lawyers relentlessly attacking the validity of Aram's claims. Aram never lashed back and was always polite.

Given Aram's cool demeanor, Mark was not about to try making Aram angry or upset. It just would not work. Instead he would relinquish to Aram in a rephrase of the question with the intention of forcing him into a gradual surrender of legal ground. Mark posed the question.

"Have you ever seen a case of such a large financial magnitude that supported such a drastic change in the Will ... so close to one's passing?"

Aram knew exactly how to handle the question but also knew that doing so would likely lead him down a path of no escape. Mark would do everything he could to assure this, but Aram told himself, not without a fight.

The real question on Aram's mind was how long he could last under Mark's questioning. Fighting back against his once friend provided Aram for just a brief moment the feeling of being a real lawyer once again. He answered the question.

"To know one's death ... my belief is that only God knows."

Mark could see he would have to slice away at Aram's responses. He knew the drill. So be it as he rephrased the question yet again.

"Your belief is not in question here. Simply I ask you ... was the time between John Avedisian's passing and the writing of the Will unusually short ... especially given the large financial magnitude of the estate?"

Aram countered back knowing he was really pushing it this time.

"Certainly the estate is large. No one in this community or in the entire world would disagree. However ... to say that there has never been an estate of such a large financial magnitude where a new Will has been written shortly before the estate holder's death ... that I can not say."

Mark was enjoying Aram's challenge as he posed his next rephrase.

"I will be more specific then. Has there ever been in your memory ... in this community of Fresno ... a case of such a large financial magnitude where the writing of a new Will was commenced so shortly as for John Avedisian's estate?"

Now this was a question that Aram could appreciatively live with. He had forced Mark to so specify the question that cross-examination will relinquish at least some of the gains made. With professional acknowledgment Aram responded.

"No ... not really."

Mark would have appreciated a straight no but decided the impact of his argument, while diminished by Aram's clever play on words, still held. He addressed Judge Connors.

"No further questions of the witness your Honor."

Pleased with Aram's response, Tom Lawrence walked to the stand with confidence for an intended brief cross-examination. To the point he asked Aram.

"Is it your professional opinion Mr. Tertanian that there could be examples of financial estates approximately the size of John

Avedisian's estate ... where the time between the writing of the
Will and the passing of the estate holder was roughly equivalent
to the time between the writing of John Avedisian's revised Will
and his passing?"

Tom's question came just as Mark expected based on Aram's
previous testimony with him. Could they have planned this from
the start? Mark looked to see the expression of Judge Connors
for any sign that Tom's question may have mitigated the impact
of his own argument. Judge Connors was careful not to show
any expression. If the testimony of Debra and then David were
to be completed today as planned, then Mark would likely get his
answer soon enough.

Following the dismissal of Aram Tertanian from the stand,
Debra Avedisian was called by Tom Lawrence to give testimony.
Tom knew it was risky business to call her to the stand because
Mark Kerkin would certainly grill her during cross-examination.
The risk, Tom determined, was outweighed by the benefit of
Debra telling her story of a last minute change of heart of her
father.

Debra's testimony was especially necessary because Tom knew
most assuredly that David would be called to testify regardless.
For Judge Connors to hear just David's side of the story would
surely prove detrimental to the acceptance of the revised Will.
With this in mind, Tom asked his first question of Debra.

"Can you describe your father's state of mind in the last week
of his life?"

Debra glanced at David just before answering.

"My father was quite lucid. His mind was as clear as I've ever
known."

Tom paced just a few feet then turned in the direction of
Judge Connors before asking Debra the next question.

"What was your father's disposition towards you in that last
week?"

David watched in disbelief as his mother wiped a tear from
her face.

"My dear father said he loved me."

Debra choked up.

"He said he was sorry for how we lost connection with each other but that there was still a chance for us to ..."

Debra now broke out in a sob.

"To prove how he really felt ... he was revising his Will."

Debra wiped tears from her face then looked directly at David.

"He told me ... this was not against David ... just that it was to show his love for me. Oh Daddy ... I miss you."

Tom Lawrence addressed Judge Connors.

"No further questions of the witness your Honor."

David was incensed at what he absolutely believed was a total lie.

Mark showed no emotion as he approached Debra for cross-examination.

"Can you describe your relationship with your father during the course of your life?"

Tom Lawrence thought to himself, here it comes. Just how far would Mark go after Debra, given her very emotional previous testimony?

Debra looked at Mark in a way that a sister looks at a brother.

"You know the answer Mark. He was my father. I loved him and he loved me."

Mark was taken by surprise that Tom did not coach Debra better. Tom already saw his mistake. Mark very gently continued his questioning.

"I guess I'm a bit confused. You mentioned in your previous testimony that in the last week of his life your father expressed regret over the connection lost with you. How can it be that you loved your father and he loved you and still there was a lost connection?"

Debra was caught off guard with the question.

"Well ... he loved me. That's all I know."

Mark hesitated for a moment before asking another question. He then decided Debra's answer was more than sufficient for the purpose he intended. Mark addressed Judge Connors.

"No further questions of the witness your Honor."

Debra looked to Memet. He gave her a sympathetic gesture. David took note of this.

Tom Lawrence exchanged a brushing glance with Mark Kerkin as he approached the stand. It was damage control time.

Within just a few minutes Mark had managed to turn Debra's compelling testimony into what appeared to be an outright lie. Whether or not Debra was lying, Tom would not allow himself to consider. He purposely did not want to know whether the new Will was a fake or not. That was not his job. No, he told himself. His job was only to make sure the process of law was carried out. In this case to make sure the new Will got a fair hearing. Still, if he thought about it just long enough, he knew what conclusion he would come to.

It was the thinking bit that Tom had trained himself over the years to shut off. If not, he figured his career as a lawyer would well be over. Perhaps if he was older, like Aram or Mark, he could take a chance to allow himself to think about such matters. They have had their careers, managed to somehow get through the ethical issues a lawyer must at some point face, or not, and ultimately come out with a belief that what they did with their life was indeed worthwhile.

For Tom, he dare not take the chance of moral implication in the dawn of his career. Someday maybe he would. For now he must fight the battle at hand, specifically to do his best that the new Will be accepted. With this in mind Tom approached Debra.

"Do you love your son?"

Debra was caught off guard, David even more so. The mother and son took a good look at each other as Debra answered.

"Very much."

Tom then looked at David as he asked the next question.

"Do you think he loves you?"

This time her tears were real.

"I hope so."

Tom had made his point as he addressed Judge Connors.

"No further questions of the witness your Honor."

Having secured a victory over the opposing side, Mark Kerkin was now reaching his stride. He had become noticeably older in recent years. Those in the Fresno legal community had begun to ask if the Mark Kerkin so renowned for his able service to John Avedisian throughout the years, still had what it took.

Some had even thought that with the passing of John Avedisian, Mark would call it quits and retire gracefully to his small farm in the nearby town of Sanger. Mark loved his farm. For him it was a relaxing getaway from the intensity of legal practice. John Avedisian had taught Mark many farming techniques. Mark liked to call these old country secrets. They were in a way, a connection to his father, Mark Kerkin Sr. This was especially important to Mark, because although he and his father did communicate, because of the divorce, there was never the father-son relationship that Mark had always wanted.

Mark did dream of retiring someday, perhaps sooner than later. For now though, his job was well laid out. Just as he had served John, he now served David. Mark reminded himself of this as David was called to the stand. This time it was the young man he remembered from the day of his birth that would be depending on Mark to do what he did best, be a lawyer through and through.

As he approached David on the stand Mark's aim was clear. Bring the final push of doubt to Judge Connors so that he would call for further investigation of the revised Will.

Mark was reasonably sure that with proper investigation the said Will as such would be declared a forgery. David would be declared once and for all the rightful heir to John's fortune.

Debra would unfortunately be found out. Glancing at her, Mark felt real pity. For despite Safe Harbor protection of her small part of the estate, by testifying to the authenticity of a forged Will, Debra had opened herself to charges of perjury. David of course would not seek prosecution, but the shame of the matter would be more than Debra could take. A real tragedy, Mark thought, for a woman who once had such potential.

Debra's ruin ran through Mark's mind even as he asked David a first question.

"Was your grandfather, John Avedisian, a decisive man? That is, did he stick to his decision once made?"

David responded without hesitation.

"He was the most decisive man I have ever met ... especially what he cared about the most."

Mark continued the questions along the lines that he and David had prepared for in detailed coaching sessions.

"In your opinion ... what was it that your grandfather most cared about? A few important examples will suffice."

Although David was ready with a rehearsed answer, he felt an emotional pull from the question that he had not anticipated.

"Most important for him was family. He would do anything possible for me and ..."

He glanced at his mother before continuing.

"My mother."

David paused for a moment before continuing.

"Then there was Armenia. Ever since the country gained independence, my grandfather's dream was to see Armenia prosperous and strong."

Mark now came to the crux of his entire argument, that which would unite previous testimony into a single cohesive objective.

"Having read through the new Will, would you say that it reinforces or detracts from what your grandfather cared most about?"

David answered without hesitation.

"It absolutely detracts from my grandfather's wishes."

Mark deliberately looked Debra's way before asking the next question.

"Why do you say this?"

David glanced at his mother before continuing.

"My grandfather would never give the money to my mother because she does not care about Armenia."

Hearing David's words, Debra put her head down. She couldn't bear to look at her own son. It seemed the very shame Mark had considered was already taking its course on Debra. Mark knew this had to be one of the most terrible moments of David's life. It was clear to him that neither Debra nor David could continue with any more of Mark's questions in this direction.

At this point, Mark had achieved his aim. He addressed Judge Connors.

"No further questions of the witness your Honor."

Tom Lawrence considered the strong testimony given by David. The question he had to wrestle with now was to what advantage could any questions he asks bring to the side of the case for the revised Will? Asking questions that had already been asked could actually reinforce the opposite side's case. Judge Connors especially looked to Tom Lawrence to see what he would do. A decision had to be made, so he made it.

"I have no questions of the witness your Honor."

As he spoke his words, Tom could almost know for sure exactly what was to happen next, almost as if he was planning it himself. He heard the words of Mark Kerkin.

"Your Honor ... may counsel approach the bench."

Judge Connors acknowledged.

"Both counsels come forward to the bench."

Mark Kerkin and Tom Lawrence both approached Judge Connors. Tom could hear Mark's words even before they were spoken.

"Your Honor ... on behalf of my client I request that a one month recess be granted to check for possible forgery evidence concerning exhibit B, the revised Will."

Tom knew this was the only chance he would get to make some kind of difference in favor of his client.

"Your Honor ... one month is more time than is necessary for investigation of any forgery evidence. Surely two weeks is enough."

Judge Connors took a moment to decide how much if any time should be given for a court recess.

"It seems apparent that some reasonable doubt has been brought to light such that a court recess is in order to further investigate possible forgery associated with exhibit B, the revised Will. Therefore, I will order a court recess for a period of three weeks."

Judge Connors words rang hard in Tom Lawrence's ears. Given the turn of events, Tom was glad he had not asked the question of whether or not the client he served was part of a forgery scheme. If so, then it was for another lawyer to defend.

CHAPTER THIRTY-FOUR

David glanced at his mother as everyone was preparing to leave the courtroom. It had been an arduous day and according to Mark, successful. David was not sure. What he did know was the gnawing feeling deep in the pit of his stomach that this whole mess was far from over. Especially seeing his mother just on the other side of the courtroom with her new boyfriend. The experience was sickening to him.

Mark could see that David was becoming more agitated by the second.

"Don't even think about it."

David looked back at Mark who was gathering various papers.

It just burns me up.

"Look at her over there with that guy. What did you say his name was?"

Mark sighed,

"Richard Davidian. Really though David ... I think I know what you are thinking and ... just don't. It's not worth it."

David couldn't even hear Mark's words as he was now becoming so incensed watching his mother being comforted after lying so blatantly. Without thinking he rushed over to his mother and Memet.

"How could you ... how ... could you lie like that?"

Memet stepped closer to Debra who was visibly shaken by David's confrontation. This brought David's ire up all the more.

"Here we go. The new guy standing up for his soon to be rich girlfriend. How really pathetic this all is."

Memet kept his cool but Debra couldn't handle what was happening. She started to cry.

"David ... I'm..."

Tom Lawrence came on the scene and pulled Debra away before she could say anything that could incriminate herself or damage the case.

"He's just upset."

Debra was now sobbing uncontrollably.

"But he's my son. I feel..."

Tom pulled Debra further, away from where she could be heard.

"Careful Debra. You must not say anything that could incriminate you or damage the case."

Debra became slightly more controlled over herself.

"I just can't believe what I've done."

Tom was alarmed by Debra's words. Indeed they confirmed what he did not want to think about, that this case was rife with fraud.

Mark rushed over to David. Memet and Tom escorted Debra from the courtroom. David knew he over reacted.

"Sorry Mark. I was out of line there."

Mark was sympathetic.

"It's understandable given the situation."

David shook his head.

"It's just that this whole mess and..."

David caught himself. Should he mention to Mark his perceived attempts on his life? Mark noticed David's hesitation.

"What is it?"

David hesitated to say but could see that Mark would persist until he had an answer.

"I didn't want to say anything about it ... I mean your focus was on the case."

Mark could see David's reluctance.

"Better just say what it is."

David gave in.

"I think someone is trying to kill me ... but ... maybe its just coincidence."

Mark became alarmed.

"An attempt on your life. This is serious. You absolutely should have told me."

Mark caught his own reaction, that David was far more to him than just a client. Regaining composure he continued.

"Tell me what has happened."

Mark glanced around the courtroom and noticed that he and David were being observed.

"Not here though."

Leaving the courthouse, Mark and David were mobbed by reporters. Just ahead of them was Debra. Tom and Memet were escorting her. Mark could see that the sight of his mother with her new boyfriend once again agitated David.

"Easy now David."

David kept his composure.

"It's okay Mark. I got it."

Mark made a way through the reporters so David could pass.

"No questions please."

They made it past the reporters to where Mark's car was parked.

"There's a new Mexican place on Blackstone. How about dinner there?"

Having not eaten much at all that day, Mexican food sounded good to David.

"Lets go."

David and Mark got in the car and headed out to the restaurant. Mark started up the conversation while driving.

"Tell me about these attempts on your life."

David rubbed his face with his hands.

"Okay ... but just realize ... I'm not claiming anything for sure just yet."

Mark stayed serious.

"We're just talking at this point. But ... it's important that I know ... at least the facts of what happened."

David waited for a stoplight before speaking.

"The first time ... I didn't give it much thought. Kalesh and I were on our way to Karabakh when the SUV suddenly lurched to the right. We just about went off a cliff. Fortunately Kalesh managed to keep the SUV under control. Kalesh had a look under the front axle and found a loose bolt. Nothing really surprising except that the SUV, a Hummer H3 was new. I just chalked it up as some kind of factory defect. That is ... until the other day when I came home to my house in Fresno."

Mark interrupted.

"On Van Ness?"

"Yes ... the old family house. Anyway, when I went into the house something just did not seem right. I walked around a bit and then I heard something. As I was walking towards the back room a man suddenly came out with a knife."

Mark was shocked.

"What ... David ... you should of told me about this right away."

David was apologetic.

"You were so busy with the trial ... well ... I figured I would tell you about it after."

David paused.

"Like right now."

Mark quipped back.

"Fair enough. Please just continue."

David went on.

"I fought the guy off. He ran out."

"What did the police say?"

David hesitated.

"I didn't report it."

Mark was holding back his expression.

"Why not David?"

David again hesitated.

"I thought it best to wait ... until the trial ... you know ... the controversy."

Mark pulled into the parking lot of the Mexican restaurant.

"Actually ... that was a good idea. Probably it's best now to not mention anything to the police at all."

David went silent. Mark knew there was something more.

"And ...?"

David reluctantly continued.

"I don't know Mark ... if it's just my imagination ... the two events. Maybe they are just coincidental. Then ... well ... I didn't want to say but ... on the plane there was this guy. He looked Armenian or Turkish ... Middle Eastern of some kind. The way he was looking at me ... unusual. I don't know ... am I going paranoid?"

Mark waited until he was sure David had nothing more to say on the subject.

"Others can speculate ... myself included ... but David ... these are critical times. You can't afford not to be careful. In ordinary times ... well yes ... perhaps it could be called paranoia but not now ... not with so much at stake."

Mark took the car keys.

"What's important now is that you be very careful. Do not assume anything."

David and Mark got out of the car and headed towards the front door of the Mexican restaurant, a place called Las Olas. Mark pulled David aside before going into the restaurant, checking to see no one was watching.

"Does anybody else know about the guy attacking you at your house?"

David could see the seriousness on Mark's face.

"No one yet."

Mark went deadly serious.

"Good. Tell no one except Kalesh ... and my father. I suggest you do this tonight. There could be a connection to this in Armenia. Meanwhile I will get a private investigator on this tomorrow. We've got to find out ... especially while the court case is pending. There is a lot of money involved. Likely that's what they are after."

David looked at his watch as he walked into the house, 10:17 PM. It was a good time to call Armenia due to the time difference, 12 hours ahead of California. He scurried through some papers in his still unpacked suitcase to find his great aunt Anna's phone number. David hoped Kalesh would still be at the house this late in the morning. The phone rang three times before there was an answer.

"Hello."

David was relieved to hear a man's voice and the English word 'Hello'. He knew it was Kalesh.

"Kalesh, it's David."

There was a hearty response on the other side.

"David ... how are you?"

"Okay ... considering. Probably you have not yet heard about the court case ..."

Kalesh interrupted David.

"No news reports yet. How did it go?"

"Mark was able to get what they call in the United States a recess. It's a waiting period while the Will gets investigated to determine if it's a forgery."

Kalesh considered what David was telling him.

"This is good news?"

"Yes ... I think so. The judge seems to have his doubts about the forged Will. It looks favorable to us."

"And your mother? Sorry David ... if I'm being too direct here."

"It's okay Kalesh. We are family after all. My mother ... well ... it's not good. She lied outright in court about my grandfather. I don't know Kalesh ... how she could be so low?"

Kalesh could tell that David was distraught.

"People can behave strangely ... even terribly ... when they are desperate. Remember David ... no matter what ... she is still your mother. Do what you must ... but remember that."

David hesitated to say anything more. Kalesh somehow sensed there was more.

"What else happened David?"

David sighed.

"A man with a knife ... he attacked me in my house. He looked Armenian or Turkish or something... Middle Eastern type for sure."

"Are you okay?"

"I'm fine Kalesh ... but I think Kerkin should know."

"I will speak with him today. Does he have your phone number?"

"He does."

Kalesh knew that Kerkin would take swift action to find out who was trying to kill David.

"Good then. Be careful David. By the way ... Ani says hello."

David's demeanor dramatically improved with Kalesh's word about Ani.

"She does? Please give my greetings to her ... that I hope to see her soon ... in Karabakh."

"Very good David. We will see you soon then."

"Okay Kalesh ... bye now."

David hung up the phone just as the jet lag was beginning to get to him. It pushed him onto the bed where he just laid down in the clothes he was wearing. David was fast asleep within five minutes.

The phone rang, waking David up in a half dazed state.

"Hello David ... it's Kerkin. Kalesh told me what happened ... in Fresno."

"What do you think?"

"I believe the attack on you in Fresno is connected with what happened to you and Kalesh on the way to Karabakh."

David was relieved that Kerkin did not think he was crazy.

"So it's not just my imagination?"

"Make no mistake here David. You are too important these days to assume otherwise. Maybe it is just coincidence ... but I really don't think so."

"Can we do anything?"

"Yes we can ... but it's going to require risk ... risk on your part David."

"What kind of risk exactly?"

Kerkin hesitated for just a moment as he knew what would be asked of David was dangerous.

"We need to set you as bait."

"Bait?"

"You are not obliged to..."

"No ... it's all right ... if it's the only way."

"Just what your grandfather would say."

David had made his decision.

"Tell me what I must do."

"Come back to Armenia right away."

"Easy enough."

Kerkin now became matter of fact serious.

"It's important that you publicize this. Mark can work out the details ... something like you are confident that the outcome of the trial will be favorable and therefore you will go back to Armenia to start some kind of fund ... say a trust ... to assist Armenia ... especially Karabakh."

"This is the bait?"

"The start of it. I suspect that you will be followed to Armenia or ... maybe they will already be waiting for you here. We can't know at this point."

David began to feel some stress over the situation.

"Will you talk with Mark or should I?"

"I will call him now and likely he will call you in a few hours. For now ... just get some sleep."

Chapter thirty-five

The Fresno Bee headline read,

John Avedisian's Grandson Establishing Trust Fund in Armenia.

It seemed the newspaper was everywhere at the airport that day as David was preparing to fly back to Armenia.

Mark had certainly done his job well. In just two days, he had the word out that the case was going in favor of David. The publicity drove the message that David would be returning immediately to Armenia to start a trust fund. This was to benefit Armenia, especially Karabakh. Mark made sure that his contacts at the Fresno Bee would get the details straight on the matter.

The opposing side also had their article with claims that the investigation would prove beyond a doubt that the new Will was indeed valid and that by consequence, Debra Avedisian would inherit almost the entire estate of her father.

Such a turn of events would almost certainly be the end of any real help to Armenia or Karabakh, at least that's what Adem and Memet were counting on. In reality though, Adem and Memet both knew that the court recess, with the purpose of investigating possible forgery of the new Will, was not in their interest in the slightest.

Memet and Adem knew there was no kidding about the truth of the matter. For although the probate lawyer Aram Tertanian was one of the best at what he did, including in this case hiring a top notch forger, the new Will after all, was a fake.

Of more immediate concern to Adem and Memet was that the forgery investigation gave further support to Teshkur's plan to simply kill David outright. Adem himself had to admit that the death of David would at least solve the problem temporarily and maybe permanently, of aid to Armenia and Karabakh through John Avedisian's estate. The problem with this, as Adem had maintained all along, was that the accomplishment of the killing could necessarily implicate the Turkish MIT. This solution, in Adem's mind, was worse than the problem.

As Mark had expected, the lure of David going back to Armenia proved too difficult for the Turks to resist. With Teshkur's go-ahead Salem would follow David back to Armenia. There he would plan David's killing, then execute it. This was in fact why he was at the airport now, watching David prepare to board the plane.

David's continued evasion of previous attempts on his life had given Salem a certain respect for the young man. That he was now going to Armenia himself to make sure the job was done right, in some sense gave Salem reason to equate himself with David. He had decided to put his own life in jeopardy. It was a kind of even deal, either David's life or his. Once on the plane with David there would be no turning back. Either he or David would die in Armenia. Only one will survive.

Salem kept his distance from David, about 100 yards back. David got in line to go through airport security. It was important that Salem remind himself to just lay back.

Don't give him any reason to suspect.

Then it suddenly hit Salem.

Is this a set up?

Could it be that Salem was now the one being hunted? Certainly the newspaper article was in their face so to speak, as if to say come on, follow me to Armenia. Salem finished the thought.

There we will hunt the hunter.

Salem had never concerned himself much with death. He figured that sooner or later he would meet his end, likely on the job. But to die in Armenia, the history of the people being as it was; for Salem this was not very appealing. Nevertheless, the task at hand was too important to risk it with others. Salem was the man for the job and he knew it. This ran through his mind as he prepared to go through the metal detector in the security line.

The metal detector beeped as Salem went through.

Annoying machine.

Salem motioned to the security officer.
"I have nothing metal on me."
The security guard pointed at Salem's chest. Then Salem realized what he forgot. He was wearing a silver cross, part of his attire to blend in with Armenia.

How could I be so careless?

Salem knew that he had better get with it. He could not afford to mess up like this in Armenia. Salem demanded this of himself as he passed through security, now in route to board the plane that David was on.

~~~~~~~~~

Waking from his sleep, Salem heard the voice of the plane's captain announcing that they would be landing in Yerevan in just about 10 minutes. It had been a long flight, almost 24 hours if the layovers in Los Angels and London were included.

Salem was sitting just three rows behind David. He had not planned it that way. In fact Salem would have preferred to have more seats between himself and David. Nevertheless, Salem would not allow himself to be distracted by what could be interpreted as either coincidence or some kind of destiny, the hunter and hunted sitting within speaking distance of each other. Neither case mattered to Salem. He only thought in terms of the reality at hand, that was to make sure he took David out.

A chaotic crowd waited just outside the airport exit. Kerkin and his private security personnel met David immediately.

"How was your flight?"

David glanced around before answering.

"Not bad ... but I think ... you know..."

Kerkin got the hint from David that he thought he could have been followed from Fresno, the killer maybe even being on the plane. Kerkin took a look around.

"Could be."

There was no one waiting for Salem. He made sure of this as he did not want to attract any kind of attention. Instead he caught a Taxi to the Hotel Yerevan in the heart of the city center.

It had been almost 15 years since Salem had been in Yerevan. That was during the time of the Karabakh war. He was part of an advanced Turkish reconnaissance mission to prepare for a full Turkish invasion. The invasion never actually happened due to the failed coup in Russia against Yeltzin.

That reconnaissance mission was however successful in a way that would now assist Salem in his mission. The success was due to the recruiting of an Armenian woman with the code-name Olga. Since that time, Olga had provided information of use to Turkish and Azeri Security forces while she remained entirely secret in her identity.

Olga had good reason to be secretive. This was mostly due to Armenia being a small country where anything much out the ordinary would bring attention relatively quickly. She made sure that the only way of contact with her was through intermediate contacts.

Salem did not like this arrangement but understood he had no choice in the matter. Either work with Olga as she dictated or don't work with her at all. The latter choice offered no other outcome but failure. All Salem could do was go to his hotel and wait for Olga to make first contact.

Salem was very exhausted as he entered his hotel room. All he could think about was falling onto the bed. That was until he heard the ring of the phone only minutes after entering the room. Salem knew the reason for this call. The voice on the line confirmed it.

"Meet me at the Mashdots Cafe ... on Bagranian street ... tomorrow morning at 8:00 AM."

Salem posed a question that he already knew the answer to.

"How will I know who you are?"

The answer.

"I will find you."

David woke up. He was still feeling tired from jet lag. Having not really recovered from his last trip to Armenia, he felt as though in a daze. He was staying at an apartment set up by Kerkin. Security personnel were in the house to make sure that any attempt on David's life was only presumed to be a surprise.

David got up and showered. The hot water running down his face provided him a respite from anxious thoughts that were swarming through his mind.

How has it come to this?

David knew that he was likely being hunted but that there was no idea as yet, to know who the killer could be. Relinquishing that last bit of water as he turned off the shower, David considered that he had no choice in the matter. That is what really made him mad.

All David had wanted to do was carry out his grandfather's wishes, a simple endeavor really. Instead he was caught in the middle of this mess, not only about saving his life, but also his own mother using whatever means available to wrest his grandfather's financial legacy from him. If it turned out that the two parts of the mess were connected, then David conceded to himself that he would be devastated.

David's anguished thoughts were interrupted by a knock on the door. Kalesh stood at the door when David opened it.

"There you are ... my cousin from America."

David was thankful to see Kalesh again and, despite the circumstances, with a positive and friendly demeanor. David motioned for Kalesh to come in but Kalesh motioned otherwise.

"We have a busy day ahead. Come on downstairs for some breakfast. Kerkin has much to discuss with you."

David acquiesced.

"All right then."

David followed Kalesh downstairs to an inviting spread of food laid out on a table where Kerkin sat. Seeing Kerkin there, David couldn't help but think, this is the man that proved himself so important to his grandfather and now, even though much older, he is proving himself yet again.

For men like Kerkin age only changed the implementation of their methods, not their resolve. This came clear as Kerkin spoke to David.

"There are important matters to discuss."

David spooned up some eggs onto his plate.

"I'm here to do what it takes."

Kerkin waited for David to take a taste of the eggs before speaking.

"We must find out just who it is that's trying to kill you."

The word kill went deep into David's psyche.

"What must I do?"

Kerkin glanced at Kalesh then looked directly at David.

"You and Kalesh must again drive to Karabakh. This time though, it will be known throughout Armenia that you are doing so. If the killers are here, and I believe this is so ... then you will almost certainly be followed ..."

David interrupted.

"Killers? How many?"

Kerkin chose his next words carefully.

"An attempt on your life here ... if it happens ... will not be taken in the chance that it does not succeed. Whoever is behind it will want to make sure of that. They will arrange as many for the task as can be managed."

David sighed.

"Not to succeed. Please excuse my concern ... but what assurance do I have that ..."

David did not want to say the words. Kerkin continued for him.

"We will make sure that any force they bring will be matched ... and then some."

David was concerned.

"So that I will not be killed?"

Kerkin took a drink of apricot juice before continuing.

"I will not lie to you. This is not without danger. I cannot guarantee you more. What I can say is that we will draw the killers out. That much is certain."

CHAPTER THIRTY-SIX

"There are problems." spoke a hushed woman's voice directly to Salem's hotel phone.

"Who is this?"

The voice came back.

"It doesn't matter ... not now. What matters is this David ... and those that work with him. A trap was laid for us and now my cover is in jeopardy."

Salem was seething.

"The plan was not followed ..."

The woman interrupted.

"Your plan was flawed."

Salem took offense at the accusation.

"You did not provide enough men to ..."

Again the woman interrupted.

"The restaurant was too small."

That was it for Salem.

"Look Olga ... yes ... I know it's you. I've paid you good money and..."

Salem stopped himself from saying something he would regret or at least what could jeopardize the mission.

"Look ... we are getting nowhere with this. What happened at the restaurant was a complete failure. So be it! Let's just make sure we do it right ... this time."

Olga would not take an offer of peace from Salem. Instead she wanted to rub the failure in Salem's face.

"This failure jeopardized many interests. I can not allow this ... I won't allow this."

Keep your mouth shut.

It was no use. Olga was pushing too much. Salem could not hold back any longer.

"You assured me there would be no problems and now you shove the blame ..."

Olga's hushed voice became more hurried.

"You should stop talking now. Remember that you are in Armenia ... a very dangerous place ... for a man like you."

Salem hated Olga's words because he knew she was right. He was a Turkish MIT agent in Armenia, completely vulnerable and dependent on a secretive Armenian agent that was a traitor to her own country.

The latter point stuck particularly uneasy with Salem. Even though he was in some sense appreciative for the services of Olga, if he admitted honestly to himself, he found her abhorrent. Olga was after all, betraying her own people. How could she do this? For Salem, it was simply incomprehensible. Probably it was for money. Greed was the usual reason.

It occurred to Salem that the people who opposed him here in Armenia, this Kerkin he had heard so much about, could at least be respected. They worked for their own people. Salem wondered about the old agent Kerkin. What had he seen in this life, adventures in the least, virtues at most?

~~~~~~~~

Kerkin sat in an old rocking chair. David and Kalesh entered his office. The old chair was out of place in the modern office, but its purpose was not to look appropriate. This was the chair that Kerkin used when contemplating a problem. He had it shipped from Fresno, a memento of a life past when he was married. Once again it served his purpose in finding a solution where there appeared none to be found.

The attempt on David's life at the restaurant did not bring the results that Kerkin had wanted.

Opportunity missed.

What should have been a successful operation was fumbled. Was it through lack of planning? Kerkin concluded, not so. The plan was well laid out. David was in full view at a well known restaurant, 'Old Yerevan'. As predicted, the assassins showed up. It was obvious who they were.

The assassins made their move on David. Kerkin's men came in fast. But then, the problem. Too much effort protecting David. Not enough effort capturing the assassins. The result; all the killers got away. No information was obtained.

Was it a mistake to protect David at all cost? Kerkin did not want to ask the question. The answer, he knew, would most certainly have put David in too much danger. It was an unfortunate reality that would have to be executed if the next attempt at finding out who David's killers were was to be successful.

The problem to solve now was how to draw out David's killers. What bothered Kerkin was the implication of an agent here in Armenia that played a significant role in the attempt on David's life. How long had this agent been in place and how well connected was he or she? These questions haunted Kerkin. It was no longer simply a case of finding the one who wanted to kill David. Rather, there was a serious security breach in Armenia. Kerkin was determined to stop this at all cost.

David and Kalesh entered Kerkin's office. They were still a bit stressed from last night's close call with what seemed sure death. Today however they were alive and in the reassuring presence of Kerkin who motioned for them to sit down and have some wine to drink. Lifting his glass Kerkin toasted.

"It was a close call last night ... no one could say otherwise. I commend you both for staying steady under the pressure."

The three men clanked glasses and gave the Armenian word for cheers, "kenats't."

Kerkin took a drink then continued.

"We have need of some significant information about the would be killers. I'm starting to suspect that there are two parties at work here. One is Turkish and the other, I regret, could be Armenian."

Kalesh reacted.

"Armenian ... how can that be?"

Kerkin sighed.

"We have all fought so hard over the years for what we now have, a free and independent Armenia. Yet, there are, and I suppose there will always be, traitors amongst us. This traitor has managed to operate undetected in Armenia. It suggests that she, yes it is a woman, has contacts, perhaps powerful contacts. That she operates under highly secretive cover could offer some explanation why these powerful contacts assist her. They may simply be naive to what she is really doing. In any event, she has, through her involvement in the attempt on David's life, revealed her presence. We must capitalize on this. It's an opportunity that we can't afford to not make the very most of."

In Fresno Mark Kerkin had just finished a rushed report from the private investigator concerning the attempt on David's life at his house on Van Ness Ave. in Fresno. Owing to the fact that one of the perpetrator's gloves was pulled off in the skirmish with David, fingerprints were found.

Unfortunately these fingerprints could not be matched to any police records. This bothered Mark because he reasoned, that if it were a standard burglary then one could assume that the perpetrator would have some kind of police record.

Mark was looking exactly at this kind of negative evidence. That is, the perpetrator was not in the house to steal, but rather was there to kill David. Mark concluded that if this were so then it would account for the perpetrator having no police record. Then again, if he were a hit man, it would also stand to reason that there would be some kind of police record. But there was not.

How could this be?

Adult criminals typically have police records. What was the catch here?

What am I missing?

The only other piece of information was that the perpetrator looked Armenian.

Then it hit Mark; Armenians, Turks, those with Middle Eastern looks, what do they have in common? They obviously have the possibility of being from another country. If that was the case then criminal record or not, the perpetrator's fingerprints would not show up on any United States based searches.

But what about international searches? Mark grabbed the phone to call the private investigator. A receptionist answered.

"Jenson private investigation."

"I need to speak with Dean Kerns."

"May I ask who is calling"

"This is Mark Kerkin. He knows who I am."

"One moment please while I connect you."

Dean Kerns got on the line in less than 30 seconds.

"What do you know Mark?"

"Can you check the fingerprints with Interpol?"

"You think this could be international?"

"I'm beginning to suspect so."

"Okay then ... I should be able to get you results by say ... tomorrow morning."

"Much thanks Dean."

"All in a day's job. Talk to you tomorrow then."

"Tomorrow."

Adem was furious. He had just found out through sources close to Teshkur that there was a failed attempt on David's life in Fresno. From what he has heard of the brilliant performance of Mark Kerkin in the court room, Adem made the mental jump that this lawyer would not let go of an attempt on David's life in his own backyard of Fresno. It most certainly would be investigated.

Once such an investigation commenced it was only a matter of time, likely a very short time, Adem reasoned, that a connection would be made to Turkish interests. If that happened, Adem was convinced that the entire court case could be blown, a complete catastrophe. Something had to be done.

It was near panic for Adem. He thought about what to do to mitigate the situation. More information was needed, but how? Was there anyone who could get this information? The only person available was someone Adem was reluctant to ask. It was Debra.

Adem was reluctant to ask Debra for two reasons. First she was not likely to be able to get Mark Kerkin to answer any questions. If by some chance he did answer then there was the very real possibility that this would give the lawyer reason to be suspicious. Also, he didn't want Debra to know that an attempt had been made on David's life. She may then change her mind about going ahead with the new Will.

All in all, getting Debra involved was a risky proposition. It could also most surely blow Memet's cover. If that happened then the repercussions would be dire. One could only imagine how Debra would react, especially if she discovered that her efforts were assisting foreign agents. That those foreign agents were Turkish would add fuel to the fire.

Considering both reasons for his reluctance to involve Debra put Adem in a no win situation. To ask Debra to help, point blank, was inviting almost certain disaster. On the other hand, to do nothing was to wait for disaster. What could he do? Adem tortured himself over the decision. The only remedy he could think of was to call in Memet. Perhaps the two of them could figure something out.

"I don't know Adem. To ask Debra ... it's going to be difficult."

Memet's mention of difficult here was almost more than Adem could take.

"I know it's difficult but what else can we do?"

"I just don't know Adem. Debra and I are just now..."

"Debra and I ... what is this Memet? Are you falling in love with her?"

Adem realized he was becoming far too irritable.

"Sorry Memet. I did not mean to imply..."

"It's okay. I understand the seriousness of the matter."

Memet paused for a brief moment.

"There is a something ... maybe."

"What?"

"The other night at Debra's house. She was almost in tears when she talked about David. How she felt terrible about her testimony in court ... how she felt that David was being directly hurt by her testimony."

"For good reason I suppose."

"Well yes. That's when I suggested ... and sorry ... I don't know why I did this ... I suggested that she contact David ... try to talk with him. I realize now that it was a bad idea but..."

Adem became encouraged at a newfound possibility.

"Wait one minute here ... I think I see where you are going ... and yes ... not the best of ideas. With that said though ... maybe the idea of making contact is not so bad. Do you think you can get her to contact Mark Kerkin with the idea of starting some kind of communication with David?"

"It's just what I was thinking. I think there's a chance."

"The beauty of this idea is that it does not give you ... or us ... away."

"Exactly."

Memet admired yet again the spectacular view of the lake as he walked up to the front door of Debra's house. It was almost dark. He and Debra had set a dinner date for the evening. Debra had promised Memet a home cooked meal. Memet relished the thought of delicious Armenian dishes even as he inwardly rehearsed how he was to convince Debra to contact Mark Kerkin.

The overt contradiction bothered him enough that for a brief moment he thought about forgetting the entire deal and just simply enjoying the wonderful meal he was sure Debra had made for him. It was only a brief moment though, nothing longer. Memet reminded himself of the job to be done. That's why he was here. He kept telling himself this right up to the front door.

Memet entered the house.

"Hello Debra."

Debra came out of the kitchen wearing an apron. She looked so beautiful. Memet couldn't help but smile at her.

"The chef for the evening?"

"Well I hope your are hungry my dear."

"I purposely did not eat anything today ... just thinking about how much I'm going to enjoy tonight's dinner."

"I hope you're going to like it."

Memet paused, caught in a moment of Debra's beauty.

"Guaranteed."

Chapter thirty-seven

David helped Kerkin to walk up some rocks that ran along a shoreline of a small stream just outside of Stepanakert. Kerkin took a breath.

"I can still remember a time when I did not need help up those rocks."

He paused for a moment.

"Old age comes quicker than I could have imagined David. There is no stopping it."

David felt something between sympathy and respect for the legend that stood before him, a man that was not without troubles throughout his long life. He never was able to reconcile with his wife. His son, though he did his best to be a good father, remained distant.

It was with these thoughts of the real man before him that David brought up the information Mark had discovered.

"Do you think it was possible that my own mother could be working with the Turkish MIT?"

Kerkin carefully stepped onto a nearby rock.

"If there is anything for certain in this world ... it is that anything is possible. Is your mother working with the Turks? I can not say for sure. What I do know is that your mother ... whoever she really is ... is good. Do you believe that David?"

David would rather not answer any question about his mother. She represented for him a kind of distaste, an awful hurt that goes down deep into a son's soul, that the very one for whom there is supposed to be trust has instead betrayed.

"I want to believe it ... but..."

David choked up a bit "What she is doing ... with the Will and the trial ... I just don't know Kerkin."

"What your mother is doing ... I suspect ... is not because she is conscious."

"Conscious ... she is alive ... she must know."

"That's just the point David. To be conscious ... your mother must see life as it really is."

Kerkin paused for a moment to watch the stream of water running over some rocks.

"The water flows where it will. I can wish for the water to go here or there but it will go in the direction that nature ... reality ... dictates. So it is with your mother. She may wish for her life to have gone in a direction she had imagined ... but that does not change reality for her. Do you know what I'm saying ... about her?"

David did not want to answer but knew he had to.

"You mean my father."

"He was a good man. Your mother loved him more than she could know. He was your mother's intention ... what she wanted from life. But when he died ... your mother could not see the reality. She would not accept it. This David ... was her fall."

"I get it Kerkin ... but to deny me ... her son?"

"When a person denies their reality ... all manner of trouble follows them. Take for instance what is happening even now. Your mother seeks to create a reality of your deceased father. She will do anything ... in this case finding a boyfriend to harm you and prevent the good intentions of your grandfather."

David was shocked at Kerkin's accusation.

"Are you saying that my mother's boyfriend is somehow connected?"

"I am indeed saying that. How he is connected ... at this point I can't say. We need to find out more."

David had climbed up to the top of a rock ledge that overhung across the stream.

"So this is no longer a question of just finding out who is trying to kill me."

David reached out to pull Kerkin up onto the rock ledge, then heaved him up.

"I know now that the stakes are much higher."

Kerkin grabbed onto David's hand.

"True enough.   What is of most concern is a possible connection between Turkish interests and a certain Armenian agent."

"Armenian agent ... who?"

"We don't know much ... only that her code name is Olga."

"Can you get to her?"

"Maybe ... if..."

"What?"

"We have to make her desperate enough."

"Desperate ... how?"

Kerkin hesitated to answer.   David sensed that Kerkin did not want to involve him.

"David you must understand that this time you may not be so fortunate. If we are to take down Olga then we will have to up the ante ... again with you as bait."

From atop the rock ledge David could see the entire path of the river.

"For me Kerkin ... there is no choice. If we don't take her out ... can I ever be at peace?"

Kerkin took in the view of the river that David saw.

"It's the same conclusion that I and ... your grandfather would have come to."

David knew right then and there, that just as the river had it's reality of direction, so too he had his reality.

"Then it's settled."

Two days later David arrived back in Yerevan with the purpose of setting the trap for his killers. Kerkin decided that the Armenian capital was the best place to lure the elusive Olga to take a chance at becoming the hunted instead of the hunter.

Olga would do this, Kerkin reasoned, because of the high visibility of Yerevan. Her reputation was at stake in the city. If she did not take the challenge then word would get out quick in Armenia's criminal underground that she backed off. This could end her career. Kerkin was betting on this.

Kerkin also knew it went without saying that setting a trap for Olga was akin to a chess match. She knew that a trap was being set for her. Her challenge would be to discover the trap, avoid it, and make the kill. All moves, hers and Kerkin's, were in plain view. What was not, were the moves of each opponent in reaction to the other. Possibilities could be entertained, but the eventual outcome would only be known when the game was over.

Kerkin also believed, but was not certain, that Olga herself would not be doing the actual job. One or more of her agents would see to that. Still, if any of these agents could be apprehended alive, then given the proximity to Yerevan, Olga could be tracked through these agents and/or their contacts.

Certainly this was not a perfect approach, but it was the only approach available. The main drawback, which Kerkin alluded to in Stepanakert, was that David had to be used again as bait. It was the only way to draw Olga out. He would have to be put in real danger, enough danger that he may not be able to escape unscathed this time.

The plan was simple enough. David would go about Yerevan to various social gatherings, both publicized and non-publicized. He would purposely draw attention. Undercover security people would be in place to protect David when the killers struck. In the end it would be a match of Kerkin's forces versus Olga's forces. David and even more so Kerkin were counting on the former.

~~~~~~~~~

"Can you kill him?"
Olga's words resonated with Krug.
"It's what I do."

Krug Hasian knew he was a killer. He had been trained in Sambo, a martial art that was developed for the Russian Army Special Forces and Rapid Reaction Police known as the Militsija.

Krug had learned Sambo when he was in the Special Forces. He had been part of a special team responsible for finding Chechen rebels. Krug had enjoyed practicing the techniques of Sambo, supposedly designed for special defense, but that could kill very quickly. In fact he had been discharged from the Special Forces because he was considered difficult to control and therefore dangerous to his comrades.

Having returned to Yerevan after being discharged from the Special Forces, Krug was befriended by Olga, an Armenian woman of questionable origins. Despite a mutual distrust on both their parts, in time Krug and Olga developed a kind of alliance. She gave him money and he protected her. This included Krug taking care of anything, or anybody, that caused Olga a problem.

With their mutual advantage in mind, Olga approached Krug as the means to kill David.

"I can pay you $100,000 for a confirmed kill."

Krug nodded his head to acknowledge the deal, but with adjustments.

"I will need to use four associates to make sure the job is done without incident. This will cost $150,000."

Olga had no hesitation concerning the extra money Krug had asked for. She knew all too well that her reputation was on the line.

"The funds will be deposited in your Swiss account."

Krug kissed Olga on her left, then right cheek.

"Very well then."

Olga was satisfied with the deal she and Krug had worked out. There was however one important element that was, from her intention, beyond negotiation.

"It must seem to independent witnesses that David had started the fight."

Krug had killed too many times to disagree with Olga's request. He would not say it, but for Olga to even have to ask for the appearance of David as the instigator was taken by Krug as an affront to his skill. He was not just a hired killer, but also a professional hit man. That was Krug's mantra.

"I will make sure that David has a knife in his hands when he challenges me."

Krug laughed in a kind of manipulative delight.

"I will then be forced to kill him, hand to hand, out of self defense."

Satisfied that Krug would get the job done, Olga called Salem.

"It has been arranged."

The morning hour was very early, still dark outside, when Salem heard Olga's words over the phone in his hotel room. Groggy, Salem tried to orient himself before answering.

"Who ... Olga?"

Olga was impatient.

"Who do think it is?"

Salem took half a minute to make sense of what Olga was saying to him. Olga's impatience was increasing.

"Are you there?"

Having come into a waking state, Salem now became cognizant of what Olga was indicating.

Who does she think she is?

Second upon second pushed Salem into a confrontational stance with Olga. Knowing how she had reacted to him so far, Salem was sure that an argument was coming.

So be it.

"We need to meet."

Olga knew Salem's request was inevitable. Given the failed attempt on David's life at the restaurant, how could she expect otherwise? Still, she was being forced to compromise her cover. This bothered Olga immensely.   For 10 years now she had managed an arrangement with foreign agents where her concealed identity was accepted. Now the Turks wanted to change this.

Olga considered the consequences of revealing her cover. Short and fat, at least from her perspective, Olga's 55 years of age were showing. Although many women of her age in Armenia still had good skin features, Olga's complexion was looking worn out. Was it the smoking or the drinking or the late nights? Perhaps all of these were to blame.

The reality of the matter though, was that Olga lived for the pleasures of life. It's how she became involved with the underworld in the first place. From her earliest memories she wanted the good life. To have that back in the days of Soviet Armenia meant to bend the rules. For Olga, the choice of a harsh but compromised life or one of opulence with consequences, was easy. It was never a question for her.

It was natural then for Olga to drift into the world of prostitution. By age 13 she knew well the seedy side of Yerevan. Such a profession in Soviet days, if found out, could have lead to severe punishment, possibly a trip to Siberia. It was only natural then that Olga would gravitate to the secretive side.

Through the cultural awakening of Armenian nationalism, to the fall of the Soviet empire and the Karabakh war, Olga's cover of secrecy evolved. As the years followed, Olga's youthful beauty transformed into the guile of age. She learned to trust no one, not even herself. This she believed was her strength, a pure survival instinct where the only reason to continue was simply to get the most of what is.

Was this the life Olga wanted for herself? The question often came to her mind. She made her choices, be they good or bad. The answer was of no matter to her. This was her life, simply as it was. As the saying went,

You make your own bed. Now sleep in it.

CHAPTER THIRTY-EIGHT

Krug and his associates sat in a silver BMW 6 series on Abovian Street in Yerevan. They were waiting for the phone to ring; a call from Olga's informant, that it was a go.

Abovian Street in the summer was a busy place. Krug knew that when the call came he would have to move fast. Even a few minutes delay would give David and those with him the chance they needed to escape or even worse, to take himself down.

Just outside the Armani shop an old man gave a flower to a young couple. Krug had seen this old man nearly every day, since his arrival in Yerevan some five years ago. There was simplicity about the old man that Krug could appreciate. He was not interested in fame or fortune. His only place in life, as far as Krug could see, was to remind lovers, young and old, that what they had, was to be cherished. It was only a dream for Krug, one that he knew was out of reach, but to watch that old man, the smile on his face as he gave out a flower, that was enough for Krug.

The phone rang. Krug picked up to a serious – no frills message.

"He's just now coming out ... walking past the Hrazdan river gorge ... just outside the Yerevan winery. Hold on."

Krug silently waited for more information. The voice came back.

"There is no one near ... within 50 meters."

Krug's driver headed in the direction of the winery, just one block down Abovian street. Two of Krug's associates readied their Beretta Tomcat semi-automatic guns. Krug checked his knife, a

Cold Steel Brave Heart. He rubbed his left hand over the handle to the razor sharp blade.

A clean cut today.

That there was no one near David made Krug suspicious. Either this would be a trivial kill or it was a trap. Krug leaned toward the latter. It did not matter in the end to Krug if it was an easy or difficult job. Whether he succeeded or failed did not matter either. No, the only real matter for Krug was the fight itself. How would it be for him to fight and to kill David? That was the motivation, the excitement for Krug. It's why he loved his job.

David was within sight. The voice on the phone came back. "It's a go. Take him down. I repeat. Take him down."

The car slowed to almost a stop, about 25 meters from David. Krug left the car while his other two associates, with guns, traveled another 75 meters, just past David. They readied their guns just in case of trouble for Krug who was fast approaching David from behind.

Now just a meter away from his prey, Krug slipped the knife into David's belt. He meant David to feel the knife being put into his belt. David pulled the knife out of his belt. It now pointed to Krug.

"He has a knife." Krug shouted out.

For a split second David was caught off guard. He reacted to the situation in a kind of shock. How could it be that he had a knife in his hand? Then he realized the game was on.

Play it man.

David knew at that very moment he could just drop the knife and run. But then, that was not how the game was to be played. The objective here was to take the hunter. Make him the hunted.

David gripped the knife even as he glanced around to see people all around watching. If the situation went bad, that is, if he was killed, no one would say that David was innocent.

Kerkin's associates were fast approaching. Krug could see this as well. The trap, as he suspected, had been set. His associates came in fast to take their part.

Krug threw a Sambo knife defense technique on David. His focus was to gain control of David's knife hand while simultaneously taking down David's body. This way he could use the knife that David wielded against David himself.

David could see from Krug's stance that he would be using Sambo techniques. He prepared himself for the first blow.

Krug pushed the hand with the knife away to David's right. David almost dropped the knife as Krug hit him hard then began to wrestle him down. David knew that he couldn't let go of the knife. If he did, he would be finished. Krug was now pulling at David's knife hand. If David was not careful the knife would be pulled into himself.

Kerkin's associates were now on the scene. Their guns were pointed at Krug. However, because of the close proximity of fighting between David and Krug, taking a shot would be putting David in real danger. All they could do was stand guard making sure that no one else interfered. If it did look bad for David then they would have to decide if taking the shot was worth the risk. This was all made worse when Krug's associates drew their guns.

Krug was surprised at David's agility with the knife. Twice during the fight, David managed to press the knife against the skin of Krug. Blood was now on the street and still, David had not lost control of the knife.

It was now clear to Krug that this young Armenian American could really fight. Krug relished the thought as he made his big move. He intentionally eased up on his resistance to David's knife hand. In the moment of reaction David followed through with the knife stopping just short of Krug's throat. The knife stopped only because Krug again put up resistance. The advantage for

Krug was that he could use the momentum of the forward lunge to flip David. Krug was now on top, putting leverage on David's knife hand.

The situation looked bad for David except that Krug had now positioned himself so that a clear shot on himself could be taken. Kerkin's associates were waiting for the word to take the shot. Krug's associates knew the drill. They prepared to defend.

From the side, Kerkin watched as the knife pressed into David's side. Kerkin gave the word.

"Take the shot ... but do not kill."

A shot was fired. It hit Krug on the side. Krug's associates took their shots. One of Kerkin's associates pushed Krug to the side then covered David to protect him from being shot. Another of Kerkin's associates positioned himself over Krug with a gun. Seeing that the situation was lost, Krug's associates ran from the scene back to the car, which then took off.

Kerkin stepped onto the scene. Motioning for David to stay down just in case there were still attackers present, he stood over Krug.

"Who are you with?"

Krug's expression was that of nothing. It was as if he anticipated what would happen next. Then it came. A single shot was fired. Krug went down. There was a bullet hole in his head.

Salem stood at a distance, a smoking gun in his hand.

~~~~~~~~~

Memet could see that something was bothering Debra. He tried to cheer her up.

"It's such a beautiful morning. Why don't we have our breakfast on the patio?"

Debra nodded okay without saying anything. She took a bowl of eggs out to the patio.

It was a strange demeanor that Memet found Debra in, as if she was in another world, separate from the reality of anyone else. He did not want to admit it, but deep down he knew the likely cause. Debra was after all still a mother and despite her conflict with David, he was still her son. Memet knew that for Debra to be the kind of woman she was, a good woman, she could not shut herself off to the needs of her son. That would make her far less of a woman than she was.

What was she thinking? It was driving Memet to utter frustration to see Debra across from him at the table on such a beautiful morning and yet not be able to have any kind of conversation. This was too much for him. He felt compelled to do something and this he knew, was dangerous. Any wrong word here could launch a direction of thought beyond which he could control, something an experienced agent as himself did not want.

But this was exactly the problem Memet found himself in. He had in fact, fallen in love with Debra. How could it have happened, he asked himself? After all these years on the job, the many women he had seduced, manipulated, and used. Now he found himself here, in Fresno, in love with an Armenian woman.

Admit it – I love this woman.

Memet braced himself with this understanding as he opened up a conversation that he knew, there would be no turning back from.

"Is it David?"

Hearing the word David was like a siren to Debra's ears. It woke her up from the self-oriented reality she had placed herself in.

"I'm so worried about him."

Memet tried to console Debra.

"Of course ... he is your son."

The ring of the phone broke an awkward silence. Debra picked it up.

"Hello."

"It's Mark Kerkin."

Debra was shocked. She whispered to Memet.

"It's Mark Kerkin."

Memet tried not to show his surprise.

"Be careful Debra."

Debra took a deep breath before speaking.

"Mark ... I'm surprised."

"My apologies Debra for calling ... but I thought you should know."

"Know what?"

"It's about David."

Debra became concerned.

"What has happened?"

"There was an incident. David was hurt."

Debra became agitated.

"Hurt ... how bad? Tell me."

Mark wanted to calm Debra as best he could.

"David is recuperating from a knife wound."

"A knife wound ... how?"

"He   was   in   a   fight   ...   in   Yerevan."
"I knew he should stay away from Armenia. It's a dangerous place."

"In all honesty Debra ... it goes much deeper than that. An attempt on David's life was also carried out in Fresno."

"How ... why David?"

Mark collected his thoughts before answering.

"Please know that before I say anything more ... I'm speaking to you as your friend. Okay?"

"Thank you Mark. After all that has happened ... well ... it's good to hear. We are still family. Now please ... tell me about my son."

Mark answered as calmly as he was able.

"We think that Turkish and/or Azeri agents are trying to kill David because of the money."

"How do you know this?"

"At this point the information is very preliminary. Mostly it's a conclusion based on motive. If David helps Karabakh then that could be perceived by Azeri interests and by extension Turkish interests ... as not good. It's more than conceivable that such interests would determine that killing David would be the easiest solution."

Debra was incensed.

"The easiest solution. That's my son they are trying to kill."

Debra broke out sobbing.

"We have to do something. Is David safe now?"

"He's safe ... at an undisclosed location."

"I need to talk to him. Can you arrange it?"

"Yes ... I can do that. Give me a few hours. I know David will be glad to hear from you."

"I hope so."

After hanging the phone up Debra fell into the arms of Memet.

"My son ... they tried to kill him."

Memet was torn with a guilty conscience. Here he was comforting a woman that he is in love with while at the same time keeping from her the very information that could save her son.

How can I do this?

Memet held onto Debra tightly as she expressed her regret about David.

"I've done this to David ... the trial. I should have never challenged the Will."

"You must not do this to yourself. None of what you are doing with the trial could have caused what happened in Armenia."

"Why couldn't it? They are trying to kill him to prevent help to Armenia?"

"Maybe ... but what you are doing with the Will and what's going on in Armenia ... how could they possibly be connected?"

"How are they connected? Isn't obvious? Besides that ... there was also an attempt on his life here.... in Fresno."

Memet went deafly silent when he heard that there was an attempt on David's life in Fresno. The situation was clearly getting out of hand and he was right in the middle of it. He was starting to feel as though Debra was looking at him ... was it suspiciously?

Does she know?

Memet began to seriously wonder if Debra thought he could be involved? After all, the trouble started just as he and Debra began seeing each other. Then again, maybe she would just think it was coincidence.

Does she see the connection?

The situation was becoming intolerable for Memet. This was a woman he loved. He had to take some action. The trouble was that the action needed was entirely serious. Memet was talking Turkish national security here.

Should I tell her?

Memet could not believe he was even considering the question. He could end up in prison, or even worse, for acting on this.

What am I going to do?

Debra sensed that something was really bothering Memet. "What's going on Richard?"

Memet was caught by Debra's question. He had a choice, right then and there, to tell the truth, or to lie.

"David is in serious danger."

"I know that."

"No ... you don't know what I know."

Debra was scared by Memet's statement.

"What you know. How? Is there something ... about you ... that you're not telling me?"

Memet could feel the anxiety pulsing through his body.

I'm found out.

"Debra ... I love you ... you know that."

Debra looked at Memet suspiciously.

"There's something you are not telling me."

Memet felt as if he was in some kind of nightmare with no escape, except to tell the truth.

"I'm not who you think I am. My name is Memet. I am Turkish."

Debra was incensed. She slapped Memet on the face.

"You liar! Who are you? What do you want from me?"

Memet felt smothered by the shame of betraying the one he loved.

"I'm sorry ... really ... I did not intend for this to happen."

"Not intend for this to happen. You lied."

Debra suddenly made a connection to Memet and David.

"You are Turkish and Turks are trying to kill my son."

"Hold on Debra. It's not what you think ... believe me."

"Tell me then ... Richard ... or Memet ... or whoever you are."

I could just leave right now.

The thought was extremely enticing. He could just run. No harm, no foul. If it were only that simple. His cover was now blown regardless. No, there was going to be fallout no matter what. He was going to lose his job. That was a fact. He would be lucky if he did not end up in prison or worse.

Unless there was a way to cover his tracks. The only way now was to give Debra what she wanted, the truth. Maybe then he could salvage the situation, maybe.

Memet braced himself for what he was about to say to Debra.

"I can help your son."

Debra was furious.

"Why should I believe you?"

"Because I work for the Turkish MIT."

No turning back now.

Memet's words put Debra into near shock.

"I can't believe this. Were you just using me all along?"

"No ... please ... I love you."

"Just forget about love. I don't love you. Get that in your head right now."

Memet took a deep breath.

"Okay ... but please ... just let me help you."

"How?"

"It's complicated ... but just give me some time. We can figure this out."

"Figure this out. This is my son."

Debra was completely furious to the point of a tirade. She screamed at Memet.

"Get out ... get out now."

All Memet could do was leave, and in a hurry. Strangely, he no longer felt the intense anxiety. Perhaps it was about telling the truth. He could not know for sure. Nothing for that matter was for sure now. All he could do was try and somehow salvage the situation. Maybe Adem would know what to do. He hoped so.

CHAPTER THIRTY-NINE

"I'm sorry Mark."

Debra's words were enough for Mark to know that she really was sorry. If her actions cost Debra the relationship with David remained to be seen. Mark thought that with enough understanding and patience of both David and Debra, reconciliation could take place. This would however likely take some time. Unfortunately, time was not something readily available. A crisis was at hand. Only swift action could save the day, maybe.

Mark had to take any information he could get, be it from Debra or his father Kerkin, or Turks, or whom ever, to try and salvage the situation. His main objectives were to keep David safe and prevent the new Will from taking effect. The safety of David was for the most part, out of Mark's control. He would have to rely on his father for this. Preventing the new Will from taking effect was an objective that Mark could significantly effect. That was the aim he would pursue with all the skills and experience that he could muster.

It had been a while since Mark and Debra spoke in person, not counting the recent trial.

"Is David safe?"

Debra asked the question as any mother would for her son.

"Rest assured. He's safe for now."

"For now?"

"I will be honest with you. Right now David is recuperating in a small village in Karabakh. He is being cared for by what I'm told is a wonderful Armenian girl. Her name is Ani."

Debra sensed from Mark's expression that Ani could be more to David than just a nurse.

"This Ani ... who is she? How did she meet David?"

Mark felt a sense of relief that at least there was something positive to tell Debra.

"I don't know a whole lot about her ... just that Ani is a beautiful and smart girl and that David likes her very much. Oh ... also ... Kalesh is her Godfather."

"I suppose I don't have a right to say much ... about her."

"Of course you do Debra. David is your son."

"The way I've treated him ... and you ... the whole family ... I'm not sure."

"It's all in the past Debra. What's important now is that we all work together ... to make the situation right."

"Can you tell me Debra just what Richard ... sorry ... his name is Memet I believe ... told you? A feeling of sadness came over Debra when she heard Mark's question. She really would have preferred to just forget about Richard, or would she?

Just forget about him.

The problem was, Debra could not forget about Richard. If she was honest with herself, Richard was the best man she had met since her deceased husband. He was kind, smart, and handsome. What more could a woman ask for? Oh yeah Debra reminded herself, honesty.

Debra knew she had to put feelings of Richard, positive or negative, aside. What mattered now was making sure David was safe. Whatever information she could offer Mark to that end, was what she would do.

"Richard said he was with the Turkish MIT."

Mark already suspected the connection of Richard, but even so, to hear it again, caught his attention.

"Did he mention anything about David?"

"Only that he could help."

"Help ... how?"

"Something with the MIT ... I'm not sure exactly. Do you think the MIT is trying to kill David."

"I'm not sure. The evidence suggests yes. On the other hand ... Richard has offered to help. It could be that there is some kind of internal dissent over killing ... sorry..."

"Don't be sorry Mark. I can handle it. Just tell me what I can do ... to help David."

Mark knew this moment was coming for Debra. She would have to put herself on the line. Mark's job now was to lay out a plan for Debra so that she could mitigate the circumstances that she created.

"Here's what you can do Debra. First we need to let Judge Connors know that the new Will is a fake. This will stop all financial issues dead in their tracks. Secondly, we need to work with Richard if it's possible. How do you feel about both of these? Can you manage them?"

Debra had no problem asking Judge Connors to throw out the case. That was easy. What was not so easy was calling Richard, then asking for his help.

How humiliating.

It does not matter, Debra reminded herself yet again. The priority here is David.

"When can we see the Judge?"

"You won't have to."

"How is that?"

"I've already spoken with Judge Connors. He has agreed to close the case provided you sign an affidavit affirming that you are no longer contesting the Will. Can you agree to that?"

"Of course. Thank you Mark."

"Think nothing of it ... all in a days work."

Mark now prepared himself to ask what he believed to be the more delicate question.

"How about contacting Richard?"

"It's kind of ... no it is ... really embarrassing."

Mark reassured Debra.

"Believe me when I say this Debra ... you have nothing to be embarrassed about."

"But how could I have been fooled by him?"

"You must remember ... he's a professional with years of experience. Just about anybody could be fooled by such a man."

Despite Mark's words of encouragement, Debra could not get the feeling of embarrassment out of her head.

How could I have fallen for him?

The question bothered Debra. Had she become so desperate for love that she was gullible, to the point of falling for a Turkish spy? Debra had to laugh at herself for just a moment. Leave it to her to fall in love with such a man. Par for the course of her life these days.

The real question though, the one that Debra did not want to look at, was if Richard really did love her? He said he did but then maybe that was all a big fake, just a way to use her. The easy answer was to just say yes, Richard used her. End of story! But that was not the answer Debra wanted. If she was honest with herself and perhaps that time had come, Debra wanted to love Richard. He had the qualities that Debra admired in a man. True, there was the problem of him being Turkish, but that could be worked out.

Stop this nonsense ... now.

Debra could not believe herself. After what Richard did to her. No, Debra knew what she had to do. Just call Richard. Get information from him. That's it.

That evening Debra made the call to Richard.

"Hello."

Debra almost hung up the phone.

"Richard ... it's me."

"I'm so glad you called."

Debra could not hold back her resentment.

"Don't be."

"Sorry ... it's just that I ... missed you."

It was hard for Debra to hear Richard's words. She could feel hope surfacing into her consciousness.

Be strong.

Debra remained resolute in what she had to do.

"What do you know about David?"

Memet knew he was stepping way over the line by helping Debra, and now by extension, Mark Kerkin. He had discussed the matter with Adem who, as could be expected, was extremely disappointed. Essentially they had lost any opportunity to save the case. The new Will would most certainly be thrown out. What remained was a salvage operation to contain the damage done. This mainly had to do with shielding the MIT from implication in the sordid affair. Secondary to this was to keep David alive. There was no point now in killing him. At least that's what Memet and Adem believed.

To the point of Debra's question, Memet could not take the chance of speaking about it on the phone. The lines could be tapped. They would have to meet in person.

"Can we meet tomorrow?"

It was hard enough for Debra to talk with Richard. She could not imagine how it would be to see him.

"I don't think it's such a good idea."

"Please Debra ... I don't want to hurt you. It's just ... I can't say it over the phone."

The message between the lines came through for Debra. This was too confidential for the phone.

"I understand. How about 7:30 A.M. at my place?"

"Sounds good."

"See you then ... tomorrow."

As she hung up the phone, Debra could not tell if she loved or hated Richard. He betrayed her and yet his actions even now told of a good man. Was she being fooled again? Perhaps. This time though, she would see Richard with eyes wide open. That's all she could do.

The next morning Memet drove up carefully into Debra's driveway. He wondered if this would be the last time he could admire the beautiful shoreline view of the lake? Who could tell? At this point, the best he could hope for was to have a civilized conversation with Debra. If he could have that then at least he could help Debra to keep her son safe. That would offer him some kind of solace.

Memet knocked on the door. There Debra was, standing in the doorway.

"Come in."

Memet could feel the tension in the air.

"Thanks."

"Would you like some coffee?"

Memet smiled as he took Debra's cue to sit at the kitchen table.

"It would be nice."

Debra brought two cups of coffee, then sat down at the table.

"Tell me ... what do you know about my son."

Memet could find no fault in Debra's direct approach. This was about her son. Any mother would not be expected to do otherwise.

"Please know that what I'm about to tell you is highly confidential."

Debra knew that Richard was putting himself on the line by giving her information. Unless it was some kind of trap, he was doing this to help her, certainly not himself. Debra could not help but appreciate what Richard was doing.

Memet took a sip of coffee as he started to divulge what he knew.

"There are those I work with that have decided ... your son should be taken out."

"You mean killed."

Memet was reluctant to agree to the semantics of the phrase, but knew he must.

"Yes ... killed. This was never my intention. I hope you can believe me."

Debra could see that Richard was trying to take her feelings into account. Whether he was faking it or not, she could not know. For now though, at least she would give him the benefit of the doubt.

"I believe you."

"Thank you. As you know, several attempts were made on David's life. He managed every time to escape these attempts."

What was coming next was information that Memet had obtained from Adem. How Adem obtained it demonstrated yet again the resourcefulness and intelligence of his colleague.

Essentially Adem had convinced his boss Ali that he was abandoning his plan in favor of Teshkur's plan. He did this by explaining that since the court had gone into recess to test the new Will for forgery, it was unlikely that the new Will would prevail. The only alternative then, was to proceed with killing David. It all made sense. Indeed the new Will, almost surely, would not prevail. Adem could conveniently blame the failure of his plan on the lawyers. He would take some heat for this but not so much that his career would be severely damaged.

"Those that want your son killed are going to try again."

Debra was slightly confused because she knew that David was being hidden in Karabakh. However, she was not about to give this information, or any information, away. She would just continue to listen.

"They know where your son is ... in Karabakh."

Given the seriousness of what Richard was saying, Debra decided to ask a question that she hoped would not give any information away that Richard did not already know.

"But how can they know?"

"They have people in place ... to find out. Now what I'm about to tell you is extremely important. The person in charge is a woman. Her code name is Olga. This time Olga will be supervising the mission directly. The day of the planned kill is July 10."

There it was. Memet gave Debra all the details she needed to take Olga down. David would stay alive, at least for a while. If it was believed that the failure of Olga's planned mission was due to bad luck, then all would be well. Memet knew that in that case, he could come out unscathed. Adem was actually taking the biggest risk as some might suspect the coincidence of his newfound support of a plan that would ultimately fail.

Memet quickly drank the rest of his coffee.

"Well then ... that's it."

Debra felt sadness run through her as she heard Richard speak those words.

Will I ever see him again?

Memet stood up from the table.

"I guess it's time for me to go."

"Okay ... let me walk you out.

Memet took one last look at the lake.

"A beautiful view."

Debra and Memet looked at the lake together for just a brief moment.

"Thank you for doing this ... really."

"I had to. There was no choice for me."

Memet turned from Debra to unlock his car. He started to get in when something told him to turn around. Debra caught herself looking at Richard's deep blue eyes.

"Keep in touch."

Richard smiled.

"I will."

~~~~~~~~~~~

It had been a long drive from Yerevan. Olga was tired, but not so much from the drive. Rather she was tired of life. That David had continually managed to avoid being killed was wearing on her. She would not admit it to anyone, but Krug's death during the last failed attempt on David's life, had hurt her. What particularly made this difficult was that the very cause of Krug's death, Salem, was sitting beside her and was in fact driving the car she now rode in.

Salem had insisted that he accompany Olga on this mission. He had no qualms about telling Olga flat out that she was not living up to expectations. She had no choice then, but to allow Salem to ride with her. It was humiliating.

"Do you think we are the hunter or the hunted?"

Salem wondered why he even bothered to ask Olga the question. As he expected, there was no reply.

What if she is the last person I ever talk to?

The thought was nearly unbearable for Salem to contemplate. Was this what his life had come to, how it would end up?

Salem never had a chance to answer the question. Instead his focus completely changed to six cars quickly approaching from a side road to his left. A thought quickly went through his mind of how Olga objected to any backup support to escort them through Armenia into Karabakh. Olga maintained that such support would alert suspicion. Salem did not like the idea. Too risky he thought. Now that risk had turned into a life threatening reality.

Olga showed no emotion at the sight of the cars. How could she not be concerned Salem wondered?

"They are going to box us in."

"Did you expect anything different?"

"You expected this?"

Olga gave no answer.

The cars approaching from the side had, just as Salem predicted, boxed them in. Three cars sped in front of Olga and Salem's car. There was of course no turning around. The hunters had made sure of that by positioning three more cars behind Salem and Olga's car.

Olga was somehow not surprised by the situation that she and Salem now found themselves in. She knew this day was coming for a long time, ever since she was 13 years of age, ever since she started down the road she was on.

How did I get here?

This was the only question Olga wanted to ask. Could her life have been different? Perhaps if she had not been lured by the money of prostitution, Olga would have stayed in school, gone to university, married early, had two kids, and so on. But that did not happen. Instead she was about to fight it out with this old man Kerkin whom she had only just recently learned about. Recently meant for Olga only enough time for Kerkin to set the trap that she fell into.

Had Olga just accepted that the young man David, whom Kerkin protected, was somehow untouchable, Olga would never have found herself in the situation she was now in. This she knew beyond a doubt.

How could I have not realized it?

The answer was so obvious in hindsight. That anonymous call to the MIT, about where David was hiding, was like a piece of cheese set for the rat to eat. It was there in plain site, only waiting for the rat to take the bite. Once the bite was taken, it would be too late. The trap would snap down, like the gun SHOT she just heard.

Salem almost lost control of the car when he heard the shot. He remained steady despite feeling a desperate loss of control. For the first time in a long while, Salem was exposed. He was not orchestrating how the situation was playing out. All he could do was drive while trying to avoid being shot. But where was he driving too?

"Your son has done good work Kerkin."

Kalesh spoke as he and Kerkin watched the road ahead. Kalesh was driving the lead of the three cars that were ahead of Olga and Salem's car.

"I never really have known him."

"Could you have done anything different?"

"I used to think so."

Gun shots were coming from both the front and back of the car. Salem knew that if he did not continually veer the car right and left then very soon one or more of the tires would be blown out. If that happened then it was over. He checked his pocket for the gun.

They can't take me alive.

Salem felt the fear that comes when death is close. He had hoped that in his case death would be without knowing. To die in his sleep, that would be the best death. But that would not be the case here, today, for him. He was going to die an agent for the Turkish MIT. No one, not even his family would know the circumstances. An obscure way to go, he thought. Then again, there were worse ways to die, say of a chronic disease like cancer. It was the way of life, then death. No one could choose either.

Olga was becoming panicked.

"Watch where you are going."

Salem had reached his breaking point with Olga.

"Shut up NOW ... before I ..."

Olga interrupted.

"Before you what ... kill me?"

Salem almost lost control of the car, partly because of his veering, but mostly because of his burning anger towards Olga. He reached in his pocket for his gun.

Who do I kill first — me or her?

Kerkin sent a message through his walkie-talkie to all cars in the chase.

"We are coming up to the bend now. Make sure they are forced to the left."

Salem was forced to almost slam on his brakes to avoid hitting the car in front of him. There was not enough time. He could not react fast enough. Salem and Olga braced themselves for the crash.

To Salem's surprise, the car in front of them had suddenly sped up, veered to the right, then again slowed down. The car was now side by side to their car. Olga could see the gun pointed at her through the side window. She ducked as the bullet proof glass was hit.

Olga felt a fear deep within.

Dear God.

Huddled down, now shaking in terror, Olga understood that her life had gone terribly wrong. She was going to die. There was no getting away from that fact.

Salem was now being forced to the left by the car to his side as well as the cars in front and back of him. They were boxed in. The only way was to take the bend to the left coming up in less than a 100 meters. Even as he made the left turn at the bend, Salem knew that he was following the path of the trap. It was no surprise to him then, that the pursuing cars did not follow.

Kerkin watched as the the car carrying Salem and Olga continued down the dirt path they were chased onto.

"It's good justice that they drive into the very mine field that would have been cleared by John Avedisian's money."

Salem took some comfort in knowing that he would not be taken alive. He looked down at Olga, huddled in fear.

"You can get up now. No one is chasing us anymore."

Olga would not hear Salem's words. That was okay by him anyway. What did amuse him slightly though was that he would die with an Armenian. How perfectly ironic for an agent of the Turkish MIT.

Such is the life – and the death.

His thought ran clear as the land mine exploded.

~~~~~~~~~~~

David could not speak a word when his mother approached. This did not hinder Debra. All she could think about was that her only son, her little boy, was alive. In tears she wrapped her arms around David.

"I'm so sorry David."

Those simple words melted David to break his silence.

"I love you mom."

Debra could see, just off to her side, a beautiful Armenian girl watching in appreciation, love's healing between a mother and son. At that very moment Debra knew that Ani would be David's wife, here in Karabakh.

Thoughts of her father ran through.

Now it's David's turn.

About the Authors

Leonard Howard is an engineer currently living in California. He is the author of various short stories. His interests, which include the history of the Caucasus and the Ottoman Empire, inspired his enthusiasm for writing Safe Harbor.

David Deranian, PhD is a physicist currently living in California. An author of various articles concerning Armenian issues, he is also a student of history. It was the intersection of history with Armenian issues that motivated his writing for Safe Harbor.